Quake

A NOVEL BY
Auður Jónsdóttir

TRANSLATED BY MEG MATICH

dottir
press

NEW YORK CITY

Published in 2022
by Dottir Press
33 Fifth Avenue
New York, NY 10003

Dottirpress.com

Previously published as *Stóri skjálfti* by Mál og menning in Iceland in 2015. Translated from Icelandic by Meg Matich. First published in English by Dottir Press in 2022.

First printing

Design and production by Drew Stevens
Map illustration by Noelle McManus

Trade Distribution through Consortium Book Sales and Distribution, www.cbsd.com.

Library of Congress Control Number: 2021941909
ISBN 978-1-948340-16-8
eBook available

ICELANDIC LITERATURE CENTER   *Quake* was translated with generous support
from the Icelandic Literature Center.

MANUFACTURED IN THE US BY MCNAUGHTON AND GUNN.

In memory of a literary friend,
Elín Oddgeirsdóttir

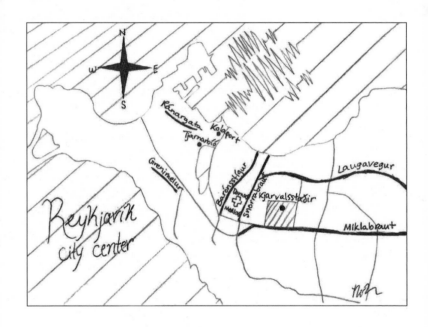

1

"What's your name?"

Unfamiliar eyes stare down at me.

"Name? My . . . name?"

"What's your name?" the voice repeats.

"Whose name?"

"Yours," the voice says. "Your name. Do you know your name?"

"Me?"

2

"Do you remember what happened?"

A kind face looks down at me. A man in a winter coat helps me to my feet. My legs are limp like dough. I falter, grab him to stop myself from falling. Strong hands in stiff gloves steady me. He smells of something familiar, something sweet—what bees make. His presence is muffled, soft-edged.

"Can you tell me what happened?" he asks again, but words stick to my palate and gum together in a creaturely moan.

His eyes try to make sense of me. He huffs steam, as if he's been running. We're standing just outside of the park next to a two-lane highway. I recognize everything around me. The snow on the sidewalk has been trampled to a hard white carpet. I know this sidewalk—it leads past houses with big windows that glow in the low light of winter— but why am I *here*, across from this man, by myself?

In this weather, the fields are indiscernible from the path that runs through them. Cars rush past us like a plague of hissing locusts.

"Are you okay?" he asks.

"I . . . don't know," I say slowly. The muscles in my mouth won't move properly.

"You landed on the pavement, and you're badly bruised," he says. He must be right because it hurts when I try to smile. "Can you remember anything that happened?" he asks once more, tightening his grip on my arm. Blue eyes, ruddy cheeks.

I can't turn away from his concern. The world lurches, but I manage to mumble, "There was a red bus here—a bus on top of a bus." I stop. I have to sound normal or I'll never get away from him. Him who? Away where?

I need to sleep, to fall asleep. Find the word—find it now.

"T-two-s-story?" I stutter. "Like . . . buses other places."

"Now you're imagining things, my friend," he says, as if he's talking to a child. "Double-deckers are in a lot of places, but not Iceland. Except—well, were there tourists in it?"

"Já, Ívar saw—"

The sound is a shard, the screech of a seabird. We both brace ourselves. The scream seems to have come out of my body, and I can't catch my breath. Another scream is coming. Another scream wants out.

"Where is he?"

"Who?" the man asks.

"My son—here. Pointed to bus and he—where?"

He looks confused. "Where did you see him last?"

Exasperated, I force myself to shout. "Here! Before I woke up. Did you see him?"

"He was here in the park?"

"Or—the entrance—" I scan the road, frantic. I resist the urge to faint as I spin to face the park. Small footprints wash together with a smattering of larger ones. I cup my head in my hands, squeeze my eyes shut to bring my surroundings into focus. I open them again. I wave the man off. "Run—there, the trees! Go! I'll be there at the bus stop, there—the shelter. We'll—"

"How old is he?"

Remember, remember.

"He's only little," I wail.

The man takes off toward Kjarvalsstaðir, the museum across the park, calling Ívar's name, jacket flapping against the back of his knees. My feet have lost their bones. They wobble under my weight, but they don't falter, though I feel myself edging toward a fall. I run, I trip.

"Ívar, where are you? Mamma is here."

I taste blood in my mouth. My thighs and butt are cold and sopping wet. I've wet myself. The pain in my forehead is worsening; I can feel each blood vessel constricting. I am limp. My body has wasted its energy, but I hold myself— all of myself—together. Firm. No blood in my hair, only the thrum of a headache. I've gotten off lightly. But him?

The memory slips into my periphery. We were walking. I was holding his little hand. He laughed. *See, Mamma, look at the cars!*

Yes, I laughed—or not? I laughed, and the red bus drove past. I said, *Ívar, look! The bus has two stories!*

As the pieces gather, their edges misalign. Did Ívar chase after the bus?

Each second teeters on an axis. I run along the edge of the park, past traffic, but he's nowhere to be found. I run back and back and back. I need to get to a phone.

I trip over my own feet, scramble out of the fall. Slip, scramble, slip to the far side of the park. That building. My heart is hurtling, but it won't burst, not now. It hastens me over the snow, which elongates even as I cross it.

I throw myself against the doors, stumbling into the bright, warm space. My violence shocks the room. Eyes gape at me over cups of coffee, forkfuls of delicate shrimp.

I'm shrieking.

3

"Did you hear what I said, Saga?" The voice is attached to a bulky torso in a white smock.

Saga! I'm Saga. Relief pervades me. I remember my name.

"Já, I heard," I mumble.

"You were in danger." His breath is humid, like it's been marinating in coffee for half a century. Each word drips hot and fragrant. Everything is white, even the bed and the blinds that hang over the window. The air is an opaque white haze. My hand hurts where a needle's been stuck into the back of it, slipped under the skin. Actually, my body is one big ache—upper arms tender, hips stung by pins and needles. A machine counts out my heartbeats, steady and strong.

"Ívar?" I ask the doctor, my heart rate rising. I pause, reaching awkwardly for more words. "My son. Ívar is my son."

My son. The words clunk around in my mouth like shoes in the washing machine. I can picture him in glimpses that vanish into white stretches, but he is not a dream. "My son, Ívar—he was with me," I say.

"Wait just a moment," he says. "I'll speak to the officer outside."

"Why are the police here?" My heart rate continues to climb.

"Don't worry. Don't excite yourself."

Time is hulking, hefty. The seconds slow to a slog; they don't want to press reality forward. A veil obscures the line between the imagined and the actual.

We were going for a walk. The memory strikes me, sudden and precise: Ívar was excited to go out. *Come on, Mamma,* he'd said.

You want to go out in the snow? I'd asked, shivering to make him laugh. Bursting with joy. *There's no leikskóli on weekends, our days to sing together and see the world. What then?*

It's too much. I force the memory out as a lump fixes itself in my throat, every cell frozen. A strange image: a frightened girl in a gingham apron, soup in a black crock, slices of delicate cake behind a glass case, shrimp like flower petals on smørrebrød. Did I make her up? No. I called out—right? Kjarvalsstaðir. Café. Everything went black.

Now everything is white, blank.

I need to find a way out of myself, out of this gargantuan grayness, to find Ívar.

I tear the needle out of my hand and clamber out of bed. Dizzy and drained, I steady myself on the bed's loose railing. The machine beeps quicker, quicker.

Another man barks, "Not so fast, my dear."

The harsh voice belongs to a man in a black uniform. He's younger than the doctor. Thank god he's being so loud, I think. If it was bad news—the worst news—then he'd speak softly. I stare at the air in front of him, waiting for him to continue.

A stern pause, and then he says, "I'm told you suffered two seizures in a row. They could have been fatal."

"But my son?" I hear myself as he must: shrill, stuck in my dread that I'll never see Ívar.

"We found him in one piece," the officer says, minimizing and jocular. "It's lucky we got there when we did."

My relief is inexpressible. "Lucky?"

"The little tyke made it all the way to Snorrabraut. He was waiting for a chance to cross the road. He'd already crossed a few streets on his own. I don't want to know what would've happened if he'd made it to the main road. Just lucky that man acted as fast as he did."

"What man?"

"The bystander who called us. I understand that he called the police, anyway. A little bit later, a girl at Kjarvalsstaðir called us, too, to say you'd collapsed in the café."

I close my eyes and try to recall the chain of events. Memories flash and fade, maybe fictions. I can see myself running in the snow, but I can't be sure of how much is real.

"So you found him?" I ask in a muted tone, relieved to hear myself form a complete sentence.

"We did—me and Dröfn, my partner. The boy handled himself well. He told us he was on the way to find a doctor for his mamma. I think he was trying to go to Domus Medica," he chuckles.

"*What?*" I snap.

"Já, he was determined to find a doctor. He's got an unusually strong sense of direction, and he's got grit for such a young kid. I tip my hat to him."

"Where is he?"

"With his father."

"He's okay?"

"I'd say so. He seemed pretty pleased with his ride in the police car," he says, adding charitably, "But he'll be happy to see you, of course."

4

He stands by the side of my bed. Laughter lights up his face, his golden locks. His baby teeth graze my cheek, little nips of love. Wasn't he going to the doctor? Or perhaps he was using the occasion to explore, like Palle when he wakes up alone in the world?

He laughs, and I am above the clouds on a peak at the edge of a precipice, where rock crumbles and tumbles into an abyss. But I'm surveying the beauty of the world—how the deep valleys, guarded by basalt bluffs, seem to glitter when the sun shines, and I see, I see the immense beauty of it all. The beauty is pain in my heart. One misstep, and everything is nothing, nothing if I fall.

"Mamma is here," I whisper as I breathe him in greedily, draw him into my arms, still uncertain whether he's a dream or flesh and blood. It's enough that he's here, my Ívar, in this strange room in which he doesn't fit. In which I shouldn't fit. He should never find out how frightened I feel, stitched into this sterile landscape with hypodermic needles.

"Come on, we'll let your mamma sleep," his pabbi whispers. I'm still floating in this new vision. The sensation is intense. Though short-lived, it stirs and settles throughout my limbs. "Now you know that Mamma is here," he whispers. "She just needs to nap."

"Mamma home!" Ívar objects.

His pabbi ushers him out with the promise of ice cream. The sound of them is swept away like shadows. No, no, stay, I long to call out, but I'm paralyzed in near slumber. My lips are stuck; my eyelids won't budge.

In this half sleep, I struggle to remember: Is he four? No, he must be three. He's three years old.

But didn't he just have his birthday?

A thunderclap rocks through my head; the ache in my shoulders intensifies. Somebody replaces the needle in my hand and tips a glass to my lips, but I sink despite my demanding thirst.

Darkness swells and melts together into a hard core that surrounds me as it forms little by little, a thick tube. The cylinder looks solid; it gleams pitch black in the light. I grab onto it, but it's made of something slippery and it rolls out of my fingers across a bleached floor. The light cuts into my eyes, then a shock of pain pierces my forehead and the nape of my neck.

I wake up crying. Somebody gives me an injection and adjusts the needle in my hand.

A man's voice: "Was that her third seizure in twenty-four hours?"

A woman's voice *mm-hmm*s: "And grand mal too."

I sink deeper and deeper into the hot dream until I glimpse bottom, the cylinder waiting there for me. Distracted by its mass, I can block out the light. It will burn my eyes. But I can't resist instinct.

My eyes: burning suns.

5

"Lost?"

"Já, elskan. I thought you knew—Bergur said you knew. He said you talked about it when he came with Ívar to visit you."

My heart is hammering. Acid is swimming in my stomach as I stare at her, my mother, who is torn to rags as she says, "They came yesterday morning, and thank god they were gone by the time you had your third seizure. Bergur said you were so happy to see Ívar."

I must look confused.

"Love, the police found Ívar. Don't you remember?"

"Wait. Is Ívar okay?"

"They extended your stay another day after the third seizure, but he's safe at home with his father. The last I heard, he and Bergur were having a boys' night, watching *Frozen*."

I watch my mother watch me while I try to make sense of all this information. Her eyes are decisive, but searching, and right now she can't hide that she's in pain in her arms or calves—somewhere. My mother is always in pain when she's tired. The worry lines over the bridge of her nose make her green eyes somehow seem more dramatic. She's thrown her usually carefully arranged hair—light red with little sprinkles of gray—into a careless topknot, braced with a claw clip. The bun sways above her white eyebrows and thin, freckled skin.

She looks at me affectionately as she pulls my sweater over my head and tinkers with my hair gingerly, saying, "They decided against sending you for more tests. I find it strange, although I guess it's because you have epilepsy."

"I don't remember much," I say, sighing into a slouch. I should have just lied.

"But you will remember eventually, I'd think. It's been over a decade since you last had a seizure," she reminds me, "but I remember you needed to sleep a hell of a lot after one. And back then, you only had one at a time. You must be exhausted after three. That's why your memory is fuzzy."

"I don't know, Mamma." I collapse into her embrace like the child I once was.

She's taken aback but wraps her thin arms around me as she asks, one last time, whether we should speak to the doctor. "I don't know how you were doing when he discharged you," she says, "but I'm sure you'd be allowed to stay another night if he saw you now."

"Maybe I'm improving. I think I'm starting to remember lots of things. But when I try to hold on to any one thought or memory, it slips away. I'd even forgotten how old Ívar is—but I remember now, I think. He's three, right?"

The lines in her forehead deepen as she tries to make sense of me.

"Right, Mamma?" I say, my voice cracking. "Is he three? Ívar? He's three, right?"

"Yes, elskan. Ívar is three and a half."

6

On the phone at home, days later, I try to focus on what is right in front of me. My apartment is different—I remember a Persian rug on the floor by the telephone bench, or something? It hurts to try to recall.

"We could buy some sort of GPS for Ívar," Bergur is saying. He tries to modulate the emotion in his voice as he rattles off increasingly condescending ideas on the other end of the line. "A specially fitted GPS armband, or something sewn into his clothes?"

Tears gather at the edges of my eyes, ready to push their way out. A pain shoots toward my head, and my stubbornness, a part of me for so long, can't keep it at bay.

"We'd keep the armband a little loose, of course," he continues, "considering how quickly he seems to outgrow his clothes." I shift on the telephone bench. I'm having trouble answering his questions because I can't make myself concentrate. I want to ask him why he isn't with me.

And why is he talking like everything is *normal*? I called him automatically—muscle memory and speed dial—to make sure he understood that I'd had another seizure. I have to talk to someone about it, and he's the most important of anyone.

"Is that so?" I mutter during an expectant pause in his monologue. The GPS idea is unlike him, to put it mildly. Under typical circumstances, it'd be me trying to sell him on safety gadgets for peace of mind, and he'd mumble nothing in response. He is the calm one; I, the stressed one.

A feeling surfaces of being slanted and skewed after my seizures in the old days. I don't remember the seizures themselves, but I remember the pervasive sense that everything around me was odd, far-off. I glimpse our family portrait in Ívar's toy trunk. He must have been playing with it. I bend toward the chest, tug it along the floor, and set the picture on the sideboard of the bench, leaning it against the wall. A bite of pain shoots through my body.

"Where are you?" I ask.

"At home, of course."

Of course. I feel a sudden tightness in my chest. In my mind, he's smiling at me with his Bergsvipur, that Bergur look, his good nature showing through as he winks, but the facts are becoming clearer. The Kodachrome slideshow in my head is flashing so fast I can't make out any individual image.

"Saga, are you listening to me?" Bergur asks. "Should we buy him something?"

"Isn't that just"—I inhale, exhale—"a false sense of security?" I put great care into each word. I'm still struggling to articulate my most delicate thoughts.

"No, no. We'll keep our eyes on him too," he says. "I'll just pop out and grab one."

I open my mouth to protest, but an oppressive drowsiness bears down on me, even bending my neck. I move to the recliner, where panic that I'll have another seizure seems to stiffen each limb in my body. Bergur sighs in resignation, asks why I always need to make all the decisions.

"How's that?" I say, the heaviness in my neck already gone.

"You're always so afraid for him—I can't understand why you're against this. We can't risk him wandering off again."

I want more than anything to tell him that I am not at all against the idea, but the accusation in his voice sets me off. "Don't you trust me?" My tongue is sore and swollen and tastes of old blood.

Silence.

"Bergur?"

"I trust you." He pauses. "I just don't trust your body."

"Served you two well enough so far." This comes out sharp, as if the words bit their way out.

"What served us? Your body?" he asks.

"Yes!"

"Okay . . . but you think it's acceptable to leave your son's life hanging in the balance between your ego and your next seizure?"

"Yes, I do," I snap, ferocious. He's so sanctimonious— our son's life in the *balance*? The old Bergur understood me well enough to pivot away from an argument with a quip. But this Bergur is stumbling, unsure of how to play this. And his hesitation pleases me. In our way, we're like a big sister and little brother, and we look that way in the family picture. His dark eyes gleam like Ívar's when he's joyful; my red hair twisted up and pinned in licks of fire. I look happy. This happier version of me deflates me.

The picture was taken on the day our son received his name—not at the hospital, but later, as is tradition: Ívar Bergsson, Bergur's son. We're holding him between us. He's tiny in his white baptismal gown. It was a sunny day, I remember—yes, I remember—and my blood starts to pump with health at the thought. It's clear as crystal, this solitary memory, settled, if a little fuzzy around the edges.

Bergur heaves a sigh. "I know it's difficult for you to talk to me with the way things are, but bickering helps no one," he says, "least of all Ívar."

Why am I acting so hostile toward him? I'm starting to feel dizzy. I need to ask him to come to me, but first I have to tell him that I don't understand why he's not here.

"Why don't you get some rest?" he says, his voice more conciliatory.

"I'm fine," I sigh, too tired to draw out the argument further. I try changing the subject. "Say, who picked me up from the hospital?"

"Today?"

"Yes."

"Don't you remember?" he asks.

"After a seizure, you're confused for a while," I say, defensive. "It affects your short-term memory."

"Are you sure that's normal?" He lowers his voice. "You don't sound like yourself, Saga."

"Yes, it's normal," I huff. "Who picked me up?"

"Well, your mother, of course."

He's barely finished the sentence when I remember my mother's strange tangle of hair at the hospital, how uncharacteristically unkempt and flustered she looked. I rock in my seat, searching for words, and settle on saying, "I'm fine; it's normal. I remember now. She opened the car door for me, fastened my seat belt, and smiled to put me at ease. She said something about Ívar. Ívar is with you, right?" I ask, careful to sound steady.

"Yes, but he's in leikskóli today. He's been with me every minute other than that, and I told him I'd pick him up after school. I thought that was the best thing for him, to keep him here, to keep things calm. He was really sensitive at first, as you might imagine." Bergur pauses. "Saga, you really don't remember how you got home?"

"No, no, I *do* remember it, I'm just a little confused. My memory is . . . taking a while to catch up. Because I just woke up." I can hear how slow my speech is, and it makes me worry that Bergur is going to accuse me of being abnormal again.

"Well, you had three major seizures. Do you remember anything that happened that day?" he asks.

"I remember almost everything," I snap. "And the rest is coming back. It was like this before. I haven't had a seizure in so long, so I forgot how they affect me."

"You never had one when we lived together," Bergur says, sounding wistful, even guilty. "Why now, Saga?"

24

"I don't know."

"Look, just don't work too hard. You need to take it easy."

"Right," I say, but I feel a new panic rising. Wait—work? Where do I work? What is my job? I put my hand over my mouth to stop the question.

"You have to think about Ívar," Bergur says, this time without accusation.

"I'm *only* thinking of him."

"I know, I'm sorry. That sounded too harsh," he mumbles, chastened. "I just think—well, I think it's a little more than just odd that you don't know how you got home from the hospital. Should you really take care of Ívar in this state?"

"Well, do you remember the name of the midwives who took care of Ívar when he was born?" I snap, realizing the question is going to sound just as ridiculous to him as it does to me.

"What are you talking about? Why should I remember that?"

"Their names were Hrafnhildur and Anna María," I answer with great seriousness, though I can tell I'm in free fall.

"Is that so?"

"Yes. I thought of them earlier, perhaps because I'd just gotten home from the hospital."

Bergur laughs. "You're right, I don't remember their names," he admits, chuckling when he says that that proves it—my memory is just fine.

"See?" I say. Meanwhile, these names repeat in quick

succession in my head, almost clanging in my skull. "The strangest thing is"—I pause to find the right words—"I don't think I remembered them before now."

"What do you mean?"

"Maybe because I . . . never really thought about it, but it just surfaced in my brain."

"It's probably because you were just in the hospital, like you had been after his birth," Bergur says, playing along. His voice softens. "Maybe I don't remember the names of the midwives, Saga, but I will never forget him lying there, still bloody from birth, across your chest. I remember when I held him for the first time, and the doctor hurried with him to the neonatal ICU."

"We remember that," I say, and my love for my son floods over me like a warm bath.

"Yes," he says, "we're not free from heartache. We have that. But now you have to lie down. I'm serious. Listen to me."

"I'm listening."

"Well, that's new," he snarks, then jumps to make up for it. "I'm sorry, I didn't mean to bring that up."

"It's okay," I say, bewildered. I don't want to fight with him. I just want to talk to him. Most of all, I want to ask him, Why aren't you here with me? But I can't do it. I don't want him to know that my memory is like scoria, full of holes and rust, or so it seems to me.

Now they're overtaking me, the names of the midwives: Hrafnhildur and Anna María. I hurry to say goodbye.

• • •

I hang up and look in the mirror in the entryway. The mirror I can trust. I smile at it. It smiles back at me, just as unnaturally.

"I came home this morning," I recite to my reflection, as clearly as I can. "Mamma picked me up. Ívar is with Bergur. I had three seizures. Mamma ran home to grab kjötsúpa. I don't need to be afraid. She's coming."

My mirror self stares back at me, harnessed in its heavy frame—a frame that Bergur found at Kolaport and refinished in our backyard on Ránargata on a warm summer day. "I remember that," I say smugly to the mirror, and the mirror seems to brighten.

Now I strain to open my eyes wide, to make sense of the distorted face that's supposed to be mine. My right eye is swallowed by swelling; the mossy-green circle at its center has sunken into a thicket of thorny red vessels. I stare, feral.

With all the melodrama of a teenager in love, Bergur often said that I had turbulent eyes. His words echo in my head now, conjuring him. This phrase of his has managed to survive inside of me. I feel like it's been so long since I've thought of it, recalled these words, but they're right here, unbidden.

I examine my features more closely. My lips are clownishly red; I'm not sure why. Lipstick? No, I see the outline of a rusty cut on my lower lip, where I must have bitten it. I don't notice the pain until I see the wound. It reminds me of ground beef still wrapped in its package of blood at the supermarket.

Truthfully, I look like I've been beaten. My forehead is

a deeper shade of purple than the cardigan Mamma knitted for me, my face swollen. The bridge of my nose is wide, too wide. It has always reminded me of a ski jump for ants, but it seems flatter now that it's sunken into the swelling that leads from my right eye to my left cheekbone. My hair is disheveled, especially my bangs, which lick upward instead of falling in a straight line over my brow. I look like a monstrous guinea pig—a sorry sight who hasn't got the faintest idea about anything, except a gut pain when I think about Bergur.

I can't be alone, it's easy to believe that. There's no warning before a seizure. I could collapse on the stairs. Somebody will have to check on me—knock on my door at least once in the morning and once in the evening—to make sure I'm safe, that I haven't lost consciousness and my capacity to call for help. But who should I call? And how? I lost my cell phone with all my contacts during one of the seizures that sent me to the hospital. There's nobody. No constant ringing, no incessant chatter. It isn't reassuring. Maybe somebody needs to reach me now, but all I have is a cordless phone with an unlisted number. I'm alone in the haze, on a strange planet.

7

There are white long-stemmed roses in a crystal vase in the center of the telephone bench. My first thought: Did somebody die? The pale flowers blend in with the snowy day out the window, but they're off somehow, a yellow shade that's not quite as light as the snow—one head bent, beginning to wither. Autumn is over; today, only winter.

The light makes my eyes smart when I enter the kitchen. They're still tender. A migraine coming on, maybe? The pain in my head is constant, worsening. Road ash from Miklabraut has settled on the waterworn frame of the kitchen window, reminding me that the windows needed work when we moved in; they're old and no longer keep out the soot from passing cars, even though we replaced the panes. Nothing came of all the things we intended to do, and now the windowsill is wet and the roof is slicked black. Snow has swept in through the gaps in the window seal and it's cold in the kitchen, hard to breathe.

My head jabs and casts me into a swerve, warping. The window traps a sudden scream inside. I pick up a cloth to wipe away the dirt, another to dry the water. Hopefully, there won't be any damage. Mold, maybe, that'd be the icing on the cake. . . .

On the sidewalk, a chubby older woman trudges along through snowdrifts, dragging a sort of sled behind her, loaded with sacks of mail. Orange jacket, black cap—I recognize her, and the recognition soothes me. My memories are smearing across fresh experience. I almost certainly don't know her. A passing car driving too close to the sidewalk splashes her. She carries on as if nothing happened, making her way like a tank, unconcerned with the heavy stream of traffic, determined to do her duty as I sink into a crouch.

Did Bergur and I talk about when Ívar would come home? Not today, no. When will he come to mine? What did we say?

I can't call back. I can't tell him about the stab of pain when I think about us. Everything becomes nothing. I remember little to nothing about the events of the past week, just fragments wading through fog. For instance, did I buy these roses? In my family, we buy white roses for funerals, and nobody's died. I raise my gaze, look straight ahead. My eyes land on the vase, its water nearly dried-up. I make my way to my feet and carry the vase over to the sink.

It's heavy. My legs are shoulder-width apart. Rush of traffic, rush of water. Dirty cars blink in quick succession: red, black, blue, but really, they're all gray. They run together in their grayness, the gray of stones, a dull gray line blurring, tunneling the rest of the scene into itself until I can see nothing else. My sudden separateness from the world snaps me awake. The water overflows the lip of the vase; I fumble to tip some back into the basin. As I do, two teenage jaywalkers dart across the main road and are nearly run down by a jeep. The crosswalk is thirty feet away from them.

They could have died for thirty feet, I think. One after another, teens take off across the highway. I should stand out on the sidewalk, grab them before they throw themselves into traffic. I don't want Ívar to mimic them like a dog that learns to chase cars from the hound next door. I can feel the pressure building behind my forehead, and I know I—

• • •

Has it passed?

Even when it's passed, pain still siphons energy from the body. It makes me ache with hunger. I had the same sensation after my seizures last time. Sickness is assertive. Nothing can quite satisfy lethargy, an inertia deep in the body.

Juice, I tell myself, instead of coffee. As soon as I've gulped down a glass of heilsusafi, I search for the coffee-maker. The headache isn't from caffeine withdrawal. It isn't a migraine. It seems to intensify when I focus on certain things, when my body is stressed in a particular way.

I feel like I've climbed the seven summits by the time the dark drops begin to jump on the base of the pot. Soon the carafe is full and simmering and the strong scent of coffee fills the apartment. I should eat something. My hands shake as I pick up an overripe banana, peel it, and eat as if my life depends on it. I finish the first banana and grab another before sliding onto a barstool next to the table.

Somebody must have given me the roses. Who? Maybe I should call somebody, just to be careful, in case something should happen. When is Ívar coming? I can still smell him, that fresh baby smell. I feel him—I *hear* him laughing as he shakes his tail like a puppy, play-tooting— prumpa, prumpa, prumpa. *Here, Mamma,* he calls, *here,* meaning, *Play with me.*

But he cannot trust me. Bergur said it, and I know it. The ache in my head is hot and sharp. It feels like a fire catching inside my skull.

I squeeze my eyelids closed.

The thoughts go up in smoke.

He cannot be with me.

Burning suns.

• • •

A strained chord peals from the doorbell just as the coffee boils. I rush to turn off the machine and hurry toward the sound. The door has already opened by the time I reach the foyer.

"Isn't your phone working?" Mamma calls in a raspy sort of bellow as she tears into the room, wearing a tailored pea coat and a colorful, chunky scarf. She's always been an

32

amalgam of a sagelike old lady and whimsical girl. Even her boots reflect this dual nature: wool-lined, kitten-heeled.

"It's fine," I say. "I was just on the phone with Bergur."

"I've been trying to call you since I dropped you at home," she says. "First the line was busy, and then nobody answered. I was terrified."

"What?"

"I got here as quickly as I could. You could have had another seizure," she says, trying to compose herself. "Or—do you think you had another?"

"No, I don't think so," I say, but I'm not certain.

"Ah, then you're fine," she says, brightening. "I ran home to grab the kjötsúpa. But we have to find a way to stay in better contact right now."

"I know," I say, doing my best to sound agreeable.

"Dídí, where should I set this pot?" I hear my pabbi call from behind her. He's the only person who calls my mother Dídí—a rather sugary nickname for Kristín—because he's the only one among us who knew Dídí, the young girl.

She dismisses him with a mumble, exchanging her half-practical shoes for her indoor ones—white clogs with plush red soles. Her back is stooped, but she's still light on her feet as she jets into the kitchen. She's hardly opened the refrigerator door when she exclaims, "Saga, it's a mess in here!"

I've never gotten used to how cheerful she sounds when she draws attention to something she finds upsetting, and I'm not certain how to respond now. My sister thinks her behavior is malicious. Our mother tries to be funny, I

33

think, but she misses the mark more often than not and says something awkward or spiteful. She's the opposite of my father, who is terrified of saying anything inappropriate—unless it's about politics, of course. Otherwise, he just mumbles something nobody can make out and chuckles quietly to himself.

"Saga, is this really suitable food for a three-year-old child?" she asks with artificial kindness, ransacking my fridge with one hand as she unwraps her scarf from around her neck with the other and tosses it on to the kitchen stool. Scarf off, I smell the myrrh and ylang-ylang oils she dabs onto her collarbone. "Dear god, Saga—how long have these merengues been here, or whatever they are?"

"They're from my birthday," I say. It sounds like a reasonable explanation to me, but I can't guarantee its veracity. My friend Tedda and her new girlfriend came with gifts a few nights ago, a gathering suddenly visible in precise detail: "Happy Birthday" out of tune, their arms stacked high with sweets, a caramel-trimmed torte from the bakery, macarons in all colors of the rainbow, a bottle of pink champagne. The thought of Tedda is warm and reassuring.

"You shouldn't save these sugary things," Mamma scolds. No sooner has she finished her sentence than she reaches for her wrist, wincing. She calls this chronic stab *fluid pain*, though she seldom tells us when she's having it. The fluid in her bones is sensitive to changes in air pressure, or so she says.

I mumble instead of answering, but having produced such a clear memory of her obscure condition gives me a sense of tranquility, as if my body wants to reward itself for recalling details.

She releases a tangle of hair from under her cap and unbuttons her coat, revealing a scoop-neck knitted dress, green as a grape. She must have knitted it recently. Her sewing magazines hide some real jewels, but her sole selection criterion is the color palette. It has to be distinctive enough for a woman who loves two things above all else: her children and wacky color combinations. I shake my head, trying to stem the flow of ridiculous details. The details, these details I'm obsessing over, feel like dreams, distant from my own life.

"Tell me where to set this pot down, Dídí. If I set it down in the wrong place, you'll get antsy. I know you," Pabbi says.

"Listen to Saga," Mamma says, looking impishly at me. There she is: girlish, even lanky, despite the crook in her back. Then she turns to Pabbi, grimacing again in pain, and grabs a little plastic box from atop the pot in his arms. "It's chopped vegetables for Ívar," she says. "Carrots, peppers, and cucumbers."

"Thanks, Mamma," I say, but I don't know whether I should be grateful or offended. I mean, I can feed my son adequately without her input.

"Nothing to thank me for," she says, thrusting her hand into her coat pocket, from which she magically pulls out a tulip-yellow cloth that she wraps into an apron around her waist and fastens with a knot. She fans her swollen fingers before she takes a cake dish covered with yellowing blobs of meringue out of the fridge.

"Ívar and I were going to finish those leftover treats after our walk. But we didn't," I explain slowly, still laboring to speak in coherent sentences, maybe because I'm not sure if it happened that way or not. A feeling of guilt claws at me. Ívar was looking forward to those leftovers— and didn't I promise him cocoa? Am I remembering right, or do I just think that was the more likely scenario? The memory of Ívar butts up against one of Tedda singing at my birthday.

My mother shoots me a pitying look. She makes her way over to me and says, "Hush, my Saga. Don't blame yourself."

"I'm not," I say, she hands me her coat and the plastic box of vegetables. She's so thin and crooked, I suddenly feel as if I'll buckle under the weight of my affection for her. She's slight, but so hectic in her expressions that, despite all frailty, her presence hums through the apartment.

"Oh, yuck! It's started to mold," Mamma shrieks, winding around to face me. "Saga, let me clean out the fridge and send the boys out to buy something healthier for Ívar."

• • •

Why don't you put the book aside for now and finish your article, instead of working on the book and worrying about the article at the same time? Just keep them separate and you'll be fine.

Stop telling me what to do, Saga.

I'm not.

You are.

36

No, I'm just offering you advice, Bergur.
Isn't it hard, living that way?
What way?
Always needing to give everybody advice.

• • •

"Hello, hello, let Mamma focus," I hear from behind me. My brother Guðni has arrived with a freshly baked bread wrapped in a tea towel. "I see you two have moved in?"

Pabbi shakes his head. He is still standing in the entryway, holding the soup. Guðni dries the snow off his clean-shaven face and slides off his heavy coat, shooting me a smile.

Mamma pops her head out from behind the fridge door when Guðni walks into the kitchen. "Everything's gone bad," she fusses.

"I'm fine," I protest, but I'm feeling so emotional that the bleakness might as well be leaking out of me.

"I didn't mean that you're bad. I mean that everything in your fridge has gone bad," she says, laughing.

"But I'm not that bad. I'm fine."

"Listen to yourself," she protests, shooting me an indulgent smile, but there's fear in her eyes. She's afraid I'll see that she's afraid for me. I know that because the next moment, she averts her eyes from me and focuses on Guðni, who always puts her in a good mood.

"And Saga, how are you doing?" he asks in his cordial way, but there's warmth in his voice. He kisses me on my cheek before setting down the bread.

"I'm just fine, thanks."

Mamma pours him a cup of coffee. He's grown some peach fuzz the color of his freckles, and he's wearing a white uniform cap that hides his receding hairline. He's excellent at making peace between warring parties.

"Why don't you go to lie down for a bit? Mamma's soup will be ready by the time you're up."

"Are you working these days?" I ask, annoyed that everyone is trying to send me to bed.

Guðni narrows his eyes, lifts his hand to his cap as if he's about to take it off, and instead wraps Mamma in a hug that makes her chirp with delight. Her boy is the only one who can hug her this effortlessly and he knows it; he's pleased with himself when he finally sets aside his cap. It's a police hat, or it looks like it belongs to a police uniform. Maybe he bought it in Copenhagen. I remember he took some training course through the Danish police. Or is it a sailor's hat? I think I remember that.

"When is Ívar coming home?" Mamma asks, still digging in the fridge. I think I know for certain that she was once sincere, surrounding, and soft with me, but I can't remember her embrace. I can only feel the loss of it, as if it will never happen again.

"I don't know," I say, and the feeling that I'm a burden descends upon me.

She hears it in my voice and steps away from the fridge to get a good look. Her eyes flicker with some sort of ancient love when she asks, "Now, what's going on?"

"I just don't know," I avoid her eyes, adding that maybe Guðni has the right idea.

"What's that idea, love?" she asks, looking at my brother.

"I mean, it's a good idea for me to lie down for a bit," I say. "Wake me up in half an hour?"

"Let's make it an hour," Mamma says, frowning at the refrigerator.

8

A deep pain in my muscles wakes me, but my body slackens when the scent of kjötsúpa wafts into my room. As kids, in our family kitchen in Hafnarfjörður, Pabbi used to tell us a story about a crafty woman who claimed she could make a delicious soup from nails. One day, she put nails into a pot of boiling water and then tricked her neighbor into supplying real ingredients, like carrots, bits of meat, and rice. With each addition, the soup became heartier. In the end, the nail soup was succulent and filling, just like the woman said it would be.

Well, we were just as gullible as the man who supplied the ingredients for nail soup. Pabbi told the story each time Mamma made kjötsúpa, which was often. But he also told it when the three of us—me, my sister, and my pabbi—made soup together. His deep-blue eyes followed us as we sprinkled herbs and vegetables and anything else we thought belonged into the pot: dried blóðberg from a jam jar, chives, scallions, carrots, potatoes, turnips, and celery. Jóhanna would root through the shelves for anything that might suit our concoction. When she was older, she played both roles—the gullible man and the trickster woman—and added even more narrative detail because she knew better than Pabbi what belonged in the soup. Her gangly body moved authoritatively through the room and past the staircase as the windowpane reflected Pabbi with Guðni in his arms, looking out into the darkness. Guðni cried and cried for Mamma—he always wanted to be with her when he was young.

My head hurts. The scene tumbles over me in hyper-clarity but then fizzles away, as if I'm a television with a broken transistor. My body is heavy with sleep. Did I sleep? I feel as if I've dreamt the nail soup memory, probably because the scent of Mamma's cooking made its way into the room while I was resting. Little by little, the pain in my head gives way to strength. It's always that way with old stories—they give a sense of safety and comfort, like the arms of a parent.

The smell reminds me of "Ugluspegill," another tale my father used to tell us. The story goes that Ugluspegill grew so sick and tired of waiting for food at a boarding-house that he sated himself with the scent of food alone. Furious at the loss of income, the owner charged him a "smelling fee" for his meals, so Ugluspegill paid with the sound of money.

Pabbi loved to tell us stories—he was a bookish man who collected the sagas of the Icelanders, poetry, adventurous stories of travelers far and wide. Sometimes, he read the stories from his books, savoring every word like a hard, sweet candy while my sister and I listened, enchanted. Guðni, still quite young, amused himself in the corner with small stones, Matchbox cars, and the skulls of birds he found on walks with Pabbi on the shoreline and over lava fields. My father understood that some people find it more interesting to stack stones than to listen to stories.

He also read us the story of Nasreddin, who wanted to wean his wife from her gossiping, so he confided to her that he had laid an egg. She broadcast the scandal all around town, making herself into a laughingstock.

Did I remember that last story right? I don't know, but each memory I see through to the end seems to indicate I'm improving. Pabbi used to say that I wasn't called Saga for nothing—the name had been searching for a little girl who loved stories as much as I did. I inhaled them, savoring each syrupy word, and I built myself a nest of tales, perched in my pabbi's strong arms. Whenever he tired of doing the telling, I told him stories. I do the same with Bergur, giving him ideas when he runs out.

Saga was lucky enough to marry an author, Pabbi said in his speech at our wedding, and everyone laughed. I remember that young woman and I smile, proud of her. Bergur asked me later on whether I had ever wanted to be a writer. *No*, I told him, which was the truth. I'm just like my aunt Elínborg, who loved music but was kicked out of her choir because she couldn't carry a tune. She cried over choral music and locked herself away for days at a time with operas she'd recorded on TV. *Somebody is going to listen*, she said to comfort herself when I visited her as a little girl, Jóhanna in tow, long after Mamma had stopped visiting her own sister, who she dismissed as a "snob."·

Why am I thinking about her? I haven't thought of her in years—hardly at all since I was a teenager. She died in hospice, literally while listening to a recording of the Hamrahlíð Choir. It happened right after my mother visited her and ended all those years of estrangement. She faded away with a smile on her lips, as if she'd finally been able to become one with the music.

Elínborg spent her entire life as a customs agent and did not die alone. She died with music. If her customers had only known how that stooped-over woman, wild with curls, cried over choir music . . . maybe they would have smiled back at her once or twice. Her last smile had had a profound effect on me: it allowed me to overcome the terror—then, as now—that I would die alone with my son.

I've thought about Bergur's question.

• • •

I remember us, then.

Saga is a beautiful name, he said right after we met.

It was a Thursday. We were both working with the gardener, both in oversized rainsuits.

I think you must keep entire worlds inside of you, Saga, because of your name, he said. I smiled, so impressed with his own unabashed earnestness that it didn't occur to me to roll my eyes. We were covered in mud up to our knees, shoveling earth into a machine that separated stones from soil, but I stole a glance at him when he wasn't looking. Even then, his face was strong, his lips soft. He's always had an athletic physique; in high school, he was a star swimmer and always popular with everyone, especially girls. Later, I realized he had a blind competitive streak. But none of it made any difference to me when we'd meet up at Lækjartorg—after we'd both scrubbed the dirt out of our skin—to drink and kiss. He tasted of landi, Iceland's moonshine. I must have tasted like the Dubonnet Tedda had nabbed from her mother's liquor cabinet.

He was a seventeen-year-old romantic, determined to become an author and to be with Saga. Saga wasn't a popular name back then. I was singular; a singular story. He wrote, I read, we were *meant to be*.

I broke up with him shortly before my twentieth birthday, when I moved to Denmark to study. It was the first time in my life that I'd paid rent—and, accordingly, I wanted to try new things. I wanted a boyfriend who lived in the same city, or the same country, for that matter. I could see Bergur struggled to empathize, but he did his best. We didn't see each other for five years. We tried out new relationships, countries, fashions; music, books, movies, and plays; group exhibitions in our friends' studios. We were swept up by politics, grassroots activism, sex, psychedelics, and learning to cook: the most effective ways to feel we'd gone off on our own.

Bergur lived to the fullest: he studied English in university, then philosophy in Berlin, then Spanish in Madrid. He was a bibliophile by nature, but his interests were far too unfocused for an academic; his work as an author better suited the diversity of his callings. He'd spend one hour writing a poem about shellfish and another writing about the stacks of novels stuffed like sausages on the shelves in the discount supermarkets during the yearly autumnal bókaflóð. Once, he published a noir written as a series of sonnets. (Even recently, he called himself a *scholar of Facebook* in an interview.) Throughout his twenties, he was inexhaustible, creative, and measured— unlike me. The only thing I could think to do was go to Copenhagen.

The seizures began during those manic years. Bergur is right when he says I never had a seizure while we were together. I think.

Five years of seizures are tucked away in my memory somewhere, but the amnesia they caused purged the boring rounds of drinks, days of hangover depression. I'd wake up in the hospital, mumbling in a half sleep in clean-smelling clothes. My mother would sit by the side of the bed with a Snickers or a Coke for me. *You have to get some sugar in you, you have to hydrate,* she'd chant in a subdued coo, not at all like her usual tone. Hair knotted back, skin scrubbed of makeup, I'd felt she was vulnerable in her plainness, yet her composure kept her at a distance. Even when it seemed as if she might tumble out of herself, she lingered close to me. I took her in—scared, gentle, resigned. I sucked down the sugar. When I was in Copenhagen, it seemed like my mother had finally focused all of her energy on me. Every Saturday and Sunday, she would call me at noon just to make sure I'd answer the phone. If my flatmate, Pia, answered, my mamma would pressure her into knocking on my door, even when a stranger's boots were in the hall. I wish I could wake up in the hospital to her sitting sideways on my bed again.

In those years, I'd drink myself into oblivion every weekend, even though I knew the alcohol was likely to trigger a seizure. On those nights, which were always wild, I worried I'd collapse the next morning on the way to my summer job or in the cafeteria at university. Nights out were a game of Russian roulette. *It's better to oversleep in the emergency room than to show up at work with a hangover,* I once said to a friend. I'm afraid I wasn't being glib.

I remember.

Pia in a mossy-green sweater and tight jeans. The bike I painted pink so it wouldn't get stolen. Chugging beer at a pub in Nørrebro. Splashing in the sea in summer. The aroma of roasted almonds in winter. Bicycle lanterns like burning butterflies on a black, wind-stilled night. I remember falling asleep alone, waking up alone. Solitude.

By my twenty-fifth birthday, though, I'd had enough. I moved home. One night, at a party in my apartment, I got drunk enough to call Bergur. I'd looked him up more than once on the internet; I knew he didn't have kids or a partner. He was constantly traveling to exotic locales, and he'd published two very successful books—a novel and a book of poems. The teenager who'd so memorably said *Saga is a beautiful name* showed up to the party half an hour after I called.

The next day, he helped me to empty ashtrays heaped with cigarette butts and scrubbed the floor, sticky with alcohol from the party. After that, he moved his things out of his cubbyhole in the countryside and into my cubbyhole in the city. The seizures stopped that day. I loved living with him—he calmed me down, countering my doubts

46

with careful observations before they overpowered me. He'd tease me when I felt sorry for myself. *You are the person I'm mostly basing the character on—critical but generous.* He leaned forward to kiss me. I had leaned away, feigning indignance, though flattered.

I remember, yes, I remember.

We made recipes we'd discovered during our time apart, although mine were fewer and less gourmet than his. He introduced me to books I never had time to read, and I shared the music and movies I'd gathered in my travels. We argued from time to time, griping over the small things, but then we'd lose ourselves in kisses. We'd make love and then continue to fight, laughing, but listening to each other's arguments while moving through each other. We could always make each other smile. Once when I was listening to Jóhanna drone on about something on the telephone, he shot me such a sarcastic look that I fell apart on the spot, choking down my laughter until I could end the call and tear his clothes off. And from our love story was born another larger story, larger than us, because Ívar was born six years after we moved in together. Our happiness grew to a fever—that, I remember. What happened then?

Memory is a foreign body moving under my skin, a pressure building behind my forehead and my temples. I massage my eyes and try to bring the images into focus. But the more I try to summon our more recent past, the more intense the pain becomes, the more the memories flicker. I can think about us at the beginning, but later, everything becomes so unclear, and—

"Is Saga acting like you'd expect?" My brother's voice wafts up from the kitchen and wedges itself between my pain and the memory. He sounds suspicious.

"What do you mean, love?" Mamma inhales this question as she says it, as if it frightens her.

"Just—I'm a bit surprised that she'd actually take anyone's advice to rest."

"Oh, she's *exhausted*, Guðni."

"No shit." Another voice enters the conversation, calm and rational. Jóhanna.

9

"You've been asleep for almost two hours," Mamma hums, surveying me as I drag myself into the kitchen. She hands me a glass of water and shushes me whenever I open my mouth, meaning that I have to drink before we can talk.

I take a few big gulps, then ask, "Did Bergur call?"

"No, my love. But pull up your socks. We're heating up the soup. The kids are starving."

The kids—Jóhanna, who's nearly forty, and Guðni, well past thirty—exchange glances. He's amused, but she seems annoyed by our mother. Jóhanna swishes over to me and wraps me in a big, sighing hug. "I was so worried about you," she says.

I tell her I've come out of it all okay and she beams at me encouragingly, but the ridiculousness of my situation is starting to hit home. I feel like I've stepped into a time machine. When was the last time we were all together at the table?

Fragments of family tableaus flash through my mind's eye and land on a scene.

• • •

I'm looking at my brother in the kitchen, boyish, without the least bit of angst. He's standing in the space between the fridge and wall, eavesdropping on a heated argument our parents are having about the new power plant at Kárahnjúkur. Pabbi thinks it's an outrage, but Mamma is in favor of the plant's construction—but only if they're going to use its resources to provide power to the public and not the aluminum companies, Iceland's cash cow. She is a country girl and a member of the Progressive Party, which is in fact center-right. She hasn't yet formed an opinion about how we should protect the environment. But shortly thereafter, her environmentalist side will burst forth with a vengeance after a visit to the homeo-pathic apothecary, where an idealistic cashier converts her into a supporter of the liberal Left-Green Movement, Pabbi's party. He'd known that she'd come over to his side, because as he puts it, they both love their country and the land it stands on, as well as the bright, crisp May sunlight. Guðni, who claims to see the merits of both sides, is most interested in keeping the peace, although he leans more toward our mother's side in the end, as he often does in such matters.

• • •

This must've been over a decade ago. Surfacing a mundane late afternoon, an afternoon that didn't matter at all and from so long ago, feels odd.

With her self-satisfied look, my mother hands me five soup bowls with gilded edges, saved from her parents' farm. She turns back to her brimming pot of soup with a movement that's familiar to me: easy and purposeful. I remember the managerial poise with which she delegated chores to me countless times. I'm finding myself mesmerized by the way her nest of hair bobs in step with her movements. She has piled it in a bun on top of her head like a ballerina, her move to draw attention up and away from the fine lines fanning the corners of her mouth and eyes.

Jóhanna and Guðni gather up spoons and knives and the loaf of warm bread wrapped in a tea towel. Guðni sneakily gives our mother a sidelong glance, as if to read her body language as he would a suspect in an interrogation. He and my father wear the same expression when they worry about my mother—furrowed eyebrows and quizzical mouth—and it looks like they're both concerned about her. Or maybe it's just Pabbi's genes making themselves known as my brother ages: in Guðni's face, my mother's eyes meld with my father's heavy expressions.

They set the table in the living room and Jóhanna lights a candle. Guðni sits at the piano and taps the keys, playing by ear. He finds a melody that Jóhanna, now leaning on the top lid, can hum along with. My mother has always said that Guðni has music in him and that it's a shame she and our father were so slow to notice it, though I doubt they had the money to pay for music lessons.

The stabbing in my temples finally begins to relent. In its place, I feel the heavy beating of my heart. I blink back the urge to wrap my arms around Guðni, who's sitting with his back straight, stroking the keys as he sings. This hulking man with broad shoulders and stubby fingers is filled with music. His cashmere sweater, worn over a finely pinstriped dress shirt, looks like something intended for someone twice his age. I recall that he appreciates fine garments, colors, shapes, cuts—and as this certainty emerges in my consciousness, I wonder if my memory is trying to right itself by feeding me this trivial information when there must be consequential knowledge right there, too—but it's safer not to think about it.

I run my fingers over the tablecloth. Burgundy brocade. Mamma must have dug it out of the closet; although it's an heirloom from my amma, I haven't laid eyes on it in years. When I turn back to the kitchen, Mamma has lifted the roses out of the vase and is busily clipping the tips of their stems to extend their lives. "Who gave you these roses?" she asks.

I don't know, so I pretend not to hear her and open the refrigerator, fumbling for something to add to the spread on the table.

I find a dish of butter and I'm already on my way out of the kitchen when Mamma exclaims, "Ah! Was it that kid's parents?"

"Yes," I say, agitated at the lie but aware that she'd drown herself in unfounded concern if she were to grasp the extent of my memory loss. I don't know where the white roses came from, but if I tell her that, she'll overreact and take drastic steps like calling her former schoolmate, a doctor in Borgarnes who prescribes her pain pills.

"What do you think Ívar is doing?" I say. "Should I call? I don't want to interrupt them if they're eating dinner."

"Saga, you're in no state for that," Mamma says, taking the butter from me. "Okay, out, out!" She shoos me away with a flick of her wrist, which causes her visible pain.

"Come here, sing with us," Jóhanna calls. I'm pacing in my own living room, not sure what to do with myself. My sister reaches out her hand, as if she's going to hug me, but I hold back and so she looks down. I find vulnerability difficult. Under normal circumstances, I'd be in charge in my own kitchen. In our small household, as recently as last week, I'd be tweaking the spices while Ívar plays with his train in the front room.

With almost childlike sincerity, they begin to sing "I Dwell in Dream Mountain," and Jóhanna submerges herself in the song—certain, focused, in tune. Since they're simple childhood songs, neither she nor Guðni looks at the sheet music I dug out of the piano bench for Ívar. When I sat with him to teach him one afternoon, I discovered that he, too, already knew them. He'd learned them in musical arts at leikskóli, his old leikskóli—he's at a new school now, I remember, feeling flushed, heat rising in my cheeks. I'm sweating.

"Dinner is served!" Mamma singsongs, prompting Pabbi to bolt out of the bathroom. My siblings' song peters out as I haul myself into a chair at the table, the room spinning around me. We are a family. We were once the quintessential nuclear family. But something is wrong with us. I can't quite put my finger on it, but I know it's true. Mamma ladles out soup; I can tell she's glad we're all

53

here, gathered around the table, but she can't quite hide the exhaustion in her body, the worry impressed upon her face. Why is she stressed?

My father is staring at her. A confluence of love, shame, and fear gathers in his eyes, as if he's anticipating a storm. Mamma smiles up at him, quelling his dread like a sedative. Moments later, as she's passing the bread, a flame from the candle Jóhanna lit before dinner licks her sleeve and, like that, she looks put off. She demands to know what purpose this *fire hazard* serves at the dinner table.

"Just trying to make the room a little cozy," Jóhanna says, ashamed.

"Sometimes you're just ridiculous," Mamma huffs as she blows out the candle. She has a mischievous glint in her eye, which is her way of softening her criticism, but Jóhanna doesn't see the glint. She's focused on Mamma's movements, like Pabbi. Mamma once seemed strong—her dainty, hypersensitive body was like a ballerina who builds strength to become light. Now, she needs to use all her strength to maintain the illusion of health.

Another odd feeling washes over me. I see my sister; I feel her discomfort. Our perceptions seem to run together in a cascade of clashing colors.

Pabbi and Guðni have taken refuge in one another, engaged in a hushed conversation at the end of the table, letting Mamma's exchange with Jóhanna reach their ears and wash over their backs like water. My father is telling Guðni about his "organization," which is really a few grouchy men who meet once a week to draft a declaration protesting *the clockwork of society* and rail against bankers and politicians.

"Where are you going to protest?" Guðni asks, with the knowing caution of a cop. The old diehards have become so political that in the last few elections, they even talked each other into putting the Left-Green Movement aside to vote for the so-called Democracy Watch Party in the hope of shaking up the three-party system. They later found themselves allied with Left-Green—though Mamma was swept up by the radical Pirate Party—but Pabbi was occupied by his sense of adventure and his bosom buddy in politics, Jörmundur, who was at that time attempting to found yet another party, maybe taking the lead from Jón Gnarr's Besti flokkurinn, if I remember correctly. And I'm not sure that I do.

Pabbi is getting more animated, crossing and uncrossing his arms over his stomach. I find myself focusing on how his wine-red shirt clashes with his blue striped belt. I'd guess that Mamma was trying to dress him up a bit with the new shirt, and then he dug the belt out of the back of their closet.

"Jörmundur is going to blitz the entire thing," he boasts. "But first we have to finish the manifesto, of course."

"Alla Budda's slob of a husband?" Mamma crows, winking conspiratorially at me, as if we're comrades-in-arms in the struggle against Jörmundur. She only pays attention when my father's conversations become gossipy enough for her. "I hope you know what you're doing, hanging around with those idiots!"

"I was talking to Guðni," Pabbi says, not looking

at Mamma, but I know he took her words in. When it really comes down to it, Mamma is the idealist, the one who drives them toward voting for the greatest public good. Pabbi's gaze darts between us siblings; his eyes look soft, like a faithful dog, under his mop of dark hair, now peppered gray. The bags under his eyes are a deep shade of purple, which contrast with his blue irises. The overall effect reminds me of his clashing shirt and belt combination.

"I wouldn't give much for a revolution if that piss-poor ringleader of yours is going to—what did you say?" Mamma snickers. "I mean, *blitz*? You've started to use slang?"

Pabbi stiffens but has the sense to take a deep breath before he comes to his own defense. "Isn't it more of a loanword?"

"Why are you talking about a revolution?" Guðni asks. "The people who run this country need a break; don't you get that? The parliament is the actual workplace of democratically elected officials, and all of these mobbish protests on government grounds—Austurvöllur, lobbing skyr at government buildings, I mean—are just disruptive. They take away time from decisions, committees, actual governing. Do you want to end up like Syria, with no leadership at all?"

"Guðni, come on—they're all talk," Jóhanna giggles.

"Let your brother finish," Mamma orders, passing me a cutting board loaded with the bread she's just sliced.

"Am I stopping him?" Jóhanna glares at Mamma with the sudden defiance of a teenage girl, but our mother just shrugs her shoulders: accusation by dismissal. I hand Guðni the bread without looking at Jóhanna or our mother as the argument drags on. The merry mother, always on the offensive; the angry daughter, always on her guard. It's strange to see their dynamic because Jóhanna is otherwise trusting; her style of communicating with Mamma is usually concise and free of malice. Still, you'd hardly know they're mother and daughter; they're so different in manner, and even looks.

Jóhanna has the darkest hair in the family, even darker than Pabbi's. Our father is strangely certain that he's descended from seventeenth-century Basque sailors—or, at the very least, from the French—and says that's why Jóhanna has such dark locks. She wears it clipped short, but with bangs long enough to brush across her deep, navy-blue eyes, so dark they look almost black. Unlike the rest of us, she's built a bit bulky, even though she's been on a strict diet her entire life. She seems to gain weight every year; no amount of working out changes that.

Now she's spilled her soup, the wet rice clinging to the front of her sweater. Jóhanna is the clumsiest member of the family, Mamma always says.

My mother wants to believe we're ladylike, although she never says it aloud. Jóhanna looks down on the idea of "refinement" and would have sent her daughter, Hallgerður, to a feminist academy nine years ago, if they'd existed then. She's still disappointed that the little one arrived before the Free the Nipple campaign made it to Reykjavík. *There'll be other revolutions*, she told Hallgerður, who believes her mother knows everything.

It's nice to think of Hallgerður, my charming little niece, who looks so much like me and whose very existence gave me the courage to have my own child. But Mamma has always been critical of these feminist leanings in her daughter and granddaughter. She claims she's afraid that Jóhanna's son, Grímur, who's a firecracker at chess but otherwise very reserved, feels excluded by his mother's preoccupation with "female nonsense."

It's not like we're remarkable! We carry around a womb and all those other icky organs. Some women seem like they think about nothing else—just their little flower, all the time. Don't be like that, Jóhanna. You have to think about your little boy now, too, she said once, brimming with good intentions but leaving Jóhanna speechless for what might have been the first time in her life. I feel similarly shocked by her vehemence against her own gender, now that the sentence is replaying in my head. When exactly did she say that? I don't remember, although the image of it is tidy in my mind, like a scene from a play, almost. Slides flash at random, but the audio playing along with these fragments rushes through my brain, as if I'm listening to a radio. I choke down a moan, swallowing it so nobody will hear.

The racket in my head is growing. I sink into my chair, but the negative thought hits me over and over again: Ívar is not with me. I need to calm myself, to still the clatter.

"You've hardly eaten, Saga," Mamma says, fine wrinkles worrying her brow.

I spoon a few morsels into my mouth and smile at her.

"Why don't you settle in, honey, and eat your own meal?" Pabbi says to her, but he sinks back into his seat when she looks at him reprovingly in response. He should know better, the poor fool.

I understand my mother. But I still can't seem to shake the feeling that I'm an alien who woke up on the kitchen floor of my family's house one day and convinced them that I was one of them: my mother's beloved, wished-for alien. She and I always flipped through her *Vogue* magazines and sewing patterns she kept in a leather folder—things the others had no interest in, like keeping up with fashion, healthy recipes, decor. All the things my mother and I know spice up life.

Jóhanna loves to garden. In the summer, she lives for that garden, but in winter, when the sun hardly makes its way over the mountains, she relies on her therapist. She never bothers with therapy during summer, when the days are bright. But she doesn't understand why my mother and I talk endlessly about how to make moss soup or the next round of spring sales.

The hours my mother and I pass together are warm and full, hours that Mamma looks forward to because she only has casual acquaintances—she worked as a legal secretary all her life and has never had a close friend. I am the best friend who sits with her on Saturday mornings, chewing on nicotine gum and dishing over the tabloids with their endless supply of woefully funny scandals. (More than anything, Mamma is tickled by the kitschy rich and tactless politicians. She's also extremely contemptuous of Icelanders who know nothing about the sustainable use of Icelandic herbs.) In the olden days, she'd wear a worn plush robe during our gossip sessions. Now, she finally has the means to buy herself new bathrobes whenever she wants. I remember how she'd wiggle her lacquered toenails before painting her fingernails. I felt joy—hers and mine—watching her wrap her red-dyed tresses around hot rollers.

We used to laugh together at Jóhanna's self-righteousness. Jóhanna would want to dive into the deep end with our mother, connecting with and understanding Mamma via her own interest in psychology and philosophy. But Mamma could parry expertly; she'd ask whether Jóhanna wasn't just a little too chubby to fit on the couch with us while we flipped through *Vogue*.

My father at least somewhat made up for the rejection. Like my sister, he enjoys gardening, even though psychologists make him squirm.

"What's the plan for Saga tonight?" Pabbi asks.

"Why think about that right now?" My mother lifts her eyebrows in a warning as she adjusts her hair clip.

"Shouldn't somebody stay with her?" he asks, calm but serious. He picks up his napkin and wipes his mouth without looking at Mamma. The movements of his hands are artificially smooth and measured, like the expression in his eyes: firm but fraught, as if on guard. Sometimes I think he has to put all his energy into keeping his feelings contained. He must believe that, too—isn't that the reason he hikes in the mountains every weekend? He's an alien, too, in his way.

He named me. When I was born a couple years later, it was his turn to choose a name; my mother had named Jóhanna after her mother. He considered me for a long moment before settling on Saga. Mamma thought it was absurd—*does the electrician suddenly believe he's a poet?* But he ignored her objections and she tuckered out.

"How about Guðni?" Mamma says, looking at her son, who's busy slurping up spoonfuls of soup as if he hasn't heard a word of the conversation.

"Isn't it better if Jóhanna stays with her?" Pabbi responds, looking at his eldest daughter, who shrugs before shooting me a look that asks, *Do you want that?*

"It's definitely better than being alone," I say. I'm fully aware that it would be worse to have Guðni stay with me: we'll either talk about his sailing club or Bergur's "dangerous" political correctness, whatever that means in Guðni's world. Or he might just keep to himself the entire time, and his proximity will feel overbearing.

"All right, then. I'll call Doddi." Jóhanna sighs. "And tell him to put the kids to bed."

"Do it right away, elskan," Mamma says, ladling more soup into Jóhanna's bowl. My father and brother are back in their conversation; this time, it's about a foreign drug ring in Iceland that Guðni's worried about. Pabbi is proud of his son.

I silently count to fifty. Ívar's absence is intolerable. *I remember your expression when I ran to grab a toothbrush, and you thought I'd disappeared, and your face filled with relief when I reappeared in the doorway. We were going to go the long way, then eat the leftovers from my birthday and drink hot chocolate.* I have to call him.

"Do you want more soup, Saga?" Mamma asks, as if my house is now hers.

"No, I need to go to the bathroom."

"Are you having cramps?"

"No, I just forgot something earlier. I need to pee." I push my panicky feelings down. I can't call Ívar, not with my parents here.

When they've finally gone home, it's well past nine o'clock.

"Don't call now, Saga dear," Jóhanna presses softly. "Ívar has already gone to bed."

"It's not that late," I protest. My chest is tight.

"It is, Saga. Call tomorrow."

"Then he'll be in leikskóli."

"It's not good to wake him, you know that. Besides, you have to rest. I can see it. Come on, I'll sit with you until you nod off."

10

"None of this would've happened if you still lived at the old place," Jóhanna says, sitting at my bedside and fiddling with a book on the end table: *Makers of Modern Theater: An Introduction.* The book came from an antiquarian bookstore on Hverfisgata, Bókin Antikvariat. She and her husband, Doddi, gave it to Bergur and me as a wedding gift. I'm puzzled by the book's presence but seem to remember reading it.

By "the old place," I think Jóhanna means our old apartment. I picture the stretch along Ránargata on a summer evening.

"I came across a man with some really compelling ideas about place and destiny. I think it was an old rabbi in a Woody Allen film," Jóhanna muses. As soon as she says it, she seems embarrassed by the reference to her old idol, now accused of molesting his own child. She sighs. "No, you know, I think I saw him in an old documentary about the unequal distribution of wealth."

She smooths the light blue duvet, tucks it around me, and says that the man in the movie had said that your fate is defined by the place you settle. In a different place, you are a different person.

"I understand," I say, although I don't. I take inventory of our location: a spacious, bright bedroom with vintage night stands, a double bed, a wooden dresser under a large window, and Ívar's toddler bed, which is usually vacant because he always crawls into my bed. The room strikes me as awkward; my connection to this furniture seems to be in my imagination. The feeling of disconnection is too strange to compute. Jóhanna slips the pillow out from under my head to fluff it.

"Are you thirsty or anything?"

"No," I say.

"You and Bergur seemed fine until you found the mold," she sighs.

Ránargata! It was comfortable; I can see the warm colors and smell the scent of food on the stove. I can picture our living room, cluttered and messy but always welcoming. She must mean that everything was fine with us before we moved away from Ránargata. I have difficulty picturing us there, my memory crackling like the evening Pabbi's ancient projector broke, but I can place us in the old apartment.

In my head, we're either eating or getting ready for bed. I remember Ívar's first night in the bassinet with its pristine canopy—how Bergur watched over him so that I could sleep in the bright nights of summer. I remember my first Christmas there with Bergur, when I baked an excess of inedible gingerbread cookies because we finally had a *real* home to bake in—

"Is everything okay, Saga?"

"Yes, just a little headache. It's normal." Now, think quickly. Jóhanna will make too much out of the gaps in my memory; she won't understand that they'll be fine soon enough, that I'll start sleeping well in just a little while.

"Let me be frank," she says. "There's something to be gained from having another person look at your life. I remember, for example, how much couples counseling helped Doddi and me. You never considered going, did you?"

"We considered anything and everything," I say, and try to steer the conversation away from the specifics. "What you were saying about mold?"

Jóhanna strokes my comforter. "I think that Ívar's illness was to blame," she says. "You seemed content on Ránargata before Ívar came down with that cough. That was it, right?"

A trickle down my throat.

"I suspected that it was something more than croup, but I kept it to myself. But really, Saga"—she shakes her head—"I don't understand how you thought it was normal to rush Ívar to the ER every few weeks."

"No."

"My god, when you first moved in and told me Ívar had turned blue!" I don't say a word, so she continues, "I'm no doctor, but it was dangerous. His life was at risk, Saga."

I feel helpless, a familiar sensation of freezing.

"And I hoped so much that the mold was to blame. That the problem was easy to fix."

"Yes," I say, listening to the wind howling outside, whipping against the windows. They sound like they'll crack under its force.

"But when he had that terrible seizure, the mold was already out of the picture. You'd moved and everything." She shakes her head, a little sad. "When my kids had croup, it just came and went—they hardly noticed, I think. The doctor assured us that croup is harmless. I'd really like to know what the tests told you. Isn't he having an endoscopy soon? What happened with that?"

"Yes, that's about it," I mutter, trying to conceal the fact that my body has tensed up with anxiety. What tests? Every word sounds like a fragment of a forgotten dream; they graze the memory, glimpses of color, the rasp of Ívar's breath in the thick of night.

"Oh, Saga, my dear, you look like you're done for the day," she says with a gentle smile, touching my hand as she reminds me that we did the right thing in selling our apartment, even if the illness had nothing to do with the mold.

"It's all running together, I'm sorry. What—what were you saying about his seizure?"

"Try not to think about that," she says. "You've lost more than a few nights of sleep worrying about him."

"I know," I mumble.

"It was complicated for Ívar, changing schools and moving and watching his parents separate. All of it. But he's a trooper, and hopefully things will get easier now. Is he doing better at his new school?"

The room whirls. My stomach churns bile. I can see Ívar in his rainsuit in front of a log house, gray but for the windows with their warm yellow frames. I say, "Difficult to say."

Jóhanna continues softly, "All families struggle at some point. Are you sure the air in this part of town is clean enough for him? All that exhaust from Miklabraut must blow right into the house."

"I don't really know. I have to fix the windows."

I'm falling asleep. She pats the bed, standing to go. I want to shout at her to stay, to tell me the rest of the story. The instinct is jarring, but I manage to whisper good night to my sister.

"Good night. Sweet dreams, Saga."

• • •

I dream of the nape of your neck, Ívar.

11

There used to be more pictures; they've left traces of their frames on the wall. I pick up our family picture and measure it against a square on the wall where the paint is darker, but I jump when a woman's voice says, "Elliði isn't available."

"But I've been on hold forever. You said he was there."

"He had to take care of an emergency."

"Doesn't he do phone consultations?" I ask, irritated.

"Well, yes," the voice lurches back, "but he's assisting another doctor in a consult. You can try back later."

"I should have been in touch with him the minute I left the hospital. I'm an urgent case," I say, whispering so that Jóhanna can't make out the words as she tinkers in the kitchen, humming along with a Bonnie Tyler song on the radio.

"Tell me your name, kennitala, and phone number," the voice says. "He'll call you as soon as he can."

"How long, do you think?"

"Name?"

I cave. "Saga Bjarnadóttir." I rattle off my kennitala and telephone number. If I can do that, maybe it's not as serious as I thought. It's a new day.

"Saga, do you want me to froth some milk for your coffee?" Jóhanna calls, lowering the radio.

"Já, but not too much," I say, making my way toward her. The light of morning, a bluish-grayness, drifts in through the kitchen window. It's faint, but it still makes my eyes water. I'm sensitive to light and it hurts.

Jóhanna is wearing a light gray cardigan over a turtleneck and a pair of unflattering jeans. I want to tell her she should stop wearing those pants, but I hold back. I shouldn't tease her while she's pouring scalding milk. It's Ívar's ceramic Moomintroll mug. My sister and I have very different coffee habits; in general, I rinse down a few spoonfuls of oatmeal with a gulf of black coffee, but Jóhanna drinks coffee in name only. She adds half a liter of milk to tíu drópar.

"What are you up to today?" she asks.

"I think I'll hike up Esjan, then head to the pool," I joke.

She chooses to ignore the comment, pouring milk through a tea strainer.

"Stop, stop! Don't do that!" I say, startling the strainer out of her hands, with the unfortunate outcome of spilling the milk. "What are you doing?" I am dumbfounded.

"What's your problem, Saga? Hand me a towel!"

"Why are you using the tea strainer?" I shoot back, more baffled than accusatory.

"I didn't use it on purpose. Just bring me the towel! I'll

buy you a new one," she says, her palms pressed tightly to the edge of the kitchen counter so that the milk doesn't drip onto the floor.

"I bought it in a teahouse in Kreuzkölln," I mutter, looking for the towel, lost in a blurry memory of Bergur with the stroller in the pouring rain in Berlin. We dashed into a teahouse with a mahogany interior, a burning candle on every table. The room smelled of a hundred types of tea leaves. There, I drank the best tea I've tasted in my entire life—the airy bitterness of jasmine pearls—while Ívar slept, rosy-cheeked from the morning sun, and thunder and lightning crashed outside. The memory becomes clearer with each passing second, but my sister's irritation breaks the calm of the teahouse.

"You're never usually this petty," she says, taking our mother's approach to offsetting tension by saying something critical in a chirpy voice.

"You're the petty one," I say. It sets her off. She grabs the towel, sops up the milk, and throws the dirty cloth in the sink without once looking in my direction.

"We have enough to worry about," she fumes. "I'm *afraid*—I'm afraid for you. And you saw how Mamma was yesterday."

"What? How?"

"The pain and nervousness."

"What's new? She's always in pain. And nervous."

"Yesterday she was so ill that she couldn't hide it," Jóhanna says. "You must've seen that."

"Okay, but what am I supposed to do about it?" I ask, but I'm having trouble recalling.

70

"Saga! Come on. Don't be like that."

"How am I being?"

"Like you don't understand. You know that she can't handle these shocks. And she knows too."

"What shock?"

"Her daughter in the hospital and her grandchild missing. You know how traumatic that was for her."

We look each other in the eyes in a tense face-off, but I'm stumped. She stares a bit longer, then drops the stern attitude.

"I'm sorry," she says. "You've got enough to deal with right now. I just meant that I hope you're not always this way."

"What way?"

"Like your reality is the only reality."

"What?"

"Just—things are sometimes different than you want them to be. But we don't need to talk about that now. I'm just stressed. It's stressful to talk. It's stressful to think about Mamma."

Jóhanna keeps trying to make me understand things I don't have any recollection of. She is tired, and I have no idea what to say to her. She might think I'm being manipulative if I tell her what's going on. I wring lukewarm water out of the towel and wipe the table down again.

"And that! You act like nobody knows how to do anything except you."

"I disagree," I say, but her bearing has changed so radically that I don't defend myself further.

"It's all the same to you, isn't it? That I've dropped

everything to stay with you. Doddi didn't go to the gym and Grímur misses his mamma. Did you know that Hallgerður will miss sports tomorrow because I have to be with you?"

I blink. I didn't mean to cause any chaos, especially to Hallgerður, who Ívar and I both love dearly. But I speak in anger. "You didn't have to stay. Guðni could have stayed with me."

"*God*, that's so typical of you."

I stare at my sister, who's usually the epitome of good-natured.

"It's just that I'm doing my best. I made coffee, went to the bakery—"

"The bakery?"

"Yes." Jóhanna gestures toward the living room and says, "I already laid it all out on the table. Fresh rolls and cheese and jam and butter."

"So you left me alone?" I hiss, so that she can't hear the worry wadded up in my throat, so that she's cut off from imagining the tumult inside of me.

She looks at me, bewildered. The silence stings the air. She asks if I'm mocking her.

"No," I answer, and I mean it. "I really appreciate the breakfast."

"Sure you do."

She doesn't look at me while I mutter, "No, I swear it, Jóhanna. Why would I act like that after you've done all of this for me?"

The question fires her up. "Because you never trust anyone with anything. I'm too incompetent or whatever, god knows, to watch Ívar. Bergur and I both fall short of your expectations in the same way, right? It's remarkable that you even let your son be with his father. Did you know that you've never once asked me to watch my own nephew? And now I can't even be trusted to make you breakfast!" There's a note of righteous satisfaction in her voice as she makes the accusation: "Saga, if you can't see that what you're doing is so demoralizing . . . just listen to me for once, okay? I don't understand how you can cop this kind of attitude, I really don't."

She glares at me, smug and furious, eyes dark.

"I'm sorry." I draw her into my arms. "You're afraid, right? Afraid, just like me."

"I've got a lot of gall," she admits, forcing a smile. "I'm just so goddamn scared. If anyone should be scared now, it's you, Saga, not me."

To make amends, I paste a smile on my face and listen as she free-associates about her life. We top bread with cheese and sliced vegetables, share an orange. She jokes that if I had seizures more often, I might be more prone to take her advice, like I did the evening before when she told me not to phone Ívar. I nod along with her monologue about my endurance, strong women in management positions, an article about the psychology of leaders, how it applies to me or how it is me. I don't tell her she's describing someone I don't know. I agree with her at the right moments, laugh as if on cue. I've resolved to have a nice time with my sister. I can pantomime normalcy.

She looks so pleased now, as if she's finally entrusting me with something of substance, but what that is, I don't understand. I'm encircled by a swarm of thoughts that threaten to overwhelm me. I do not have the same memories as my sister.

"Before I forget," she says, "are those white roses from that kid's parents?"

"Yes," I answer, and hope that it's true.

12

I want to know more—much more—about Ívar's illness. I vaguely recall taking him to the children's hospital. I remember standing over him as he lay in bed, plugged into incredible devices that monitored his breath and heartbeat. Something reminds me of ice. Flashes of memory trouble my mind. Didn't Jóhanna say that Ívar was in danger, something *life-threatening*?

I try to see the events before me and it causes a new sensation, as if I'm inhaling ice crystals. My body rejects the image, this image that has no home in my head; my heart thrashes like a captive, lashed down. I try to take control of my breath but don't manage it before my body breathes the image back out.

Jóhanna is puttering away in my kitchen, unaware of the radiating panic that's begun to slash a path across the floor. I lurch toward the couch and curl up in a ball against the armrest, my hands over my eyes, petrified by the intervals of chaos that have taken over my life. My heart is thundering, worsening an already-pounding headache.

What did she say about the mold in the old apartment? We were on Ránargata. I remember moving and I remember a woman, a specialist with a collection of strange devices that measured mold invisible to the naked eye. Ívar had so much fun listening to her tools beep, I remember, but I don't remember what he said to her. It's exhausting to fish that much out of my memory, but I press myself to do it.

Bergur managed all the ruckus of moving. The buyer was a partial owner at a travel company—yes, I remember that I was satisfied with the deal. He had the materials to repair the house's foundation, and the location meant we'd get a healthy sum for the house, more generous than the realtor had led us to believe, though we really wanted more. We longed to grow, to live in a two-story house with a basement. Bergur, always so optimistic, wanted a finished basement that he could turn into an office so he could avoid renting one, and I . . . I wanted to work there, too, didn't I?

I worked in some sort of management, an organization. Something with film. I studied film in Denmark for two years, where I learned about filmography but specialized in production. A knot in my stomach. I never tried to go to a famous film school, maybe to avoid rejection; I drifted into my course of study after having worked as a coffee girl for a few years on the set of Icelandic films. Then, after Denmark, I went home and worked my way up. I stopped fetching coffee and started filling out spreadsheets, organizing schedules, stretching each production's budget, no matter how limited.

I remember those years. They were eventful and went by quickly; I went places I never would have otherwise, awash in work, a good reputation in the business. And then Ívar came along and I realized I wanted more for my life than filmmaking could offer me. I couldn't turn down income, though. So then what happened?

What did I do then?

My thoughts are too bulbous for me to think one through to the end.

I slide off the sofa and close the door to the kitchen, where Jóhanna is contentedly washing up. The woman on the phone recognizes my voice. She cuts me off before I even get a chance to stammer out my business: "Like I said, Elliði isn't available and he won't be available for the next few days, unfortunately."

"Isn't there anybody else I can speak with?" I ask, feeling my desperation grow as I count seconds.

"You can try to get a hold of Þormar."

"Who's that?"

"Þormar is a neurology resident. He's here temporarily, and we're glad to have him." Her tone is already friendlier.

"Yes, all right. A resident?"

"He's acting as a specialist. He's been in medical school for a very long time—it's a complex subject, let me tell you. The most difficult. He's with us for a bit before he goes back to Karolinska University Hospital in Stockholm."

"Okay, that's fine," I say, surprised by the outpouring of information.

"He knows his stuff—I can vouch for him, since he's my nephew. I wouldn't direct you to him if I didn't feel certain about his expertise," the woman says, now seeming to warm to me.

"I'm so lucky you answered my call, then," I say. I'm trying to be cheeky, but it comes out condescending. I shut up before I say something else stupid.

"Well, you just try to do your best in an emergency," she says, cold again. She says she has to transfer me so she can answer other calls. I'm on hold for a few minutes before I'm greeted by a young, tired voice. It's the Þormar in question.

I tell him my issue as concisely as possible: "I had three major seizures in forty-eight hours after having been symptom-free for more than a decade."

He seems only marginally interested, irritated by the interruption. Clearly, his aunt has done him a disservice by passing me on to him.

But when I tell him about the gaps in my memory, which sound more farfetched when I talk about them out loud, he perks up, his interest piqued. By the time I've reached the end of my explanation, I've lost the thread of my own narrative. I must sound crazy.

"Come and see me," he says when I stop to reorient myself.

"What? When?"

"Now, now. I have a few minutes to myself during lunch, provided nothing else comes up."

"I'll be there in a few minutes! Thanks!"

"Yes, see you soon—but take a cab or get somebody to drive you."

I tell Jóhanna I've found a doctor. She offers to drive

me and throws on her sweater and nags me to let her come inside with me. I refuse and she relents, as long as I promise I'll call her or Mamma when I'm finished. She drops me off outside the hospital with a gentle threat: "I'll sleep at your place again tonight, Saga." I am not to be alone, apparently.

. . .

The nephew is boyish, but he's got to be at least in his thirties, judging by the duration of his studies. He blows his bangs away from his drowsy eyes. His hair hangs wispy and soft and chestnut-brown above his pale face. His mouth is crooked, the right corner pulled down. The distortion gives him a stern expression.

He slips out from behind his desk to greet me and shake my hand. "Welcome—Saga, is that right?"

"Yes, hello," I say, flustered. He must think I'm a nutcase after the mess I blurted out on the telephone, but I re-blurt my symptoms nonetheless, saying that my most upsetting memories shoot up out of my consciousness for a moment, like little sardines, before amnesia swallows them whole. That just thinking about certain subjects causes me physical agony. That I'm hindered from recalling parts of my own life by stabbing pain, like an electric fence you use to keep animals from escape. That I can't say certain words out loud, but I can think them.

As I speak, I can't help but feel glad that at least my speech is clear now. Maybe my memory is coming together, too, and I'm just making a mountain out of a molehill. I pause for breath and let my eyes wander across his desk: a beat-up paperback of Chomsky's *On Anarchism* is splayed facedown next to an overripe banana. I guess that's lunch.

"Have a seat," he says in a friendly voice, seemingly unconcerned with my bruised face. "You think you remember the bigger picture of your life, but there are gaps in your memory? And this occurred after the seizures? Is that how you would describe your condition?"

"Yes," I answer, feeling focused.

"And were you sent for any labs when you were hospitalized?" he asks, probably confirming what my patient record has already told him.

"No, I don't know of any. My family told the hospital that I'm epileptic and on medication, so they probably just assumed the epilepsy was to blame."

"Do you take your medication regularly?" he asks, conducting a series of tests to check my coordination, reflexes, and strength, tapping me with a little hammer and moving his hands in a percussive choreography.

"Yes, valproate. Three hundred milligrams in the morning and six hundred in the evening."

I rattle off my medical history while he pokes and prods me and asks a litany of questions I've answered since I was a kid. I tell him I'd never experienced two seizures in the same day before; more often than not, I had two seizures a year, when I was drinking a lot. But after each seizure, the specialist just increased my dosage, perhaps underestimating the severity of my illness. I told him about the recent past: that I had been on medication when I unexpectedly became pregnant, and I went off meds during my pregnancy. Once my son was born, my normal doctor increased my dosage. "He said newborns can cause protracted sleeplessness. I decreased my dosage once my child turned one."

"Which you should not have done," he says, setting aside the little hammer.

"But Elliði went along with it," I countered. "I hadn't had a seizure in more than ten years. I thought they'd stopped altogether."

"The seizures stopped because you were taking the medication. You're probably also aware that drinking is not a good idea while on that medication."

"I know, I know," I answer. I drink wine with dinner and celebrate with champagne, though there's seldom an occasion for it. Bergur has avoided alcohol more or less since he was a teenager, so we don't often have it in the house. He says it dulls his senses and thoughts, but he'll always order himself a Maß of beer when he goes to Germany to give readings. At most, he toasts with me on New Year's Eve or orders a glass of expensive red wine with steak at a restaurant.

"And you've never experienced any type of withdrawal?"

"Not that I recall," I say, grimacing humorously, as if to say, "How would I know?"

"Is it possible that you've had additional seizures in the past few days since you left the hospital?"

"I don't think so," I say, but there's no way to answer the question, really. "Someone's been with me around the clock for the past few days."

"The memory can, of course, be a little foggy after

something like this. But gaps in your memory of the kind you're experiencing, where your mind is, um, compartmentalizing memories according to how much they hurt and keeping you from accessing even certain words—well, that is anomalous."

"Yes, I completely agree. I can't describe it better than I have, though. It's as if my mind is a mail carrier sorting my memories into *bearable* and *unbearable*, and booby-trapping the unbearable ones. When I try to fit the pieces of my life together, any difficult thoughts produce stabbing headaches."

"Is that new?"

"Yeah," I say, fairly sure of my answer—at least, I have no recollection of a pain like that from when I was a teenager.

"Mm-hmm. What's the nature of the memories you're trying to recall?"

"Well, *everything*. My head starts to throb whenever I try to understand why my husband has moved out. I try to remember the fight, to recall some rupture, but—I'm not kidding, it's even starting now!" I clutch my head and close my eyes tightly.

"Hold on, Saga." Þormar fetches a wet cloth that he presses to my forehead until the pain subsides. "The brain is a complex wonder," he continues. "Mysterious. I remember reading Oliver Sacks's story of a patient who survived a heart attack but then never recognized his wife again, though he never stopped asking for her." He smiles incredulously at this anecdote, sets aside the cloth, and takes the stance of a lecturer. "Epileptic seizures can cause brain damage. A person can have difficulty breathing right when the brain and the muscles need a lot of oxygen. That can lead to brain cell death." He pauses as if he's said more than he meant to and contemplates me. "Having many seizures in a row can cause memory loss, difficulty focusing, chronic fatigue, impulsiveness, uncontrollable crying, and hypomania, slowed response time—"

Jesus. The words whirl around me. I scramble to catch them and collect them in the sieve of a brain I'm stuck with. When his words pick up speed, I blink my eyes quickly to try to force myself to focus and comprehend.

"Not to paint the devil on the wall, but these types of changes are sometimes irreversible," he says. "But your own experience is interesting, unique. And the brain is such a wonder that sometimes its parts don't seem"—the young doctor pauses, searching for the right word—"to make much sense. The more that I study the brain, the less I know. I've stopped ruling out anything."

"I understand," I say, but I don't.

He leans forward conspiratorially. "You could be a new species."

"Why do you say that?"

"An insect hidden in the rainforest, a species that lives to avoid all discomfort but which hasn't yet been catalogued."

"Are you sure about that?"

"No, not at all," he acknowledges. "And because I'm not sure what is going on with your symptoms, I've spent my lunch hour with you. I can tell you what I'm certain of—your brain's normal functioning has been disrupted, and you appear to be experiencing something we call *functional symptoms*, which are real symptoms with no apparent cause. You may have heard about conversion disorders," he says, "which is how we refer to functional symptoms that can't be explained by medical evaluation. These disorders used to be called hysteria, or psychogenic—"

He trails off when I start to look irritated. I say, "I haven't heard anything about *that*, but I have heard that doctors stopped diagnosing women with hysteria, so perhaps it is the doctors that have the conversion disorder?"

"Excuse me," he says. "It wasn't my intention to minimize your situation. I shouldn't think out loud." He chews his lip. "People who experience these symptoms can still have a measure of control over them. Stress and anxiety can activate them. Do you think that applies to you?"

The question catches me off guard. Am I under stress? Yes, surely, now. But before I had the seizure—was I stressed then? My head starts to burn. I wince and cry out, and that's when I finally see belief in the young doctor's eyes.

"I don't trust myself," I sob, almost reaching out for his white coat. "So how can I trust myself with my son?"

"You can't. You can't be alone with a child," he says bluntly, handing me the wet cloth again.

"Then what do I do?"

"You find somebody to be with you until, hopefully, we figure out what's going on and can treat you." He sits on his stool to clarify the matter. "I can't really make a diagnosis at this stage. It could be a number of serious things—that's the bad news. The good news is that it doesn't have to be."

"So—what?"

"I'd like to do an EEG and an MRI of your brain. It's a bit unlikely that those will give us answers, but we will look at the problem from every angle. We're trying to see if there's still epileptic activity in your brain—specifically, something called a focal seizure, which causes symptoms in one discreet part of the brain."

I swallow. I'm put off by his technical way of speaking. Elliði never talks to me like this; he interprets the secrets of the body like a spiritual scholar interprets an ancient script. He shares his view, rather than a list of parts and tests and malfunctions.

Oblivious, Þormar continues his narrative in a language that's completely foreign to me. "It's probably misleading to speak about an exact location, because long-term memory is stored throughout the brain, and it really varies. But the temporal lobe, especially the hippocampus, is closely associated with the creation of memory. That also applies to the area called the epileptogenic zone, which is where seizures that occur as a result of injury typically take place."

"I wasn't injured. I'm epileptic," I say, confused. "I've been epileptic since I was a child."

He gives me a look of pity. "I'm sorry," he says. "Exhaustion-induced rambling sometimes gets me into trouble." He smiles, then stiffens into a more serious expression. "You could have an underlying illness that causes memory loss and contributes to epilepsy. Anything."

"Okay. Do I go to the EEG now?"

"No, we'll wait for Elliði. He's your doctor," Þormar says. "He knows your history. He's the more experienced one here."

"But this is an emergency," I remind him. I feel desperate for the EEG's potential to shed light, terrified to head back home. "Remember, I'm a new species," I add in a pathetic attempt to appeal to his sense of humor, but it gets me nowhere.

"Stay home for the next two days and make sure somebody stays with you and your child the entire time, or at least while we explore a breakdown in the executive center, which I hope we find. Until then, make sure you get enough rest."

"Is it possible to check me into the hospital?"

"Ask the overlords of social welfare." He smirks at me, but I'm stony and scared, too grim to laugh about Iceland's bureaucratic healthcare system. He looks out the window, fiddles with his hair, and says, "Okay. Let's try to get the EEG today. Do you trust yourself to wait here? It could be a few hours."

"Yes," I say without hesitating.

"Then just sit tight," he says. "I have to make a few phone calls." He returns to his desk, picks up the phone, and grins when he says, "If I manage to get you in today, you'll be witnessing a miracle that breaks all laws of nature."

13

A dark blue Benz with a TAXI sign waits outside the hospital, a short distance from the entrance to the juvenile wing, where Ívar slept after his birth, a tiny, sickly bundle in an incubator. All of his energy was dedicated to his rapid breathing, but I was never afraid for him. I was amazed that we both survived those horrible hours when I was completely at the whim of my body in labor. If anything, I counted myself lucky that Ívar had landed in the care of a seasoned pediatrician during the first days of his life. But once it was time to leave the hospital, I had made heavy weather of the drive home. I was terrified: How could the doctors and nurses entrust Bergur and me with someone so helpless?

This taxi smells of new leather, but also the faint odor of urine. I pinch my nose as I close the door.

"Where you going?" the driver asks, looking straight ahead.

"Miklabraut 38," I say.

"Miklabraut 38! That's right down the street."

"Yes," I say. "I'm worn out."

Before pulling out, he turns back to eye me. "You look like somebody who could walk."

"And yet you just picked me up at the hospital," I say, trying not to sound haughty.

He strokes his shiny hair, which looks like it's been slicked back with some sort of old-school gel, and rolls his eyes. We set off.

Reykjavík is sable with dirty snow—it could use a shower, I think, just like the driver. An old man pulls a little cart over the slushy sidewalk, overflowing with bright yellow plastic bags. Children throw snowballs at the bus shelter. A car with a broken exhaust pipe hisses out smoke at the red light. A fog has settled over the south of Iceland, masking the mountains. The horizon is obstructed by the airfield and Hotel Loftleiðir.

Epilepsy is anarchy in its purest form, Þormar had said. He'd disrupted the orderly functions of Iceland's clinical world when he let me cut the line for testing. Two women had smeared gel in my hair and stimulated my senses with rapidly blinking lights, a test meant to allow them to monitor my brain waves. The fine ripples on paper were the manifestation of my entire reality.

The anarchy of the world is rooted in the anarchy of the body; we have no power, but we struggle to control our fate to the bitter, bloody end. People with epilepsy are steps closer than others to the paradox, he rambled, at once jejune and sagelike, but he quieted down when he realized that I'd lost his thread once again. Then he'd said, *You live in a body you can't control; you can be conscious of the anarchy.*

Is this really the place for that? You sound like a punk manifesto.

Punk rock makes sense, he volleyed, looking young and tired. *Give punk a chance.*

Nothing makes sense, but we'll see where it all leads me. We agreed that Elliði would call me—hopefully soon—with the results from the tests, and Þormar temporarily increased my dosage to three hundred milligrams. Earlier, I'd self-administered a triple dosage to shore up against a seizure. I could tell he thought I'd done something of the sort when he said that taking extra medication would "confuse" my body and could cause a seizure as easily as ward one off. He'd guided me to an old armchair in an empty room, where I'd waited for the next few hours, and he returned to his shift, his lunch hour long over.

14

"Saga, how are you?"

"I'm fine. I was just coming in," I pant, pleased I made it to the phone in time to answer the call and plunking myself onto the telephone bench without taking off my shoes. I'm hardly able to kick them off, having run out of energy after waiting at the hospital for what seemed like an eternity.

"You didn't answer your cell," Bergur said.

"I lost it during the seizure." Seizures?

"That's the only thing that could separate you from your cell." He chuckles, then stifles the laughter, unsure if it's okay to joke.

"Is Ívar okay?"

"Já, já, there's nothing wrong with him," he answers. "Oh—there was an issue. Some kind of sewage problem at his leikskóli, so I had to pick him up around noon."

"Why wasn't I called?" I'm miffed.

"I already told them about the situation, Saga."

"The *situation*?"

"Your condition." He hesitates, as if he's surprised by his own answer, before asking, "Are you alone?"

90

"Yes," I answer, depressed at the realization that I now need someone with me even during the day.

"Is that a good idea? I thought somebody had to be with you."

"Jæja, you're right. I just got home. Jóhanna is coming—I was at the doctor."

"And?"

"He increased my dosage."

"Já, and . . . ?"

"And I think I'll qualify for the Reykjavík CrossFit Championship, at this rate."

He snickers, a familiar laugh that's more sucking in breath than voice. Then he asks if I can do him a favor.

"I have to give a reading for a hundred people in Höfði in half an hour, then back to Árbæjarsafn, and then onto a library in Mosfellsbær, and I don't know what to do with Ívar," he explains, audibly panicked. "My mom is at aerobics, so I can't get a hold of her. Are you in a position to have him with you today, or—how are things? Should I call amma Dídí instead?"

"Well, that's the question, isn't it?" I say snarkily. "*Can* I be trusted to watch my own child?"

"Don't start," he says. "You're a great mother. I'm only asking if you feel like you're up for it."

No, no way, I think, but I say, "Yes, of course. Bring him over."

• • •

The second I hang up, fear washes over me. Bergur doesn't know how impaired I really am—I don't even know why we don't live together anymore. It doesn't shock me, really, that he lives somewhere else, but I just don't remember the chain of events that led up to it. I seriously doubt that Elliði has ever met a woman who's forgotten why she and her husband separated. A part of me wants Bergur to come to me so that we can sleep with Ívar between us at night, his contented breaths lulling us to sleep, but as soon as the peaceful image rises in my mind, I am flooded with anger.

I can access a memory of the first night I settled into my new life, a strange visitor in my empty home, Bergur gone and Ívar too.

The pain in my head advances as I maneuver around my memory. Digging. Stabbing. It gets the upper hand. To spare myself, I resist the reflex of memory and think of Ívar. I am going to be with him, alone, only for a few hours, I think. It's not like I have seizures every single hour. I'll make sure that he sits with me, nothing more. We'll read a book together in the quiet and he'll tell me all about his new leikskóli. We'll be settled.

No. Þormar didn't leave any room for ambiguity in his prescription. Can I teach Ívar to call the ambulance? Maybe I should put it on speed dial. We must adapt to our new reality—and the reality is that this could happen to anybody; anybody could die suddenly of, say, a heart attack while alone at home with a toddler.

I phone Mamma, but it just rings. I call Jóhanna to ask her to come over. I don't explain why, and she says she can't come now but that she'll be here after work.

Oh, hell. Why didn't Mamma answer? I don't want to involve my friends in this mess. I need to get a hold of

Bergur and bring this misguided plan to an end. I can trust him with this news, right? We could always trust each other with anything. I can feel his embrace and the scent of spearmint, cheroot cigars, and aftershave. Yearning wants to say its part.

But yearning pierces my head, and I will myself to go blank. I can't have a seizure, not now. I should eat something; I can't think about my own husband. I can't believe I didn't follow the doctor's advice. A good mother wouldn't jeopardize her son's safety just to see him, but I really need to see him.

A compromise. After I've put my arms around Ívar and held onto him a little, I'll tell Bergur that I'm sorry, but he has to take Ívar with him to his readings. No, that's silly. Of course I'll watch him. I must have some sort of control over myself—I always have control of things, it's just who I am, even though it feels like I'm paddling in a raging river. Each day rushes me forward, sweeping storm debris along with me.

This is a mistake.

They're already here. I should invite Bergur in to talk. But where would I begin? He's in a hurry.

"There's Mamma, Ívar!" Bergur says merrily.

"Hello, sunshine," I coo.

"Aren't you going to say hello to your mamma?" Bergur asks.

Ívar looks at me for a moment, his eyes serious and dark in stark contrast against his blue toddler balaclava. He clings to his pabbi. They're standing outside the open door, snow blowing around them, traffic whizzing by. One of them doesn't want to see the woman in the doorway, while the other is staring diplomatically at her, pretending not to notice her monstrous appearance, face swollen and bruised. Bergur must be cold. He's not wearing a hat, though he's in a warm lopapeysa and his leather jacket is unbuttoned. The snow has dusted his dark hair with white.

"Ívar is a little tired," he says to smooth over this inauspicious reunion.

"Don't you want to be with Mamma, Ívar?" I whisper with tears in the back of my throat. I slip into my sneakers and step outside, crouching so that the snow touches my butt. He doesn't answer.

Bergur shoots me an apologetic little smile, strokes his hair, and says gently, "Ívar, Mamma is waiting. Look!"

"I want to go with Pabbi," Ívar protests without looking at me.

"But Pabbi has to work," Bergur says, kneeling next to Ívar, holding his little face, and looking straight into his eyes. Ívar is the spitting image of his father, and they look a little pathetic at the moment: two lost boys watching over one another.

I take Ívar's hand and kiss him on his soft, cold cheek. It's heaven. He still smells of his morning dose of cod liver oil, like he's a little seal cub.

"Hæ, Mamma," he says, sniffling. He makes a little grimace, then nearly knocks me over as he launches toward me. He kisses me on one cheek and then the other, and then repeats the game, pecking me again and again. My little beggar.

Bergur and I lock eyes—have we turned a corner?—until Ívar turns to his pabbi and waves, seemingly ready to come with me. Then he throws himself into my arms again and clings to me like he is never going to let go. I have to shake him off because Bergur wants to give him a kiss before he goes. I feel guilty about misleading Bergur, but he won't make it to Höfði in time if I tell him where things stand with my memory. Besides, I need time with my son and don't want to risk losing it.

Jóhanna will come soon, I reason to myself. Right after work, she said.

"Mamma!" Ívar laughs, radiating joy as I take off his snow boots.

"Are you hungry, ástin mín?" I ask him.

He shakes his head, rips his cap off to reveal sweaty locks of hair, wiggles out of his sweater, and runs into the living room. Hardly a second passes before he calls, "Where's my car?"

"What car?"

"The white police car," he says, leading me into the living room and pointing decisively at a building he'd constructed out of Playmobil miniatures and Lego blocks.

"I—I don't know," I sputter. "Maybe Amma Kristín put it away?"

"I want my police car," Ívar says, screwing his face up into a fierce scowl. He demands that I call Amma to ask about the car.

"Hold on, ástin mín, maybe in a little while," I mumble, before hurrying to ask him if he'd like to take off his wet socks.

"Where's my car?"

"Ívar, I do not know. Come here and sit with me on the sofa. Let's talk a little bit."

He shakes his head, still frowning, actually glaring at me. Oh my god, I do not have the energy to deal with him when he's like this. He looks around, vexed, and then says, "I'm scared."

"Scared of what?"

"Just . . . scared."

"There's nothing to be afraid of, my love. Should I heat up some cocoa?"

He scrutinizes me for a moment before nodding in assent.

"Then come with me into the kitchen."

Ívar obeys, my little fireball, the very personification of earnestness. I can always get Ívar to listen at times when Bergur thinks it's impossible to keep him under control, though a smile is usually enough to win him over. He grabs onto the bottom of my sweater and follows me to the kitchen. Now his expression is almost protective, as if he has no intention of letting me lose consciousness on his watch. I wonder what he understands about all of this. It'll take him time to trust me; I have to accept that. Ever since his birth, we've been exceptionally bonded—so close that Bergur was sometimes frustrated with our intimacy. He demanded that I stop breastfeeding Ívar before he was even two years old. It feels good to think about those times, but it's essential to remain calm, to proceed steadily. I'll make us some hot chocolate, then we'll sit on the sofa together until Jóhanna comes, which I hope is sooner rather than later.

Ívar sits next to the refrigerator, my little watchdog. He usually likes to hang around when I putter about in the kitchen. Today, he doesn't take his eyes off me while I combine milk, cocoa, sugar, vanilla.

"Is everything okay, Ívar minn?" I ask, a little concerned.

He nods and looks down quickly.

"What, ástin mín?"

"You not my friend," he mumbles angrily.

"What do you mean?"

"I don't want to be alone! The bad men will take me! You not my friend!" His voice is shrill.

I run to him, wrap my arms around his stiff body, and try to soothe the anger in him. We sway, squeezing each other. I bury my nose in his hair until he pulls away to peek at me. He's waiting for me to smile—proof that he can be himself once again. I assent and watch relief spread across his little face.

"Pabbi buyed the penguin movie for the TV," he says, lamblike again, as if that frightened outburst didn't happen.

"Wow, your very own copy?" I say, remembering our trip to the movie theater, just the two of us on a Sunday afternoon to see the animated film about penguins. Ívar lived for that movie, babbling about it long after it was over. That was probably in September, I think. I thought it would be a good idea to start off autumn with a trip to the theater; I told him that winter, fast approaching, was the coziest season for movies. Now he owns his very own penguin movie and he's glowing with pride. I stand again. "Everything is fine, darling. Nothing bad will happen. Let's think about *other* things you love, like dinosaurs and froskaís popsicles."

"Dinosaurs can't go to the playground because they're extinct, right?" he asks.

I love where his mind goes.

"True, they are," I say. "But they wouldn't be allowed on the swings anyway."

The wind has stirred up a powder cloud of snow; the air is saturated white. A car seems to have gotten stuck at the traffic light. A white gust obscures my view. I think about poor Bergur driving in this weather, but it immediately triggers panic. What if he's in an accident? What if he doesn't come back, and I have a seizure, and Ívar is by himself?

• • •

I will myself not to slide into this chasm, telling myself: Then Jóhanna would come. Calm yourself. Reach from breath to breath to keep from slipping. Steer the breath and the body will obey.

Unmedicated during pregnancy, I reasoned with my body and it settled, satisfied. When I was small, I spoke to this body, too—turned my awareness inward to face it, holding its gaze in the soothing split-second before I lost consciousness. The moment would ebb tidal as colors crashed into a single omnitone, as if I had been swept into a Van Gogh. Sometimes my seizures would catch me off guard and I would make a fool of myself, stumbling during class, dumbstruck, and waking to the sound of my playmates' laughter. I'd forgotten the sensation that now advances upon me, intending to overtake me. But I know it. I know how to face it.

Breathe. Slow exhale. Hold. Slow inhale. Slow exhale.

"What are you doing, Mamma?"

"Ocean breaths."

"What's that?"

"Just—yoga breaths. Do you remember your yoga class?"

"Should I do yoga too?"

"Yes, we'll breathe together. Breathe out—keep going, keep going, keep going. And in. And breathe out."

We breathe in time together until he says he's bored with breathing and points out that there's a bad smell coming from the stove.

"No, no!" I say, running for the stove. I can't do anything right. The cocoa is scalded, and that was the last of the milk. We can't even go to the store to get more.

Foolish to think that I could act like nothing happened, that we'd pick up where we left off before the seizure, despite our very changed circumstances. Now we just have to sit and wait until somebody comes for us—though the waiting is itself a danger. We are bivouacked.

I can't wait for Jóhanna. I have to call my mother. Or the police? I was just talking with Bergur . . . and then what? Where did I put the phone?

I can't remember where I put the phone. I can't trust my body. My body can't be trusted with Ívar. I run to the front door.

15

"Hey, wait up! We're neighbors, right?"

"Um . . . you mean me? Jú, my grandma lives next door."

The girl is not dressed for the weather—she's wearing a canvas jacket and a keffiyeh, both now damp. She's trying to work out what I'm after; I must look a sight, panting in the doorway with a child glued to my leg. Fortunately, she looks puzzled, rather than alarmed.

"I see you here all the time," I blurt out, sounding like an ass.

"I stay with my grandma sometimes."

"What's your name?"

"Lilja Dögg."

"I'm Saga. How old are you, Lilja?" I fear I sound very creepy, but I plow ahead.

"I'm seventeen."

"Odd question, I know, ha—say, do you happen to be free right now?"

"Kind of—"

"Could I talk to you for a second, then?"

"But we're already talking, aren't we?"

"Well, yes, but would you like to come in?" I sound like a murderer in a bad horror film, but she nods her head and plods through the deep snow and up the stairs to my front door. She's tall and sturdy with broad shoulders. Her eyes are blue, and her pale face is streaked with mascara dripping down to her dimples.

She stamps her feet to get the snow off in the entryway before turning to me. "How did you get the bruises on your face?"

"Don't worry, I haven't been beaten up," I say, but she seems to want a real explanation. All I can think to say is, "I need help, I just really need help," and mutter something about sleeping badly.

She must be content to live with a little uncertainty because a few minutes later, we've made a deal. I will give her whatever cash is in my wallet, and she will watch over Ívar (and me) for the next few hours.

"Well, you're a gorgeous guy," she says to Ívar. She takes off her beat-up Doc Martens—one is spray-painted silver, the other gold—and slips off her jacket, revealing a strapless dress that looks like it's made of sealskin. Her upper arms, the creamy white of turnips, are covered in goosebumps, and her breasts spill out of the bodice of her dress like a pirate lass. She kneels next to Ívar as she stuffs the six 1,000 krona notes I gave her into the pocket of her tight dress. Is it even a dress? It barely reaches the top of her thighs, which are covered by ripped up leggings over fishnets. Ívar smiles at her as if she comes over every day.

"Were you on your way somewhere?" I ask.

"Heading to my school up in Hamrahlíð," she says, unwrapping a stick of Extra gum and popping it in my son's mouth. He smiles and giggles.

"Actually, he's never had gum before," I scold, but she shrugs her shoulders as if approving treats with me is below her pay grade. After a short pause, I say, "So you're studying there? At the high school in Hamrahlíð?"

She nods.

"Do you enjoy it?"

"Sure, sure, especially now that I'm helping my friend with his essay about democracy in the digital age. He reads all sorts of scholarly articles about the most extraordinary things, and this one is so interesting."

"But why doesn't he write it himself?"

She laughs as if I've said something ridiculous. "He's studying democracy in *practice*," Lilja says. "He believes the best way to write about democracy is to talk with someone who thinks differently than he does about freedom and rights."

"Ah," I say, a little taken aback by this chatty creature.

"You know," she says casually, "things like 'Should alcohol be sold in grocery stores?' or 'Should Iceland legalize marijuana?' 'What is citizenship, and should it be abolished so that we can move freely across borders?' All kinds of things! We talk about what should be available on the internet—private data and stuff—but mainly, we debate whether humanity jointly owns all intellectual property and what the role of the individual is. If intellectual property isn't freely available to all, many people will never have access to the things that can change their lives for the better. Something as simple as a song can inspire people to fight a dictatorship. So, anyway, we talk and talk until he knows how the essay should be, so he's not only *talking* about democracy, but he's also *using* a democratic method himself. But to be honest, I guess there's a flaw with his approach, because we pretty much agree on everything—"

"What about you?" I interrupt, confused about why she devotes so much energy to this guy's writing ambitions. "Don't you want to write your own essays?"

"Jæja," she says, turning back to Ívar, who is running around the room, presumably to find things to show her. Her answer is so clipped that it doesn't occur to me to continue the conversation.

"Can I offer you something to eat?" I ask after a moment's silence.

"No, I ate at my grandma's—liver and hearts," she says in the same noncommittal tone, sauntering over to a corner of the living room. Ívar wobbles toward her, holding a huge box of Lego blocks. "Don't you want to take time for yourself while I'm here?"

"Yes, of course," I say, as if dismissed. I stand to leave the living room.

"You need to work, don't you?" she asks. I open my mouth to say yes, but something holds me back. Lilja combs through the pile of Legos; with each sweep of her arms, her breasts nearly pop out of her dress. Ívar is staring at this, too, baring his milky teeth like he's remembering his Edenic life before he was weaned. I shake myself out of the reverie and give myself a pep talk: I've lied over and over again to my family, my friends, Bergur. For

6,000 krona, I should be able to come clean to this teen-ager. Besides, she needs to know what's going on in case something happens.

"I have epilepsy," I blurt out to a total stranger. I tell her about my recent hospitalization for grand mal seizures and that I can't be alone with my own child, that I think I'm divorced but I'm definitely separated, that my ex-husband is busy with work and I'm uncomfortable burdening my family with my problems, since I don't even understand these issues myself, and—

"Sit down," Lilja interrupts, pointing me toward the sofa. I obey automatically.

She looks at me with greater compassion than anyone has shown me since I woke up in this nightmare, and her kindness clicks me into reality. I start to feel the weight of exhaustion on my body.

She glances at Ívar, who's concentrating on building a fire station. Turning back to me, she says, "My little sister gets seizures too. Nobody knows why."

I am surprised and (selfishly) relieved. She must know what to do if something happens.

"How old is your sister?"

"She's eight. The doctors hope she'll grow out of it. I do too. It's really freaky."

"Freaky?"

"Yes. Have you ever seen anybody have a seizure?"

I'm about to tell her that I have, but then I realize it's not true. She's too busy with her own story to notice when I don't answer.

"The doctors were afraid she had a brain tumor. They

did a bunch of tests when she was just little. Luckily, she didn't have anything like that. Wait—do you have a brain tumor?"

"No!" I say. "Or—I don't think so. I mean, I hope not," I add, thinking about the tests Þormar mentioned.

"That's something you'll have to find out," she says.

An ache slices through my head. I try to generate a good reason why it's not a tumor, but the pain clangs louder than my thoughts. I have to say something, *do* something, let her know I might have a seizure—now. In my panic, I try to stand.

"Sit down, close your eyes," she comforts me. "You definitely need to rest. We'll be fine."

My submission is entire. I sink into my chair to wait for the pain to abate, so drained that saying even a single word would take too much energy. I listen to them play. Ívar giggles, monkeying around, no longer skeptical of this visit. He has completely forgotten me.

Thank god.

16

When did we last make love? I remember our first time, but every other time runs together into a singular feeling of having slept with Bergur, and I have little memory of particular episodes. With that feeling comes a quiet reminder, too, that a long time has passed since the last time, so long that the mere thought makes my body thirst for intimacy. He wanted to sleep with me; I'm sure about that. But what about me? I don't know. I contract into myself and close. The thirst for closeness quickly gives way to a strange need to flee.

I dreamed that I was lying on his broad chest, the smell of him mingling with my own scent after sex—but we hadn't made love. The dream was a moment I'd lived. I relive it in my half wakefulness, and it's so consuming that I long to climb back into it. No matter how hard I try, the last time we made love isn't any clearer to me than our quarrels—but we must have fought furiously, since the dream isn't anywhere near our reality.

I shouldn't think about this now. It hurts. How long did I sleep? I feel like the doorbell rang. Yes, the door's opening. Ívar is still playing. I stand and see the Lego blocks spread out like saplings across the floor, punctuated by a few buildings. The girl, yes, I remember as I head toward the door, dread now sweeping over me. There is a strange girl here and she built an entire Lego city with Ívar. I can hear Jóhanna peppering the girl with questions, but I'm having trouble waking, getting to my feet, going out to the foyer to explain things to Jóhanna.

"Saga, what the hell is going on? We have to talk. Now."

Jóhanna looks horrified. I wonder what I'm doing or look like that is so bizarre.

"Mamma's gone!" she blurts.

I stare at her. What? I must have misheard.

"What do you mean?" I ask after a long pause, shaking my head and trying to respond in a way she'll deem normal.

"Don't be like that," Jóhanna snaps. "You know *exactly* what I mean."

Do I? Well, yes and no. She says that Mamma's gone, and while I know what those words mean in general, I don't have any sense of why she'd go, or where, or what it means. Reality is a little absurd for me right now, a movie with an incomprehensible plot that seems to have no ending, but I sense this response is not going to fly with Jóhanna. "Where'd she go?" I ask. I'm an imbecile, powerless, unable to access my own backstory. Dread wraps its arms around me.

"I don't know. She's just *disappeared*," Jóhanna says, as if nothing could be more self-explanatory. "She was so afraid for you—and Ívar. It set her off again. We should've seen it coming this time."

I feel ashamed for having caused this and for falling short of my sister's expectations, but I didn't suspect anything was awry; I don't even know if I should've suspected something. My entire existence is fog, I think, straining to overpower panic with logic. But I can't.

"Do you think Mamma's in danger?"

"I hope not. If it's like before, she'll come back. It really comes down to her state of mind," Jóhanna says, trying to calm down. She sighs dramatically, as if in surrender. "Who's this, then?" she inquires archly, gesturing at Lilja Dögg, who hovers near us with Ívar glued to her side.

Her real question is obvious from her expression: *Why is this strange, grimy-looking teenager playing with my nephew, when I, his aunt, have never even been allowed to babysit?*

"I got some help," I answer, my voice steady.

"Help?" She sounds doubtful, then she asks with strange formality, "Do you mean from the Department of Welfare? Is she a home health aide for you?"

"That's uncalled-for," I snap. "I can take care of myself. Look, the fact that I hired the neighbor girl to watch my son while I rest is hardly more pressing than our mother running off. Jóhanna, what can we do?"

"Let's go to the kitchen—we'll have a cup of coffee," she says, glancing sidelong at Lilja Dögg. When we're out of earshot, she whispers, "Saga, are you sure that everything's okay?"

"No," I admit.

The answer catches her off guard. "Right, well, you

need to call the doctor, then," she says, sounding strained and powerless. She can't stand being unable to fix things. My heart sinks for her.

"There's nothing doctors can really do, Jóhanna. I just need time to right myself. But what about Mamma? No one can get a hold of her? I've tried, actually—"

"It's just ridiculous nobody told you Mamma was missing. I gave Pabbi a lot of shit for not telling me as soon as he found out," she says. "I guess they didn't want you to worry, given everything else. She snuck out while he was asleep last night. I don't know what he thought—maybe he figured he'd just dash out and find her. Anyway, now you know."

I'm itching to fill in the blanks, but asking a lot of questions goes against my better judgment. She'll start suspecting that things aren't quite what they seem, that *I'm* not quite what I seem. The last thing I need is to be peppered with questions I can't answer.

"We'll figure it out," she says, transitioning back to her usual role of the big sister who reassures the rest of us. "Guðni is out looking for her—ah, it is what it is. Same thing as always."

"Are you sure?" I ask doubtfully.

"As much as I can be," she says. "But I don't understand why you aren't at the hospital if you're feeling so weak? It seems safer, even if there's nothing they can do."

"Ask the Ministry of Health," I say, stealing a line from Þormar.

This gets her going. "Damn the ministries and the ministers. Are they going to keep cutting our healthcare till there's nothing left? Doddi says that they've been making cuts since the early 2000s—"

"Jæja," I say. This seems to satisfy her; she switches back to monologuing about Mamma.

"I expected this, though it's been a long time. Did you see how she looked at dinner? That should've raised some flags. And Pabbi, too—he had his eyes glued to her! She really seemed keyed up, you must have noticed that, like she would snap if you said the wrong thing. Except she was nice to you—understandably so. Maybe that's why you didn't notice something was wrong. But you don't usually notice, anyway."

"Jæja," I repeat, nodding along with this characterization of me, even though I do remember. Mamma buzzing around, Pabbi taking cover with Guðni, Jóhanna trying to cheer Mamma up, me, out of it. Perfectly dysfunctional, as usual.

"Saga." I hear Lilja's voice through the kitchen door. "Does Ívar have a potty?"

17

After pelting me with the news of my mother and tapping my remaining energy stores, Jóhanna leaves. My mother's disappearance is (to her) much more urgent than watching over me. Before she left, she shot a suspicious glance at Lilja Dögg as she pulled up Ívar's yellow Angry Bird underpants. She acknowledged that it was somewhat of a relief to know I wasn't alone, but I could read the resentment in her expression. My sister wants to be one-of-a-kind, irreplaceable.

"My mother is gone," I say out loud.

"I heard," Lilja Dögg says.

We make eye contact for a moment, and I can tell she senses I've been emptied by this news. I've always seen myself as a shrewd woman who can think on her feet, two strings to her bow, who can overpower any problem—but now I'm pathetic. I mumble, "I feel like she's always getting lost."

"What do you mean?" Lilja asks, her voice neutral. Maybe she sees me, Saga, and not just some crazy woman.

"I don't know what I know," I say slowly, enunciating each syllable so that I can register their full meaning. "I can only half remember most of the details of my life. I don't know why I'm telling you this, I admit—maybe because I haven't told anyone yet."

"Why?"

"Why what?"

"Why can't you tell anyone about your memory loss?" she asks. I'm impressed with her mature tone; she has the clinical distance of a psychologist with me. Meanwhile, her hands are busy building a firehouse for Ívar, who's thrilled to see his dream come to life.

"Because I have no friends, even in my family. Except, well—him," I say, trying to sound amused as I point at Ívar.

"But he's three years old." Lilja Dögg's solemn Bambi eyes are reproachful.

"Almost three and a half now," I counter.

At his age, I thought my sister, Jóhanna, was the be-all and end-all: sister, friend, sometimes-mother. She plans to come back this evening, and though I'm less than enthusiastic about it, I know I can't be without her. But I can't imagine having her here, either, even if Mamma is gone. Maybe *because* she's gone. I don't know. I don't know anything.

Exhibit A: What the hell did Jóhanna mean that Mamma snuck out in the middle of the night? It's winter; everything's covered in snow. It was punishingly cold last night.

Don't worry about this, Jóhanna said before she left, strangely grounded. *Guðni will figure out what's going on.*

But what can I do? I'd asked desperately.

Just take care of yourself, Saga. Since this girl is here, I'm going to run home. I have to check on my own family. But I'll be back.

Just go. I'm fine, I'd lied.

I'll only be a bit, she said in the same voice our mother used to use when she needed air.

• • •

I look at my son. He's holding a red Lego out toward the teenage girl who's puzzling over me. Ívar obviously trusts her; maybe he trusts too easily? What if she can't be trusted?

"You've got to talk to someone other than this one here, Mister Three-Year-Old, and this bossy sister of yours."

"You thought she seemed bossy?"

"Don't you have any friends?"

I do. I mutter something about calling Tedda to ask her about . . . myself. If anybody can describe me back to myself, it must be her, my lifelong friend. The revelation of my amnesia doesn't seem to faze Lilja; she doesn't question my credibility or treat me as if I'm exaggerating my condition. She looks thoughtful, as if she's working out the possibilities.

"Do you have a computer?"

"Yes, of course. A laptop."

"Have you checked it out to see if there are clues in your desktop files or by Googling your name?"

I think for a moment. Where's the computer? Probably in the bedroom. Did I use the internet to find the phone number for Landspítali? No, I reached them through 118.

"Are you on Facebook?" she asks.

"Yes, but I don't think I'm very active on it," I answer, remembering.

"Still. Maybe it could help you figure out who you are." Lilja links a red block to a yellow chimney. "And your computer should have clues about your job, at least."

The girl's sharp. Now I just have to figure out where I left my laptop. Habit triumphs over memory; I find it in my bedroom. I bolt downstairs, so overwhelmed by curiosity that I open it in mid-flight. Once the computer boots up, I put in my password (I remember!) and search through the files on my desktop:

> *Applications and budget*
> *We Can Never Forget*
> *Press: Memory of the world/our role*
> *Health*
> *Goal*
> *Household budget*
> *Journal*

"Click on *Journal*!" Lilja barks, full of anticipation. She and Ívar have come over to sit next to me. He reaches for the computer he never gets to touch, a device full of forbidden amusements. I do as she suggests and let out a wail of relief when I locate a file that seems as if it could be about my life.

It's called *Saga: Chronology.*

18

We snuggle up to one another. Because it's gotten late, the dramatic B movie on television makes me think that one day, we're both going to die—one before the other—and that the moment will arrive sooner than we think, and that this moment, right now, will become nothing more than the echo of a thought. I commit the moment to memory. I want to outlive him, my Ívar, and not the other way around. I can't bear the thought of losing him, so I press myself closer to him and say, *We'll always be together.*

He smiles a little, his eyes glued to the people dying on screen. *Okay.*

The ease of the observation comforts me. *Okay*, he said.

• • •

I can't find Ívar.

He doesn't look up from the television, the crack of a smile frozen on his face when he says, *What? What?*

Bergur, where is Ívar? Where is he? I scream.

Come on, he's with your mamma, he says, a look of disdain straining his face. *Isn't that what you wanted?*

● ● ●

"Did you have a bad dream?"

God, she's maternal for a teenager. For a moment, she reminds me of the man who saved me.

"What happened? Did I have a seizure?" A feeling of sunkenness permeates my whole body, as if I've been hit by a truck. I lean into the crook of the couch. I know I've slept, but I feel like I've been awake for days.

"You got super tired all of a sudden, and I asked if you'd like me to stay longer so you could get some shut-eye, and you passed out," Lilja answers, tucking her hair behind her ear, her eyes worried and drawn against her young face. "I just let you sleep—you seemed so tired. My sister is exhausted for a long time after she has one too. She's always passing out."

"Where is Ívar?" I whimper. I'm still logy.

"He's sitting on the kitchen floor, eating the kjötsúpa I heated up."

"Alone?"

"Yes. The turnips were soft, but I cut them into pieces just in case. He didn't want any meat. Is that okay?"

"Yes, yes, of course," I say, but nothing is okay. I'm relieved he turned his nose up at the meat because he tends to put too much food in his mouth at once. Dinner has been a constant argument for about six months now. And didn't somebody say something about difficulty swallowing, or maybe croup? Wait, *regurgitate*, isn't that what the doctor said—

The girl shushes my thoughts. "They haven't found your mother."

116

"They haven't?" I croak. My mouth is so dry.

"No. I'm so sorry. Your sister called and said she would be a little bit late, if that was okay."

"And?" I sound sharp, but I'm feeling overwhelmed as I remember Johanna's earlier visit. Some things are more strenuous to think about than others.

"And I said yes," Lilja says.

"I don't have any more cash to give you," I mumble.

"No worries," she says. "Or—sorry, of course you're stressed. After all this! But don't think about paying me right now."

I smile weakly. She's so kind, this girl. Fatigue pulls at me, but I push back and sit up so I can look her in her eyes, so sincere and resolved.

"I can stay a little longer if my friend can come by too, you know, with the essay and all," she adds.

I have trouble figuring out how to answer. Do I really want another teenage stranger here while I'm in this much disrepair?

"Maybe he can fix the problem with the computer."

"What problem?"

"Remember, we opened up Word and the letters in that document were all scrambled?" she says with a sympathetic smile. "Probably a virus. Oh, and your inbox is full of spam—you need a better filter."

Now I remember. I got a godforsaken computer virus before the day of the seizure. I haven't paid enough attention to my computer.

"We didn't find much on Facebook. I scrolled through a bit more while you were asleep. There wasn't anything about you, really, except your birthdate. You pretty much just repost sad stories about refugees and suffering in Palestine, like me. But I use Twitter, of course," Lilja says. "Anyway, it's been a long time since you've posted anything at all. Your feed is packed with birthday wishes from all kinds of people. You must know a lot of people— seems like a lot of foreigners."

"A lot of colleagues," I say, but it's a guess. I wonder how much longer it's appropriate to ask her to stay and keep an eye on Ívar. I'd think she'd be expected home eventually.

"Right. It'd be cool to have your job," she says, and before I can ask her what my job is exactly, Ívar calls out to her. She shoots me a grin and chases after him.

Then, suddenly, the scene surfaces. We had opened my journal on the computer, but the letters ran together like confused ants. My backup brain, the laptop, has revolted against me too. *It's almost too absurd to be true*, I remember telling Lilja, who answered that her friend Óðinn says that absurdity doesn't exist because normalcy is a construct.

I struggle to piece together what else we did. I think we tried everything before I finally surrendered to exhaustion. Or was it hopelessness?

Lilja returns to report that "Ívar is over the moon" to get to eat on the floor and commences with her hard sell. "My friend Óðinn is brilliant at fixing computers," she says. She keeps jerking her neck to flip the bangs away from her eyes. I want to tell her to get a barrette or something because her frantic movements are making me edgy.

"So should I call him? He owes me one."

I have to answer her, but I can't manage to see a single thought through to the end.

"Saga, should I call?" Lilja Dögg says, jerking again.

My mouth refuses to answer. I can't take a position. Should a strange boy come to my house, and should I let him dig into my computer? He doesn't know me in the least, and I don't know him. Where are the stories that can tell me about my circumstances, my life? I know they must be difficult to face, or else I would be able to access them. It's crucial that I find them, though I know to expect that remembering can bring headaches or even a seizure. Even pleasant memories build up pressure behind my forehead as they return and coalesce.

• • •

Sautéed garlic. The smell fills me with a feeling of wellness. I turn to him and wrap my arms around him. *I love you more than anything*, I say, running my fingers through his curls as he takes a sip from my glass of red wine.

That's because we don't have kids, he says teasingly. *If you had a kid, then you'd love it more than me.*

No, I laugh. *My heart would only grow.*

That doesn't matter, he says, turning to me. *You only like me for my cooking.*

How do you know? I mumble through a kiss as we tumble to the floor and let the garlic burn to soot.

• • •

I can't place these memories in time, no matter the effort. I shake my head to snap out of my reverie and answer

119

Lilja, "You can tell your friend to come if you really think he can help."

She gives me an earnest nod and steps away to call Óðinn. I open the computer absentmindedly. At least the internet's working. I click on my home page—the news section of Ríkisútvarpið—and a horrific article I read not long ago flits into my consciousness: A mother had had a seizure in the bath and died in front of her young child. At the end of the article, there was a link to another gut-wrenching report—a woman in western Iceland had died in front of her three-year-old twins.

That woman and I had something in common: she hadn't had a seizure for many years either. Maybe we both stayed up night after night, worrying over our children, until insomnia finally did us in? I have the impression I read about what provoked her epilepsy, but I seem to have misplaced these details. Now this awful story has invaded my brain, and the only way to escape is to think about something even more traumatic that'll trigger my subconscious to suck it back down.

Mamma. How is the search for my mother going? Where are they looking? I hope Guðni's figured out how to delegate. It's utter nonsense, all of it—and now I've started using my mother's old-fashioned expressions. Is she lost because of me?

"I'm full," a loud voice calls from the doorway. Hopeful eyes look up at me, flush with enthusiasm. Ívar takes off running and jumps up into my arms so that my computer falls onto the floor with a bang. "I love my mamma," he says, burying his head in my neck.

My eyes fill with tears. I hug him so closely that he squirms and squeals, "Not so tight, Mamma!"

But I don't let go. If I give an inch, I fear I'll sink deeper into this quicksand; I'll be swallowed by a stone-gray fog. I'm stranded in space and time. All I can do is tighten my grip, become a vice sturdy enough to hold onto life. I could die now. The electrical pulses in my brain are becoming so strong, my system might overload. Grand mal, petit mal . . . it doesn't matter. If I'm crossing the highway, I must run between short signals. The intensity of the attack is irrelevant; where it happens isn't. If I were to die now, I would never hold my son after this, this moment, this one, the last time I'd take in his honeyed scent, his wet breath in my nose and mouth. His smile, my life force. And what would he do without me? Of course, he'd live on, but I would never see him again, so he would die to me. His path would change.

I can't think like this. I'm dooming myself. I'm losing. Losing what? Him, my body—

My heart hammers as if I'm crash-landing a plane. I've always been petrified of landings. Bergur used to tease me about the time I worked myself into a panic on an airplane before Ívar was born. The wheels had scraped the runway at a terrifying speed, seeming to defy the brakes, the single system we were all at the mercy of. Now I'm condemned to life in the moment of landing, but this time the wheels really are broken. My body feels forever caught in that fraction of a second, waiting to see if we manage to land, but now with a child in my arms— just like when we flew home in turbulence, Ívar pressed

121

to my chest, after visiting Bergur at an artist residency in Boston.

"I sent Óðinn a text," Lilja Dögg enunciates carefully, to be on the safe side, I guess, since I'm so unresponsive. She shoots me a little half smile, as if to let me know she isn't so serious. But I've never met anybody so young who's so serious, committed, and sincere. It occurs to me that she might be—what do they say now?—on the spectrum. I've been forced to let my own absurdity guide me to set aside convention and allow another stranger into my house.

Lilja's staring at me as if she is waiting for something. "Thank *you*," I say. "Well-done!" I add, to give the guise of normalcy.

"Is everything okay?"

"Yes, perfectly. I'm feeling much better now. I just need to eat. I can't forget to eat. We can't forget that," I say. I'm still holding Ívar like a straitjacket, so I blow on his neck to lighten things up.

Big, bubbly laughs. His dark eyes glisten with elation. He wants to play helicopter, so I play along, twirling him in my arms while sputtering out the puttering noise of helicopter blades. I'm responsible for our levity, our carelessness, but what if I fall?

With this thought, I don't manage the third circle. Dizziness can cause a seizure, made worse by low blood sugar, Saga. It's time to eat.

I smile in surrender and fuss with Ívar's hair through his shrieks of giggles, which have kept him flying after his helicopter ride.

"More helicopter, Mamma! More helicopter. Mamma?"

Ívar's demands are so charming that I can hardly resist the temptation to lose myself in dizziness, to disappear into the darkness.

I'm sorry, Ívar. I'm sorry about thinking these things. I'll never leave you, I whisper in my mind, the words on endless repeat. I need to eat, but there's no chance I'll be able to stomach that oily soup, the soup Mamma made to help me heal before she ran off. She could have been hit by a car. A shiver runs down my spine. She could be in trouble somewhere. My mother is missing. And what did I do? I went to sleep.

• • •

"So, Óðinn is on his way," Lilja says, "but I think you should also call your friend."

She's right. It's time for Tedda. I step out to make the call.

When I come back, Ívar is singing Icelandic emergency services' telephone number in a bright voice. "One, one, two! One, one, two! One, one, two! Look, Mamma! I know the numbers. One mouth, one nose, two eyes. One, one, two!" Then he flips the numbers. "Two mouths, one eye! Ha! Isn't that funny?" He breaks into giggles, sticking his tongue out at me.

"Um, what song is that?" I ask Lilja.

"Just something I learned in a first aid course," she says, shrugging. "You know, for my little sister. It's for teaching kids how to call an ambulance if something happens to their parents. One mouth, one nose, two eyes—1-1-2."

She read my mind, this girl. She taught him who to call for help, rather than relying on speed dial, which could be even more confusing for him. "Thanks," I say, "I'm grateful."

She smiles shyly. "So what did your friend say?"

What did Tedda say? *My dear, how awful! In the hospital? What happened? My god! You don't remember anything? Okay, phew! Of course, otherwise you wouldn't have remembered who I was. Sorry, black humor. But you, I mean—you're not kidding? No, no, of course not. Poor thing. What's up with Ívar? The sweet baby! Huh, your mamma's run off? Are you joking? Should I come? Okay, I'll be there.*

I tell Lilja that my friend is on her way, too, and that Bergur will be arriving soon as well—Ívar can't stay up much later.

"Maybe Óðinn will get here first," Lilja says. She seems very focused on figuring out the order of arrival. Of course, Mamma could always reappear too. She could do that. She could.

The doorbell rings. "One, one, two—and turn in a loop!" Ívar shouts. He falls, laughing, on his backside. He loves guests, especially when it's almost time to go to bed. But I open the door to an unanticipated visitor.

"Hi, Pabbi."

19

"Saga, my Saga," Pabbi says. He's stark-white, standing in the doorjamb, looking lost. "You've heard what's happened, haven't you, love?" His bulldog eyes swell with dejection, a navy-blue well of emotions.

"Yeah, but I don't entirely understand what's going on."

"No wonder. We've never really understood your mamma, have we?" he says. He sounds conspiratorial, like it's us against her.

"What is it you don't understand?" I spit out, surprising myself with my intensity.

"Ah, Saga." He sighs and lifts his hands in a "nothing to be done" gesture. "Aren't you going to invite me in?"

I move out of his way. I can't tell whether it's good, bad, or inconvenient that he's showed up at my door, covered in snow. His cap, knitted by you-know-who, reeks of wet wool. He stuffs it in his pocket, runs his fingers through salt-and-pepper hair.

"Can I get you a coffee?" I ask.

"First, I'd like to see my grandson."

He's hardly finished his sentence when Ívar shrieks, "Big Afi!"

My pabbi is "Big Afi" because he has a Jeep. It doesn't matter that it's a small Jeep on its last legs; he's the most important one. Grandpa Stebbi, Bergur's father, is "Little Afi" because he drives a Renault.

Ívar's Big Afi lifts him high in the air and they both break into peals of laughter, the glee of a child and the husky laughter of a grown man, which is pure in its own way. I remember when Pabbi used to lift me high in the air—I remember joy.

"Afi, where is Amma?" Ívar asks when his grandpa sets him back on the ground.

Pabbi looks at me with shame in his eyes, and I hurry to make something up. "Amma is at the store, buying food."

"And *candy*," Ívar says, excited, since Amma and Afi give him too many sweets. They always slip him a little something when Bergur and I aren't watching.

"Uh, yes, sweets as well," Pabbi says, fidgeting. I'm uncomfortable with the lie too. But what else can I tell my son?

"I like gummy bears the best," Ívar says.

"Amma wouldn't forget that," I say, a little too good at continuing this lie. "Come into the living room, pabbi."

Lilja jumps to her feet when my Pabbi walks into the living room.

"Hello," she says, formal as a bureaucrat, and steps forward to shake his hand. She certainly knows how to behave, even if her clothes don't really imply it.

My father seems confused. "This is Lilja Dögg, our

neighbor," I say in a cheerful voice, Ívar on my right hip. I'm conscious that I'm speaking too loudly.

"Lilja, yes," my father mutters, wiping his hands on his pant leg before taking her hand. "Are you friends?"

Lilja looks at me to answer.

"No," I blurt. "She's here to help me with Ívar."

"Mm—a babysitter even when you're home?"

"Yes, while I recover from the seizure."

"Of course, of course! What was I thinking, Saga? I should have known," he says. "I'm just not myself. How are you doing now?"

"I'm getting better," I say. "Take a seat, Pabbi."

He lifts his eyebrows in a way that reveals his distaste for my furniture as he gawks at a low sofa with dark blue upholstery. The scoop of its bench is even lower than the teak coffee table and sideboard that make the set. He scans the other seating options: two stools with light blue cushions and two mid-century chairs with seats that touch the floor, arms angled sharply toward the ceiling. "Where did you get such tiny furniture?" he asks.

"A clearance sale at a little decor store I've always wanted to shop at but I never had the money to buy anything—until they liquidated," I answer, relieved that I can produce this explanation without much thought.

He chuckles, and the laughter shakes his frame, deep in his belly. I feel light. His calmness signals to me that everything will be okay.

"You've just gotten the crumbs, like the rest of us," he thunders, plunking himself down on one of the chairs and sinking way down, mouth agape at the depth. Ívar screeches with laughter at his grandpa's face as he flings himself into his lap with such force that the chair lifts off the floor before banging back down.

"What crumbs?" I ask.

"From the table of capitalism, my love," my father answers, ruffling Ívar's hair.

Lilja looks down quickly. I hope she doesn't start to laugh; my pabbi couldn't handle that right now. But she looks up just as quickly and gives my father a look that means she's taking him seriously. Encouraged, he tells her about his socialist friend Jörmundur: a remarkable person, a good friend, and the most level-headed human being Pabbi has ever met, especially if we're talking about the fight against the democratic deficit.

"Democratic deficit?" Lilja repeats.

My father perks up; her response is a magic potion that will bring on a great big lecture.

"Yes, it's a deep swamp here—complete anomie, expensive stupidity, let me tell you," he booms into her earnest face, now ruffling his grandson's hair so ardently that Ívar wriggles away from beneath his hairy hand. "It's crooked, like this goddamn chair."

It occurs to me that my fussy furniture looks like Solveig's—his mother, a woman he hardly knew. She lived in a fashionable community for seniors at the end, after an entire life spent on the flowlines in the fish processing plant.

From an early age, she watched for her husband's return from the rough waters near Stokkseyri. Short but substantial, she was a handsome woman with "Indian" hair that she cut off when she became a widow. Her eyes were stormy with sensitivity and a dark longing, and I picture her dressed in knee-length, carefully pressed shifts, either a leafy-green or sky-blue, with a white apron tied around her waist—except during long hours in the fish processing plants, when she wore white pants, a lopa-peysa under a protective smock, and rubber boots. The women in my father's stories always had "Indian hair" and wore dresses of leaves, but I know the picture of Solveig is correct, although I've hardly thought about her in years—I must have seen a picture of her as a young woman on one of our trips to the old folks' home.

I was focused on my father during those few visits. He seemed changed—reserved and restless—when we entered the room of this fragile, quivering woman with white hair bound in a bun. She always greeted him warmly: *Hello, my dear Bjarni.*

Hi, Mamma, he would say, moving toward the window, standing across from the specter of the woman who had died in his mind when he was a child, the woman who sometimes appeared to him as he told his children stories. The elf woman who spoke to the sea and could conjure almost anything with her bare hands.

She was a worker right down to the tips of her toes, but her household reaped the benefits of her artisanry. Her thumbs were leafy-green like her dress, and she'd culti-vated an unusually successful garden with little plots for herbs and vegetables. She'd dressed the yard with hand-crafted tables and chairs, where you could sit to listen to the undulations of the ocean. Her furniture could have been on display in a showroom in Copenhagen. She and her husband had made all of it during the bright summer nights before they were married; they were cash-poor but economical and artistic, and they soon became rich with children. Her husband died when their sons were still young—and after that, she saw no way to care for her youngest son. Only on special days, after she'd given him up, would she bring him to her home in the beautiful, lush countryside at the neck of the Westfjords.

People in town were warm enough to him, but not much beyond that. It was as if he had run ashore like driftwood, in a stoic village that sustained itself on the industriousness of an Iceland long-gone. They often said things like, *You're a hardworking boy,* when he actually needed comforting. At Ívar's age, he had already lost everything when his father sank into the sea.

He once brought Jóhanna to see the lambs in that village when she was ten. They ate peculiarly acrid-smelling kleinur, and she held back tears in the silent moments; I remember her telling me that. Yes, she told me that.

Pabbi told Jóhanna about the all-encompassing warmth of his mother's embrace, which he felt only in dreams, because he never held her again after he left. When he visited her and his brothers on special days, he retreated from his mother with a polite smile. She didn't know how to behave toward him, either, and met his reticence with aloofness, I imagine, although my father would never describe it that way. In any case, it doesn't matter. It's too painful for him to think of his childhood.

I never saw my grandmother when she had long

Indian hair; I only know her white knot. But I can see her. I created a composite, this glitched image, from my father's memory. The fragments of stories arranged themselves. My understanding of the world is, in large part, a result of the fictions of others. It's confirmation that writing has a definite value, an idea that would be interesting to discuss with Bergur if I remember, but for now, I can count myself lucky that my father's memories have been reborn in my mind, even though my own recollections are in a sorry state.

The guests have given the living room new life, at least: a girl with big breasts, long feet, leggings full of holes, a sealskin dress, and a sixty-year-old man in a button-down and wrinkle-free pants with peppery hair.

If Bergur were here now, he'd wave me into the kitchen and say something clever to make me laugh, to soothe me. Neither of them belongs here, in this living room that I love like Ívar loves his toys. I've furnished it so I can hear my own thoughts when I'm in it—nothing superfluous or out of place, apart from Ívar's chaotic toy corner near the balcony.

It occurs to me that my father may have felt more comfortable in the apartment I had with Bergur, amid the clash of the piecemeal furniture we collected and the eclectic art Bergur bought on trips—grotesque expressionism was his forte—and god, the junk piled around him, tomes and empty cups and half-full sketchbooks. The memory begins to go black, so I catch myself and divert my thoughts.

Didn't Pabbi love that Mexican candlestick? It was

geometric and jarring in its rainbow of colors, like a Christmas gift a six-year-old might make in school. I bought it in Nørrebro when I was still forming my own sense of style, but I'd convinced Bergur to take it with him to the new apartment, happy to be rid of it.

The candlestick or Bergur? Which one was I thinking of?

"Saga, is everything okay?" Lilja asks in a quiet voice, but the question is loud enough that Pabbi and Ívar bristle.

"Yes, everything's fine. Why?"

"You grabbed your forehead."

"I'm just tired, I think. You must be tired, too, Pabbi."

"Hardly. Guðni is coming," he says.

"Guðni—now?"

"Já, we're going to check the usual places," he explains, as if it's something they do every day.

"What usual places?"

"Places that Dídí could be," he answers, a little irritated by my officiousness.

"Don't we need to notify someone?"

"Your brother knows what he's doing," he hurls back at me with sudden brusqueness. The corners of his mouth betray his anxiety. The old volcano has been dormant ever since I can remember, although sometimes I hear crackling in its crater.

I know I should know everything about her hideouts, her "usual places." I feel it. The feeling rises from my stomach to my head; the room begins to spin; the knot of nerves in my stomach draws together. My nerves numb my limbs. For a moment, I feel as if my mother's disappearance is none of my business. I try to resist the numbness, but I'm afraid of my hands, cold and clammy. I hear hammering—my heart.

"Do you want something to eat before Guðni arrives?" I ask, retrieving the good-daughter role from somewhere in my psyche.

"I was hoping you had some kjötsúpa left," he says good-naturedly. Ívar squeals with joy.

20

Ívar giggles, exchanging glances with Lilja while I free Pabbi from the chair. "Just as well that you bought this thing on clearance," Pabbi wheezes, flushed, shaking his heavy posterior as I pull him out.

I paper over the awkwardness of the situation by asking whether he wants something to drink.

"Truth be told"—he smacks his lips—"coffee would be a real treat."

"With the soup?"

"If it's not any trouble."

I let Ívar set the table in the living room, which doubles as my dining room. He thinks it's an absolute necessity that his grandfather eats at a well-dressed table, so he's arranged the dishes carefully, bubbly with concentration. A moment later, Pabbi's slurped down his soup. He sucks the soft meat from the bone before sipping coffee from a Polish mug. His appetite, at the very least, is still strong.

Ívar follows the assault on the soup with fascination. His own plate is filled with strips of meat and soggy chunks of turnip, which he nibbles to keep up with his grandfather.

After some persuasion, Lilja eats the soup, too, smiling considerately at me. I'm grateful for her grounding presence; I hardly know where I'd be without her, although I've only known her for a few hours. It's remarkable that she simply walked into my life—in the fullest meaning of the word *walk*.

"I think Guðni's going to come along anytime now," Pabbi says, taking another sip of coffee.

The bright side of losing Mamma: I'm no longer my family's biggest concern on this never-ending conveyor belt of anxiety.

"Do you remember, Saga," Pabbi says, squirming a little in his seat, "when I'd make you meat soup as a kid?"

His eager expression reminds me of Ívar when he asks questions like whether I still have milk in my breasts. Lilja is occupied with getting Ívar to eat his turnips, spooning tiny bites into his mouth—"One for the little jólasveinn!"—that he chews willingly.

I don't know that I do remember; I sense the memory, and the sound of the words themselves is familiar. In the hideaways of my mind, there's a buried image—an image of my siblings and I circling like vultures around my mother's smoked lamb. Is this image a real memory? Or is the image the version of events that I think I should see?

"What about it?" I ask, agitated, to wrest myself from the thought, though I'm conscious of the uncertainty in my voice. I remember about the soup—we just discussed it the other day—but I want to know why he's asking.

"Jóhanna remembers," he says. "I never needed to do anything but play a game with her. I'd ask: What more can we put in the soup, little lady? Then she'd run off and grab some carrots or spices, anything she'd seen your mamma put in soup."

I'm reminded of how inconsolable Ívar is if he misses *Fireman Sam*. I don't know if *Fireman Sam* is even on today, but there's no need to take chances, so I ask Lilja to flip on the television for him.

"Can't the little one do it himself?" Pabbi asks, as if in fear that Ívar's level of independence is woefully low.

"I don't like him to touch the buttons with sticky fingers," I say. I'm grateful when Lilja leads Ívar to the television.

My father leans forward and says in a half whisper, "Is that little stinker a bit afraid around you, Saga? After everything that happened?"

"Maybe," I say defensively.

"That's only natural. But you should know—we were all scared out of our wits. And it must've been hard on him. He needs time, just like you."

"Well, I've really had enough time to unwind," I say snarkily.

"I think you're in pretty good shape now, all things considered," my father says. "Everything's coming around. Have you had any more seizures?"

"No."

"No, no, hopefully they'll stop again, like they did the last time. Everything will be fine, just like I told your mamma."

"Yes, let's hope."

"She's always so afraid, your mamma—she just doesn't know how to act in the face of everything you're going through. You know that, Saga."

"Now, weren't you telling me that I was getting better?"

"I didn't mean *that*; I meant the other thing. It hurts to divorce the father of your child, doesn't it?"

I don't have words. Pabbi probably has the beginnings of glaucoma, since he doesn't seem to see my agitation as he peppers me with upsetting questions.

"Was separating really the only option? A lot has to happen before couples with a young child take such drastic steps—"

"I don't know, Pabbi," I say, which is true. I actually do not know what led to our divorce, but I don't dare let on the extent of my amnesia to him.

Pabbi sighs heavily. The reality is that he probably misses Bergur. He loved their passionate discussions of Icelandic politics, each burning in their own way with idealism and a giddy desire to broadcast their opinions. Bergur dissected the words and actions of politicians, taking inspiration from poets and intellectuals from Latin America. Pabbi listened fixedly, nodding his head in agreement before offering something about the decline of his beloved Icelandic society into cowardice and ignorance. They'd keep their coffee cups full for hours, nodding in time with one another, both enamored of their own voices, of sacrificing themselves to the revolution—and both slightly afraid of their wives.

"You never tell us anything, Saga," Pabbi tuts. "One day,

you two are together and the next, he's moved out. We don't know which way is up. Even Jóhanna hardly knew anything—of course, your mamma tried to pump her for information. Are you sure you did the right thing?"

"What do you mean?"

"I don't like to meddle in other people's affairs, but you always have to have your way, to decide everything. . . . You're so much like your mamma. And sometimes, Saga, you overdo it."

"What do you know about the decisions I've made?" I ask, swallowing the lump in my throat.

"I don't pretend to know anything, my girl. But is it worth all this?" he says, eyes on the floor. "I wasn't always there when you were little, but I still wanted to keep an eye on my babies. You have to think about Ívar in all of this mess."

"If you're so in command of your family, where is Mamma? Why is she gone?"

He's offended. "You know better than to use that against me."

"You, too, Pabbi."

"I just wanted to know how you are—"

"No, Pabbi, I'm not letting you stick your nose into my private life. My hands are full enough without having to explain myself to you."

"Don't be so cold, my love. You and your mamma both do this—go on the attack. You sound like machine guns firing off rounds. Can't you take a lesson from your sister?" he says, sounding melancholy. "She's always so gentle."

"Sure, she gently has her nose in everybody else's

business," I snort, but I immediately regret it. He looks horrified by how mean I am. Then the phone rings.

It's Guðni. He's not on the way. He saw a light on in our mother's brother Jonas's house. Mamma knows his house is empty this time of year. Jónas is a retired ship captain who now lives in Tenerife, soaking up the sun while the rest of us slog through winter.

Guðni is resourceful, I have to say. He had the sense to call Jónas's neighbor, which never would've occurred to me.

"I'm going to head over there and check it out with my colleague," Guðni says.

"What about us? What should I do?"

"Tell Pabbi I'll call as soon as I know something."

21

Moments later, the doorbell rings again. My first thought is that it must be Bergur come to get Ívar, but through the patterned glass panes of the front door, I see a Russian fur hat. That can only mean one thing: Tedda is here.

Her face lights up when I open the door. Light locks peek out from under the gray-brown fur. Her brown eyes glitter in the light of the entryway. She has deep dimples, her upper lip pouty, her front teeth a little crooked. Her hair is unruly and reminds me of the covers of the romance novels she shared with me when we worked summers at the old folks' home in Hafnarfjörður, two crazy teenagers in mango lip gloss.

When we started puberty, boys began to look at her with the same sort of desire they'd reserved for the treat-filled chocolate Easter eggs, numbered according to decadence, only the year before. In time, I began to understand that there were also girls who saw Easter Egg No. 7 in my friend Tedda, who became more of a womanizer as time passed. But we didn't talk about it like we talked about other things. She was the It Girl, and I respected that. I was never jealous, strangely enough. Our friend-ship was never like that.

"If you love someone, set them free," Tedda would repeat affectionately to all the boys—and later, all the girls—she broke up with.

"Saga, you look *awful*!" she now says, squinting her eyes to get a better look at me. "Have you really lost it all?"

I lift one brow to indicate that she should keep what she learned from me on the telephone to herself.

"Sorry," she whispers, struggling to get through the door. "I didn't know it was a secret—"

"Shhh," I whisper in her ear. The soft scent of tobacco smoke and honeysuckle floats up to my nose. She must have started smoking again, but I don't bring it up.

"It's okay, my love, I'm not going to trumpet it to the entire world." She kisses me on the cheek. Her touch is cold and refreshing. She takes a step back, gives me a good look, and asks, "Did you find her, love? Do you remember that?"

"No," I say, "or rather, yes. I mean, we haven't found her, but I remember that she is missing. My father's here."

"Oh god!" she gasps.

"What?"

"The boy!"

"What boy?"

"I forgot him outside—" She's hardly finished her sentence before she's standing in the snow in her stock-ing feet, calling out, "Hey, kid, where are you?"

I hear a shrill voice call, "Here!"

"Well, what are you thinking?" Tedda bellows, shivering

141

in her wool leggings and her thin blouse. "Get in before you freeze to death!"

A gangly teenage boy slogs through the snow to reach my door, clinging to the handrail for dear life. Long arms pop out of the sleeves of his army-green parka. His nose is three sizes too big for his face, and his neck protrudes from his sweater like a young giraffe. He's not wearing gloves, and his sneakers are soaked. This must be the famous Óðinn. I hope he doesn't catch a cold.

"Welcome," I say, remembering for a second to be self-conscious about my battered face. "Are you here to look at my computer?"

"What's wrong with your computer?" Tedda interjects.

"It crashed, taking everything I know about myself with it," I say, joking, but they both seem confused by the statement.

"I'm looking for Lilja Dögg," he says without acknowledging my question.

Tedda giggles. She tends to laugh when others would be shocked or surprised or insulted. She's eager—even more so when there's a mystery at hand.

"And just who is Lilja Dögg, Saga?" she asks, with no attempt to hide the mischief in her eyes.

"His friend," I quickly explain. "She, um, came here today to help me with Ívar."

Tedda immediately loses interest and busies herself taking off her wet socks. But she looks up when Lilja appears.

"Hey, Óðinn. Thanks for coming."

"No problem," he mumbles, keeping his head down,

even though he's brightened up since she walked into the room. "Where's her computer?"

"In the bedroom," Lilja says before I can answer.

"You certainly have a lot of guests tonight, Saga," Pabbi says, waltzing in with Ívar in his arms. "Hi, Tedda!"

"Hi, Bjarni," Tedda says crisply. "You've got quite the quandary, don't you?"

"You said it!" Pabbi says. "Our Saga can really use your friendship now. It's all gone to hell here, but I think— well, it's private. But life seems completely different today, seeing how she is now, compared to yesterday."

"Oh, my dear." Tedda heaves a sigh, taking the matter into her own hands. "Let's talk. Baddi, can you go talk to your grandchild while the boy and this girl, Lára Dögg, look at the computer for Saga? You know, while we take stock of everything."

"Lilja Dögg," I correct her, but it falls on deaf ears.

"Tja, he was watching some kids' show when the bell rang," Pabbi says, "about a British fireman."

"Great, so why don't you keep watching it together?" Tedda says, lovingly bossing him around. "Saga, can I borrow some socks?"

Tedda is a trip—a sly, smoking autodidact who moves between countries as casually as I go to the mall. She's been in more relationships than I care to recall and switches careers annually, so she's built up a treasure trove of skills in disparate industries. One minute, she's importing jewelry from India, the next, she's making a documentary about the destructive power of Western countries. Then she's setting up an opera with an independent theater

143

group in Egilsstaðir, or chasing down leads as a journalist for a radical online magazine, or designing book covers. I can't even remember if she's still in the job I set her up with (against my better judgment) as a production assistant on a Hollywood movie filming in Iceland. She's a gadfly, but she's also oddly successful at nearly everything she tries. Tedda published a poetry book a couple of years back, and even Bergur was forced to admit it "wasn't bad." (He couldn't bring himself to a stronger compliment because they've never really liked each other. Once, at a party, she left in a huff because Bergur accused her of being full of shit.)

It's the same story with Tedda and Jóhanna. Jóhanna finds Tedda shallow and unserious, and Tedda thinks Jóhanna is an unbearable drama queen. I think Jóhanna reminds Tedda of her own mother, an affectionate and hardworking woman who manages a gourmet shop—"She stuffs you with love and food until you throw up on her," is how Tedda describes their dynamic. Tedda claims that she is more like her father, a cocksure lady-killer who abandoned them to open a fish business in Brazil. It became extraordinarily profitable. Tedda identifies with him, but it's a bit of a mirage. She's only seen him twice since she was seven years old.

"Don't talk so loudly," I plead once I've hung up her socks to dry and we're perched on stools in the kitchen. The faint sound of kids' TV carries into the room. "I don't want my pabbi to hear this."

Tedda lifts an elegant eyebrow. "They don't know about your memory problem?"

"I hardly even know what to make of it myself."

"But how does it manifest?"

"It's like—"

"Hold on, love. Can I light a cigarette before we dive in?"

"Did you start again?"

"Just on weekends," she says, flexing her feet to admire the zany, red-striped wool socks Mamma knitted.

"But the weekend is over."

"Hey, Saga. Shouldn't we discuss more serious things now?"

I open the window wide despite the snow swirling outside, so that she can light a cigarette. I clamber back onto the barstool with an illicit clay ashtray I made for my mother as a Christmas gift when I was in primary school. She gave it back to me at some point.

The cold air plays around us as I tell her more about my mother's mysterious disappearance and my deteriorating identity. "In sum, I don't trust myself, and neither should Ívar."

Tedda smokes vigorously with her eyes glued to me, thinking and inhaling and thinking and blowing smoke, before she says, "But you've always been epileptic."

"Jæja, but I haven't had a seizure since long before Ívar was born," I say quietly, careful not to let my distress increase my volume. "But this time, I woke up in the hospital and didn't even know how old my son is."

"You don't know that?"

"Well, I do *now*. And of course, I remember a lot, but not everything. The strangest things are locked in a sort

145

of haze. I'm losing control of everything. I don't—I don't even know if I should tell my family about this," I sputter. "What if I told them today and I remember everything tomorrow, and telling them causes even more panic?"

"Well, they're feeling like shit now anyway because of your mamma, aren't they?" Tedda says, thoughtless yet down-to-earth, as per usual.

"Jæja, of course—or rather, I don't know. I don't know anything. My memory is about as reliable as a drunk politician."

Tedda squeals at the comparison. She still thinks I'm funny, which feels good because it means I'm still me. I look for myself in the eyes of my friend—*Saga with the rapier wit*. Please, let her eyes tell me who I am.

22

"Really, Saga, even *I* own three vases," Tedda says. She is rummaging in the cupboard, although I told her the white roses are currently resting in the only vase I own.

"Right, but knowing you, you borrowed all three vases from your neighbors and forgot to return them," I say.

"Your mamma always reappears," she murmurs encouragingly and winks at me as she lets water flow into the pitcher she's repurposing.

"You know that?" I say, surprised.

"Yes, you always told me when you thought she was depressed. Someone always knew when she was struggling. Wasn't she always like this?" Tedda dives back into the cupboard to look for sugar. "My amma used to say you should always give flowers a little bit of sugar."

I roll my eyes. She's so fickle. Tedda usually claims that sugar is as dangerous as heroin.

Done with her flower arrangement, she turns her attention on me full bore. "Tell me more about your amnesia."

"It's like . . . my memory flickers on and off, like a lightbulb that isn't screwed in tight," I say, not certain that I can describe it. "I mean, Bergur had to tell me that Mamma picked me up at the hospital after the seizures. I didn't have a clue how I got home. He seemed shocked—"

"Don't let him feed you information!" Tedda all but shouts.

"Shhh, not so loud! I'm just saying that I don't remember being discharged or any of it."

"Are you going to live inside of this patchwork universe that revolves around Bergur forever?"

"No, I know we're divorced. I know it well, Tedda," I say. Against my will, I'm sniffling. "But we're still close."

"Of course, and that's what he wants." She sighs. "Maybe you'll get back together." Her nose wrinkles at the thought of this.

"Would that be so bad, though?" I say, feeling my heartbeat pick up.

"I guess you don't remember the ten thousand therapy sessions we've had, when we went through your complaints over and over and how you needed space, how he did nothing but convolute your life, how angry you were at his thoughtlessness?"

"So was it me who wanted a divorce?"

"Are you kidding me, Saga?"

"I don't actually r-remember," I stammer as heavy sobs take over. Tears run down my cheeks. I'm hopelessly sad to learn this, and there's nothing I can do to change it. I use all my strength to fight back the violent dread quaking inside of me. "I just feel—" I say between sobs.

"Feel what?" she asks.

"Like I miss him."

"Wow." She puts her arms around me and whispers, "After everything?"

"I only seem to conjure the good when I try to recall our past or the reasons we've split up. My mind is like a video store that only carries rom-coms."

"I'm sorry," she laughs, ruffling my hair, "but if you're still renting videos, you really do have brain damage."

A peal of laughter breaks through my tears but quickly floats away. I need Bergur, especially now, when I'm not supposed to be alone with Ívar. "You just don't know," I whimper.

"I don't know what?"

"What it's like to be a mother and not be able to care for your own child!"

I regret it as soon as the words escape my lips. I know my friend dreams of having a child someday, despite her perpetual aversion to commitment.

Tedda stares at me, wounded. "You're right. I don't know anything about being a mother," she says finally.

"I didn't mean it like that," I say. Tedda, always brimming with life, loves children—and children love her.

"No, I know," she says with a smile. "But you're allowed to mean it that way." She reaches for two wine glasses, fills them with water from the faucet, and hands me one. "Look, Saga, it's not just one thing, it's everything." She exhales. "Ívar, splitting with Bergur, your mother . . . and you, Saga, your mind. What you're saying to me is just so strange, and I'm sorry to say it, but it's difficult for me to understand that you can't remember the arguments, all the times you called me pissed off about something Bergur did." Tedda tilts her head and waits for an answer.

"It's impossible to sufficiently explain something I don't understand myself. It takes more effort than riding a bike up the side of a mountain for me to recall these things. Everything is a fog, so thick that I can't see the details of my life. I just have this terrible ache. I think it's loss."

"Wasn't losing Bergur the point when you said that it'd be better for you and Ívar if he just vanished off the earth?"

"Bergur?"

"Yes." Tedda's eyes glint with intensity. "You said that."

I never could have said that. "What's the matter with you, Tedda?"

"When you first started talking about separating, you said you couldn't do it because you didn't trust Bergur to watch Ívar on his custody days. He'd be so obsessed with work that it would be dangerous for Ívar," she said. "You came to the conclusion that it'd be best if Bergur were just out of the picture entirely."

I'm at a loss. The words seem jumbled when I mutter, "I must have meant that it would be best if he moved far away—to Brazil or something, like your pabbi."

Tedda turns this excuse against me. "Really? Would you send Ívar to Brazil on summer vacation?"

"I don't know! I think it's toxic, putting it like that. Do you honestly mean that I want my husband to die?"

"Your *husband*?"

"My son's father, I mean."

"Oh, I don't know, Saga. You just wanted him out of the picture because you didn't trust him with Ívar. But now you want him back because you don't trust yourself."

"Jesus, I only said that I miss him," I hiss, bewildered that she's throwing my own words back at me. I'm wading through hot, viscous memories, unable to bridge the crevasses they've sprung.

"I know you want me to empathize with your current feelings," Tedda says pragmatically, "but my job is to keep your head on straight."

"Ah, but the brain inside that head has turned to sludge."

"Yes, and I think you're doing very well, considering," she says in a sympathetic voice that I find intolerable. "I'd really go around the bend in your situation. But it'll all be okay. You're just exhausted; you've overstretched yourself. You remember your birthday party, right?"

"No, I don't remember!" I nearly shriek.

"But you have to. It was the nail in the coffin."

I lurch over, short of breath and feeling like I'm going to pass out, but I push through it because I need to drive it clearly into her head: "Tedda, that's exactly the fucking problem. I do not remember."

She laughs and gives me a look of deep, loving sincerity when she begins, "Yes, of course, because—"

"Saga, Saga!" Pabbi rushes into the doorway, gasping. "Ívar peed on the sofa."

"What? But he stopped wetting himself months ago," I protest automatically. Fatigue is about to overpower me, unless what I'm actually feeling is hopelessness so complete that my body wants to be siphoned into a black hole.

"Well, he still did it, the little devil. And that girl needs to find some dry clothes for him. Where is something he can wear?"

I feel a nagging mix of compassion for my son, the poor thing, guilt and shame for not reminding him to use the potty earlier, and irritation with Bergur. Why the hell hasn't he picked him up? He's always lost in his thoughts, no matter who it affects. The complaint shoots through my mind, a sharp spear that strikes my temples and blinds me. *Is* he like that, Bergur? Lost in his own head? Yes, I seem to know that. The windowpane glints. Darkness is dilating; it washes in and swamps me. The spinning is unbearable. I need to attend to Ívar, and she's in my way.

"Saga!"

Tedda is flat on her back on the kitchen floor, eyes wide and afraid. Did she slip in those crazy socks Mamma knitted?

"What are you doing?" I say.

She props herself up on her elbows and struggles to her feet.

I try to help her, but I'm not able to get a grip on her. I am so fumbly and confused; my hands don't feel connected to my will.

"Saga, is everything okay?" Pabbi asks, trepidation in his voice. Then they're all standing there, looking at me— Ívar and the teenagers too. "Saga, talk to me!"

I rush to Ívar, who is crying and wet with piss. I hug him to me. Plump hands grip tightly around my neck when I squeeze myself to his little rib cage and focus on his heart-beat. I glance at Tedda as my father and Lilja help her up.

"Why did you shove me?" she says, more curious than accusatory, but I immediately feel defensive.

"I didn't."

"Yes, you did."

"Saga is not in control," my father says hoarsely. "If only her mother were here now—"

That computer kid is staring at me. What does he think of this circus? Lilja offers me a glass of water.

I avoid their eyes and keep hugging my wet son. "You can find clean clothes in the wardrobe in my bedroom," I say. "I'm going to lay down now. Right now."

23

Her breath plays on my senses and becomes my own breathing. I try to ease into the sounds, but she's speaking with such agitation that I can't grasp what she's saying. Her breath reeks of Camel Lights. The smell sticks to my awareness and coaxes out the unpleasant image of her lying on her back on a checkered kitchen floor, looking up at me. Did I dream that? My limbs are heavy with a soreness so acute that I'm unable to make quick movements, but the pain isn't new to me, as if it's been lurking just under my awareness since the first seizure and I've only now felt it.

Tedda pops a piece of gum in her mouth and makes a frowny face. "I know I'm letting you down—I'll make it up to you, Saga, but they're all here with you and you're calm now and there's a wrap party with the foreign crew tonight and I want to see everybody and I have to pick up the Hollywood guy. He doesn't like to be late—you know how it is, I hope! But you can call me, if that's worth anything. Even if it's the middle of the night, I'll hurry over, I promise. *Promise*. I just have to go now."

Tedda gives me a solemn look, in which I recognize the aggressive love of female friends.

"It's okay," I mumble, confused, into a wet pillow. I must have drooled on it, which means I must have been asleep. "Tedda, wait—who is watching Ívar?"

"Bergur came and got him."

I digest this, imagining the handoff: Ívar looking for me to say goodbye, but I'm unconscious, unable to be roused, shackled to the situation, appearing every bit an unfit parent. I feel like I'm drowning. "Was he sad about leaving?"

Tedda shakes her head. "I think he was just happy to see his pabbi," she answers gently.

"Did Bergur have the baby seat in his car?"

"I assume so; I didn't ask him about it," Tedda says. "But are you okay? Do you remember what happened?"

I sit up gingerly and think for a moment. A half-familiar image of Tedda spread out on the kitchen floor bursts before my eyes. "Yes, I remember you flat on your back. Jesus Christ, Tedda! You just laid there. What happened?"

"Saga, my love, you had some sort of seizure."

"I did? I don't think so. I would have been the one on the floor in that case."

"I've heard of things like this—a *partial* seizure," Tedda says confidently, "when people seem awake but aren't in control of what they do. They can bay like a mad dog, or they can cause some sort of ruckus in public, but they aren't aware of what's happening."

"Do I bark now?" I say, trying to spin it as a joke, but I guess it's too close to reality for Tedda to laugh. Whatever.

I don't put much stock in her diagnosis. "Where did you hear about partial seizures?" I ask, skeptical.

She frowns as she tries to remember and ventures a guess that it was at a Red Cross course.

"You took a Red Cross course?"

"I took it when I was trying to get involved in NATO, don't you remember?"

"No," I say. If I had to remember everything Tedda's taken up over the years, I wouldn't have space for anything else. The brain's capacity for random information is limited. "But you're sure Ívar was okay? The two of us tend to interpret behavior differently . . ."

"Yes. He was absolutely fine."

"He wasn't afraid?"

"No. When he saw me on the floor, he was mainly concerned that he'd pissed his pants."

I'm filled with sympathy for him. He'd peed his pants—and he was so proud to be a big boy. "I guess I should count myself lucky that he didn't see me lay you flat," I say. "*That* would have been scary."

Tedda appraises me, as if she's deciding what's appropriate to say to someone losing her marbles. She decides to be encouraging. "You're right. Maybe it wasn't a seizure, Saga, since you still remember what happened—or, you know, most of it."

"Yikes," I say, giggling a little. "I can't believe I pushed you."

"I'm sure I deserved it," she laughs, relieved at having landed on the right words. "But now I gotta run, hon, I'm super late."

"Typical Tedda."

"Oh, just so you know, your pabbi is freaking out downstairs."

"What do you mean?"

"Guðni called. Your mamma wasn't at her brother's. A neighbor was using your uncle's house to shelter a stray cat or something. Anyway, your pabbi's running in circles down there. It looks like he's going to explode, he's so out of sorts. And Jóhanna is here. Those weird teenagers are trying to calm him down too. They found something on your computer, but they wouldn't tell me what—they said it's personal information and that they're bound by confidentiality. Then your pabbi went on a rant about democracy. Are you really in the Snowden camp? All right, I think that's the update. I'm leaving for real now."

Tedda waggles her eyebrows as I collapse back into my pillow, chewing on this new information. She blows me a kiss and turns dramatically on her heel, so that her hair whirls in the air.

• • •

Did *I* push Tedda? She laid on the floor shouting my name, but I feel like the more accurate story is that my *body* pushed her, not I. *I* just stood there. Ívar was wailing, and Tedda said she thought I had wanted Bergur gone. I never could've said anything like that. He fell in love with me when I was at my most awkward: a gangly girl with frizzy red hair, face dotted with dull freckles, feet big enough to fit men's shoes.

He took in the scent of my body; he endured my wild emotions along with me and wasn't repelled by them. With him, I felt valid, significant. Sometimes I feel as if I didn't really become myself until we were together for the first time. I have only a faint memory of the girl I was before that.

I do remember when Tedda came into my life. She was fierce and flippant and challenged me to talk back. I began to feel as if I had control over who I was, even in the eyes of others. Tedda propelled me forward with her laughter; she thought I was the funniest person in the world. She got me to make fun of my epilepsy. I conjured a comedy routine about the weird camp my parents had scrimped and saved for me to attend soon after my diagnosis. Nobody could go swimming without a counselor, we exchanged stories of our medical adventures around the campfire, instead of ghost stories, and some kids were forced to wear helmets. I'd pantomime a girl and boy making out, both wearing helmets, which Tedda thought was hilarious. Little by little, I found space to stand outside of the thing that had defined me. This was when I'd only had absence seizures and didn't know yet that I would one day foam at the mouth or shit myself in front of my classmates during a seizure, just like the boy who'd collapsed in the canteen at camp.

After that humiliation, Tedda gave me a pep talk. We were messing around with Jóhanna's makeup, and she said I was *beautiful*. Not like how Bergur would one day say it; in his eyes, I really felt I was stunning. Tedda said it just to be nice, to praise me and quell my self-loathing side.

She could charm away all complications, all misery, with a well-chosen word. She picked me up at the hospital with a bag full of video games and candy after my abortion. I didn't tell anyone else—not even Jóhanna or Bergur knew. To this day, it's something I can't think about without my head splitting in pain.

This was shortly before I went to Denmark, I believe. I had recently broken up with Bergur and . . . I can't remember the face of the father of my child, or his name either. Just bloody gauze in an aluminum tray in the operating room, women moved through as if on a conveyor belt—but that detail might be imagined, my mind creating evidence of an intense experience I don't actually remember. If I bumped into this guy, with whom I conceived a child, today, I might feel awkward and wonder where I'd seen him before, whether he had been one of the boys who teased me in elementary school for being an antisocial nerd, or if he was the guy who sat across the desk from me at the bank when I failed, obstinate and melodramatic, to contest an overdraft. It was these itchy, shameful feelings that Tedda discerned and then so easily enchanted away.

Bergur has never seen me have a seizure. I don't know that he understands how traumatic it is, what an insult it is to the whole body. As a writer, Bergur is renowned for his wild imagination, the dry precision of his writing, and his audacity—Icelandic critics have even come up with a phrase for his style, *Bergskur húmor*. But he often focuses on the surface of things and doesn't grasp their real nature. For instance, Bergur doesn't understand that I could— unlikely, though conceivably—die. I could have a series of seizures again and not survive. And what then? Who will cut Ívar's fingernails when I die? He gets hangnails when Bergur clips them. He doesn't know how to cut kids' nails, doesn't even notice that Ívar gets hangnails. Hangnails can cause real problems—blood poisoning, even. What happens if Ívar is allergic to penicillin?

What if I die? If I die, Ívar dies.

My breathing is becoming ragged. He could have hangnails now, for all I know. What if Bergur puts him in the shower and forgets to adjust the temperature of the water? What if the water rushes over Ívar, hot, hotter, over his soft face, and he doesn't know that it's going to become boiling hot—where's the phone? I have to tell Bergur to be careful about the temperature of the water. I can't forget.

24

"Saga, it's no joke. Pabbi told me what happened. How do you know you aren't going to have a seizure in your sleep? Maybe you're having a lot of different types of seizures. What do we know?"

Jóhanna is on the bed, her cheeks still red from the snow, bleating a familiar diatribe.

"What I'd like to know is why you aren't in the hospital? You've got to *demand* that they admit you; it's serious. Mamma could be trapped god-knows-where in a ditch, in the cold, and meanwhile, you're critically ill, yet you've gone and invited a bunch of troubled teenagers to live in your house! Pabbi told me the truth, Saga. That girl isn't a home health aide."

"No," I say, "she's—"

Before I can finish, my sister digs in her heels. "Should she even be here? And that boy is so rude; he didn't even acknowledge me!"

"Jóhanna," I murmur in resignation. "I'm sorry I lied. As you can tell, I'm not myself."

"Yes, of course," she says, chastened. She presses her lips into a line as her eyes fill with tears. "There's nothing to forgive. I don't mean to lecture you. I just feel so afraid. I'm just so afraid for you both, and Pabbi is having a heart attack because of all this."

"Tedda mentioned he was really freaking out."

"Tedda!" She snorts, shaking her head, but thinks better of criticizing my best friend just now. "It's all so confusing. Pabbi and I were hoping Guðni would find Mamma at Uncle's, but we're flying blind now. So, yes, he's freaking out. And, really, Saga—call the hospital and tell them about this fit you had, the seizure or whatever it was. You could be in real danger."

I squeeze her hand so tightly that her wedding ring digs into my skin. I tell her I'm not considered an urgent case. "If I were to go to the hospital, I'd just be sent home after waiting for hours, and they'd do nothing more than advise me to have someone stay with me. Maybe they'd tell me to come for a checkup, but that'd probably mean more waiting for nothing. I don't have the energy to deal with that," I whisper. "I just don't have it in me."

I lean over to hug her. Her scent overpowers my senses: salty sweat and tropical fruit shampoo, like the sea breezes of the Caribbean. She sighs into the crook of my neck, just like she did when we were little and she was the big sister I looked up to, before we became so distant that I befriended people she couldn't stand, before we grew into independent women, Saga and Jóhanna. When we still smelled of baby powder and cheap green-apple shampoo from the grocery store. That's how I remember us.

• • •

Jóhanna, I shouted, *wait for me!* She stopped walking, her expression patient, and held her arms out for me.

Only two and a half years older than me, but still my security. She held me in her arms, even though we were the same height.

Can I come with you? I whispered in her ear. She already had pierced ears, and she was wearing earrings with green stones. I wanted the same earrings; I wanted everything that she had, to do everything that she did.

You have to stay home, she whispered, adding that she was going to a school dance that was only for teenagers.

She didn't need to tell me that; I knew it. She'd dressed up in a white jumpsuit she'd bought at the mall and was wearing pink lip gloss. That night, I struggled to keep my eyes open until she came home so that we could brush our teeth together. I missed when we danced the tooth-brushing dance, a tradition we started when I was little. She would lull me to sleep by reading to me when I could only pronounce a few words.

But everything changed when she started middle school. She wanted to be with her friends, and she'd screech: *Mamma, can you take her?* I wanted to be with the big girls, to wear fruity lip gloss and steal T-shirts out of her closet and listen to her dish about the cutest boys in school. I wanted to learn the jazz ballet steps she practiced on Saturday mornings.

She was my world. Now a grown woman, I lean into her chest, surrendering to memories tucked away long ago. I feel a sort of stinging joy when I think of the girl who was once me, who now dances awkwardly in my head.

When I hit puberty, my peers often told me that I wasn't cute, which I took to mean I was ugly. But I was clever and funny, so the popular girls at my school never turned me away, even though they sacrificed one another to the fires of humiliation. They'd do anything that elevated them in the eyes of the older boys, who didn't know their asses from their elbows. But before long, Tedda made a real place for me in middle school.

On the other hand, I still had an older sister who wanted nothing to do with me, even when her friends weren't around. The age difference separated us like a gulf when she was a teen and I was still a kid. She was always in a hurry to grow up—and when I got to the end of high school, Jóhanna already seemed to be just another square adult.

Now, Tedda, she was something else. I met her when she came to class one day, beaming, and sprinkled magic powder over me like the Fairy Godmother in Cinderella.

As soon as she laid eyes on me, she sat next to me. *Is this teacher some kind of joke?* she smirked.

She made me her second-in-command when she assumed her position as leader of the teens. She was fiercely loyal from the get-go, yet she stood shoulder to shoulder with the others in our class—maybe because she had a mystique about her and was on the border of becoming an outsider like me. One of her requests as my friend and protector was that I didn't make any demands of her. We reveled in our unconditional lightness

164

and developed our own sort of coded humor. We dedicated ourselves to answering questions with wordplay and riddles so cryptic they left those around us dumbfounded. And the way we dressed was ours, too—we wore either messy, frilly dresses or leather pants and revealing black shirts, and for the most part, we listened to rock. Our norm was rebellion. We needed to be antisocial in order to enjoy ourselves socially. We built ourselves a world—and because of it, Jóhanna was no longer my world.

But Jóhanna, fashionable and popular in middle school, became uncool during high school. She was plump; it's true. Out went the tight jeans, in came baggy, body-hiding tops. She became a size too big for the normal stores; her breasts bounced under her burgundy turtleneck and her hips fattened into love handles. She got straight As in school, which I had no interest in, and I made fun of her when she registered for university. By then, she had inherited Pabbi's double chin and was chronically uptight and matronly. Was there no end to her troubles? I had become cleverer and more adventurous throughout the years because of my alliance with Tedda. I didn't want Jóhanna anywhere near me.

Things improved between us with her current identity as devout family woman and quasi-feminist, but I remained the same rebel kid sister who regularly drank herself into the hospital. Shortly after her studies, Jóhanna was hired as an editor at a publishing house. The old me would've found that cool, but the press specialized in melodramatic chick lit and self-help books written by

American authors—so exotic to Icelanders. She loved reading translated novels about women trapped in the bonds of wifely tradition. Martyrs.

Her taste has made her the butt of more than a few jokes from Bergur, who consumes novels in at least five languages. His books were always strewn across the house, and I couldn't help but read the few I could fumble my way through. These days, I find very few books worth diving into, since I've become accustomed to reading through the lens of a critic, a quality I inherited from Bergur. We both love dry humor and the absurd. I can smell the books now, the scent of Bergur's presence: old paper, hot coffee, stale cigarillo smoke.

Jóhanna's favorite books are ridiculous—either too sentimental or too "reliant on the tired trope of magical realism," as Bergur joked when she gave him a novel about an Iranian family for a Christmas gift. Bergur can be a snob.

Do I think she's lowbrow? That'd make me pretty bitchy. Like our parents, we've stuck together in a tense relationship. We've long ceased to understand one another, but we *are* sisters, still able to clutch each other in the abyss.

"Uh, excuse me," a husky voice interrupts my reverie. The boy in the doorway takes a good look at us without venturing in, my laptop under his arm. "So—I've finished fixing your computer," Óðinn says, slowly raising his eyes to meet my gaze. "I restarted it. There was a little problem with the operating system, but I still managed to fix it, and I gave it a tune-up."

"Thank you so much. Wonderful!" I say as I take my computer from him. His long fingers remind me of a guy I danced with in seventh grade. Gangly and white as a sheet, his arms had dangled like worms from his sleeves. I'd always thought of him as "the spaghetti boy" and hoped at each mixer that he wouldn't ask me to dance again, but he always did. I was probably the only girl he wasn't afraid to approach. I'd completely forgotten about him.

"I'll just go back downstairs then," Óðinn says, shooting me a questioning look.

"Go ahead!" I say brightly, but he hesitates. He runs his fingers through his dull mop of hair, raises his chin, and opens his mouth but doesn't say anything.

"Do you need something?"

"So, listen—" he stops abruptly.

"Já?"

"I'm vegan. I can't eat your soup. You have a bag of frozen veggies in the freezer—I'm sorry, we peeked in your fridge. Is it okay if I heat some up? Or . . . do you want us to go home?"

I'm not sure how to respond. I forgot about the teenagers in my living room, and Ívar's already gone to Bergur's place. The thought of being dependent on just my family gives me pause. On the other hand, I don't know these kids and have no real reason to trust them, especially in my condition. Actually, the girl has been really nice, helpful, but I know absolutely nothing about this boy, though how bad could an essay-writing teenage vegan be? He seems polite—and he did fix my computer. He's an idealist, from what Lilja told me, someone who takes the democratic

167

method for a test drive instead of merely writing an essay about it.

"Please stay a little longer," I say. "You can eat anything you find."

Jóhanna looks at me, confused. "Saga, I'm here. I can stay with you now."

"Yes, but you'll need to go home at some point," I say.

"Pabbi is here, too, and when he goes, someone else will come."

"Okay, but Guðni is looking for Mamma, so that's two people who can't help me," I tut. I turn to Óðinn. "I'd be really grateful if you stayed a little longer. The frozen veggies are yours."

"Thank you," he says formally. "You just need to restart, then everything will be fine."

"The computer? Got it."

"No, I mean *you*. Lilja says you can remember some things, but not everything. Maybe you need to reset yourself with mindfulness or meditation or something like that—you know, empty your thoughts, then refill your mind."

Jóhanna looks at me in disbelief once he disappears down the stairs. "You're letting some random teenagers rummage through your computer? You didn't let him have your password, did you?"

"Sort of. They're in a file on the computer."

Jóhanna snorts.

"What, are you now going to go on and on about how careless I am? I'm an adult with a job and a child and a mortgage. I don't need your approval here."

"No." She laughs. "Oh, Saga, you're just—"

"What? I'm just what?" I glare at her defiantly, warily, like a kid who doesn't know if they're about to receive a chocolate bar or an onion.

"The only one of your kind."

Jesus. Why can't she just say *one of a kind* like a normal person? She thinks I trust her, even though she complains that I'm too sarcastic and nags me for not eating enough, because she's the one who will never leave me. But she's wrong; I don't trust her. She isn't lowbrow, my sister, she's just *her*, Jóhanna Bjarnadóttir: Expert in all things Icelandic, loving wife, mother of kind children, sentimental editor, glutton (yes, she's a glutton) with a love of exotic cookbooks, gardener with a green thumb, regular at the local dance studio, and frequent visitor to the shrink during the winter dark. Above all, she's the firstborn. *Frumba*, Mamma used to call her.

"Jóhanna," I say, "please help me find myself in this computer."

"Find yourself?"

"I can't remember who I am, Jóhanna. Since the seizure, I haven't been able to remember my life."

"Go on," she says. She's more composed than I'd expected. Relieved, I unburden myself to her.

"I remember most of the broad strokes, but . . . well, for example, I don't know for sure what my job is. Don't laugh! I have a hazy idea of what it is, and I keep remembering more and more, and maybe that's normal. I don't even know how much money I have. And I don't remember why Ívar had to go to the hospital—why he didn't have enough oxygen, remember, you said—" My voice breaks off midsentence. "Say something."

Jóhanna raises her fingertips to her lips, as if in prayer. "Ívar had to go to the hospital because of a swollen throat that impaired his ability to breathe. One night, it was so serious that an ambulance took him to the hospital. Bergur woke up to find him struggling."

"Bergur!" I find this galling, for some reason.

"You told me Bergur was the one who woke up."

"It's true that I'm a deep sleeper," I mumble.

Jóhanna smiles reassuringly, but she can't help me. I can't sleep with my child in the house alone ever again. I have to stay awake. The pressure is building in my temples. I hear a cry. I can never sleep again. That's what I'm calling out—no, I'm screaming.

• • •

Wake up, Saga. Something's wrong with Ívar, Bergur said. *He won't wake up, he's laboring to breathe, his chest is hardly moving.*

Call an ambulance, I shrieked. *Did you call yet?*

Aren't we overreacting?

Just call, I wailed. *Ívar can't breathe!*

But the doctor said that the swollen throat is laryngitis. It isn't dangerous, Bergur said, grabbing the phone. *Open the window. The fresh air will help.*

But it didn't help. He was turning blue. I tried mouth-to-mouth, but I couldn't get any air into him. His color deepened. *Call again, Bergur!*

They're on the way.

They'll be too late!
Look, the ambulance. It's already here—look.

• • •

"You always had to monitor his sleep when he got a cold,"
Jóhanna says. "Eventually, he had to get an endoscopy to
see whether he has underlying asthma or a virus, something that leads to congestion and swelling. At any rate,
the doctors think he'll grow out of it in a few years."

"A few years is an *eternity*," I say, "at least, to this
divorced, epileptic mother of a young child with a
never-ending cold." I don't know if my sister understands
my reality. I hardly understand it myself.

"I don't envy you," Jóhanna says sympathetically.

"Also"—I avoid her eyes to say this next part, hoarse
with the sadness of it—"I don't remember why Bergur and
I divorced. Can you tell me?"

I've hardly finished the question when everything in
my periphery starts to spin. I focus on Jóhanna to keep
myself grounded. I bite her sentences in half to swallow
individual words, forcing them down.

" . . . you said you had grown apart; you'd been together
since you were kids. You said he was still the immature
boy who got lost in Facebook rants about city planning
when he should have been playing with Ívar. He didn't
have a good head on his shoulders, you said, just a good
laptop. And you said it was no treat to live with an author,
no matter how avant-garde his work was twenty years ago
or something, because the edgier the author, the less likely

171

they are to mop the kitchen floor—well, unless they're given four free weeks to write at a cottage in the countryside, where they're forced to clean up. You said you couldn't stand his books anymore because they were so full of his bullshit idealism and hypocrisy, that you had enough to think about with work. You took care of the house and Ívar, and Bergur didn't lift a finger for you. Talking to him about this was pointless. He just pretended to listen, like when Ívar found a cigar stub by the balcony door and thought that it was candy and"—Jóhanna pauses—"you were very frustrated, but I always thought you were exaggerating too. You loved Bergur more than anything."

"Yes," I say, feeling my throat constrict at the thought. "I do."

"But you didn't usually talk about your private life with me. When you called me out of the blue a few weeks ago with this litany, I knew it was a stressful time, and I chalked your feelings up to anxiety about Ívar," she says. "Then, almost out of nowhere, Bergur moved out."

I pull away from her to arrest an oncoming headache. What kind of neurotic nag is she describing? Where is the clever hotshot Bergur always adored? This is total nonsense. I can't stand to listen.

"I'm just telling you what you told me," she says, and I can hear the doubt in her voice. "I don't know anything beyond that." Then she steers the conversation toward more practical matters: "As for your job, you don't know that you work at the Tjarnarbíó Theater? Or do you mean you don't recall what you do there?"

I shake my head. I don't know what I know. I have the distinct sensation that I didn't exactly like my work; otherwise, I would remember more than fragmented images, as strange as that sounds.

"You're the assistant director of a new performance, but you also do publicity." Jóhanna sounds like she's writing a job description. "But I understand from Mamma that it's all temporary. You told her it doesn't pay well and that it's a bit of a pain, so you were thinking about going back to school."

I shake my head, feeling lost. None of it seems to have anything to do with me. Despite the risk-taking and instability involved in the movie business, I've missed its familiar processes and lively environment. My film colleagues were like my third family; they shared a world with me that none of my other families knew anything about, not even Bergur. I had it all, and now I work in an empty office, newly divorced. "The theater isn't my home," I say, and I know I'm right. Maybe I'll work in film again when my health allows, but on my own terms.

"What about your phone? Hasn't anybody tried to contact you? Have you gotten messages from work or anything like that?"

"I lost my cell when I had the first seizure," I say. My phone and computer hold the keys to my daily life; I feel that I'm in danger of losing a big part of myself. My closest friends remind me of a hall of mirrors: their eyes show me some of who I am, but my reflection is distorted. They don't all see the same person.

"Saga, are you okay?"

"I'm okay," I say. "I'm just taking in this new information. Next question: If I wanted to go back to school . . . do I have the means?"

"I . . . think you owe a lot of back taxes," Jóhanna says reluctantly. "The apartment had to be in Bergur's name, but you got Pabbi to sign a guarantee so that you wouldn't end up in trouble in escrow. Remember? I was a witness. I don't think you wanted me to know about your financial situation—working day and night at the theater, and Bergur only bringing in money here and there. Oh, you need to make sure he doesn't stick you with the taxes."

Bergur has no interest in money—the material world is not his thing. Paying bills or keeping a budget feels like a burden. But I beam when I think back to when Bergur and I were kids. We lived for films, music, books, road trips— and we loved each other. I remember idolizing Bergur for giving a homeless person fifty euros when we were on a school trip in France. He asked me whether we had more need for this money than the old woman in the street. *No, she needs it more*, I said, and my jaw dropped when he placed the bill in her palm with a self-satisfied grin.

Then something shifted. I became the type of person who took control without a second thought. If I ever stopped to think, the house of cards would fall, and my debts would become something more menacing.

"Talk to your tax person, Saga. Tomorrow—first thing."

"I know," I say. I picture my accountant: a motherly woman in her sixties, sitting by a computer at a desk piled high with folders. She glanced at my stomach, swelling with pregnancy, and said that I was carrying a boy. *I can sense these things*, this practical woman said, turning back to the stack of tax returns. When my doctor gave me the same news at twenty weeks, I burst out that my accountant had already informed us.

It's a good memory, one my brain will allow to enter, and I hurry to tell Jóhanna before it retreats again. She laughs. Now, that's her kind of story.

I'm still smiling as I open my laptop. The computer boots up, revealing a checkerboard of blue folders. I don't know which to open first.

"Saga," Jóhanna says.

"Yes? What?" I say, slightly irritated. I wish she'd let me focus.

"Thank you for telling me all of that. I appreciate that you came to me."

"Thank you for being here for me," I say, and despite myself, I feel real gratitude for my big sister, my first protector. "I should have come to you with this, instead of Tedda."

"Oh—have you told Tedda everything?" she says. She sounds hurt.

"Some things," I say. "Look, here's everything. Where should we begin?"

"At the beginning, with *A*." That's Jóhanna, practical to the very end. I click on a folder labeled *Applications and Budget*.

25

My entire world might be contained in this computer. Jóhanna has already started to dig through my files, and I know that she, like me, has butterflies in her stomach.

The folder contains digital copies of applications and budget plans for a play called *We Can Never Forget*, produced and performed by a group called the Liars, directed by Vigdís Jakobsdóttir. I can picture a dark-haired woman with a pixie cut and sarcastic smile. It's her, Vigdís. There are a few Excel sheets and a description of the work that feels familiar but faraway—two similar summaries differing in length, probably for different applications. The opening sentences are the same in both:

> *The play* We Can Never Forget *will be performed as an improvisational piece, although the attached script will be utilized as a tool to drive the narrative. The script may be seen as a street map to guide the actors, but the actual work will unfold organically.*
>
> *The organizing principle of the work is a single concept: human memory. Accordingly, we will work from our own*

common memory of the 'guidebook' or 'script'; the perfor-
mance is a form of research into the ways that we as human
beings tread water in a sea of memories. We are formed by
our memories—or rather, our roles are. Is there a way to
escape inevitability? To be other than what we are?

The project statement is so prescient, it seems ironic.

"Are you sure you weren't a lab rat?" But Jóhanna quickly realizes the joke didn't go over well, and she leans over to hug me.

We sit there for a while, looking out into the howling dark, out where Ívar was lost, and I can sense that she's thinking about our mother too. We're wondering what's become of her. But we have to get back to our work.

She opens a file named *We Can Never Forget*. "There's nothing here, just some notes," she tells me a moment later. "Is that what you call a script?"

"It's an improvisational performance," I remind her. "Try clicking on *Press*."

She clicks on *Memory of the World/Our Role*, where we find a few drafts of short texts about the work, most of them along the same lines as the application statement. I look at Jóhanna, whose wan smile signals she's humoring me but we won't find anything useful. She clicks on the file: *Health*.

To Do:
A) Speak with Bergur about Ívar sleeping in the same room with him. Absolutely forbid him from hiring an overnight babysitter.

B) Ask Ívar's teacher to listen to his breathing.
C) Get a new inhaler for Ívar.
D) Make appointment/Domus Medica/Ívar.
E) Remember to take medication.

My to-do list reminds me that I forgot to pick up my prescriptions. In my daily life, there's so much to think about, and my work has always taken precedence. But I've always remembered to take my medicine like clockwork when I know I'll be under pressure at work—to say nothing of long night shoots, when I'd take several doses ahead of time. Until recently, I'd been able to function just like everyone else.

Could it be that I didn't take care of myself last week and forgot to take my medicine?

Then I must have been more than a little stressed; I tend to keep a better eye on myself when I'm with Ívar, given the scare we had. But long shifts with a child are of a different nature than long shifts at work, and it makes sense that I'd be sleep-deprived enough to forget. The medicine cabinet in the bathroom is full. Maybe it was already like that—or did somebody pick up a new prescription after the seizures?

I remind myself of the know-it-all teenage girl who didn't feel the need to listen to the doctor—the girl who always lied and said she didn't drink wine so that he would increase her dosage, perplexed by the convulsions she always seemed to go through after long nights of drinking she never admitted to. She felt less like a freak when she told herself that she controlled the ride. When she behaved like her medical diagnosis was a lot of nonsense, she felt that she was free from the attacker on her heels, who pursued her like a shadow and attacked from behind— threw her to the ground wherever she was, unconscious while he raped her so violently that she foamed at the mouth and pissed and shit, writhed in the stink of herself.

She longed to take control, direct her own body, her own life; to direct all of the functions of the world, if need be. She believed that the dosage he had given her was too high, that she was freer from her attacker than the doctor would let on. As long as she lied, she could live according to her own mind, manipulating her own dosage so that she was in control. She—not he, the attacker.

She was on medication when she became pregnant, although the doctor constantly reminded her that she could discontinue it during pregnancy to avoid the adverse effects, like heart defects, even though the odds were low. She made the decision to stop taking them without telling her doctor because she did not want to have to think about her attacker. She didn't want him to hover over her while she had a child at her breast. He shouldn't have been in the picture.

When she was permitted to stop taking her medication, she seemed to freeze with terror for the rest of her pregnancy. All at once, she didn't have them anymore, her weapons. The attacker could come back whenever he chose.

But he didn't come. Some believe that the body protects itself during pregnancy, even against itself. Later, when the child was born, the doctor increased her dosage again, and when she said she didn't see herself as a patient with an illness—she was used to working nights—the doctor told her that sleeping during the day and working at night impacted the body differently than snoozing irregularly night after night because of a young child with a tummyache or milky teeth coming in.

But she didn't think about the seizures. Because after Ívar was born, she felt she was free from the attacker. For the first time in her life, she saw her body as a friend, even a best friend.

It was all a lie. The attacker crept after the girl and appeared behind her in the mirror, his face distorting her own. Now Jóhanna can't make out the attacker—nobody can see him, except for me—and I blink my eyes heavily, point them out of the black windows and flee into the darkness, where snow buntings prepare for the night storm. Maybe my mother is doing that, too, wherever she is. Lost.

I recover my senses when Jóhanna says, "The phone's going to ring any minute."

"What?"

"Just—they'll find Mamma soon. She can't have gotten that far."

"No."

I try to comfort her with a smile, but the smile is so stiff that she shakes its melancholy off and says, "Well, should we take a peek at your goals?"

"Yes, of course," I say, feeling lighter now that I've given up on the idea of comforting either of us.

She does her best to lighten the mood, too, by playfully

waving her hands when we arrive at the file titled *Goal*. It's empty, except for one sentence:

Neither control nor be controlled.

"What does that mean?" Jóhanna asks. "I'm honestly curious."

Just that. I feel like I understand that sentence better than anyone else these days—without, of course, actually being able to explain it to my sister. So I say the first thing that comes to mind: "That's me. This sentence is me."

"How do you mean?"

"I don't know. I just know it's true."

"I don't quite get it . . . but let's keep digging." She sighs, seeming to sense that we've bumped up against the boundary of the personal and are now dealing with matters that aren't comprehensible to anyone other than the sister who recorded them before her memory failed her. She opens a file named *Household Budget* out of a sense of duty, but she's aware enough of my discomfort to crack a joke. "That's going to be fun for the accountant, ha."

"Yeah," I mumble as we scroll down a list of unpaid invoices and a draft of a letter I had obviously intended to read aloud to some lucky employee at customs. There, I also find out that I have a meeting next week with the realtor and Bergur.

Budgeting has always been the dirty laundry of our household, a basket of obligations and sacrifices made long ago. All the years I spent filming in the wildest, most temperamental, areas of Iceland financed Bergur's writing, even after the marriage should have collapsed. But the sacrifices don't upset me. Instead, I feel nostalgic for our sense of the future.

And I remember love.

It's a betrayal to Bergur to air our dirty laundry in front of others, and Jóhanna senses that. As a kindness, she tells me she doesn't have the nerve to plumb the finances of people who care nothing about money.

I'm grateful. And I smirk when we find my journal, and Jóhanna teases, "I was just saying you must not have a lot going on." Five short entries appear on the screen.

Turning Point
I've gotten a job as the assistant director of a new Icelandic work. Rehearsals start in early autumn. Can't imagine being away more often while Ívar is little.

This season of my life is over. I'm done with the whims of chauvinists in the industry. I've served them since I was a teenager, when I falsely believed I was the one who was in control.

Bergur made Hungarian goulash to celebrate. But the day ended in a horrible fight, Ívar crying his eyes out. Why? Why can't Bergur even manage something as simple as stew?

No, of course, because we fight about everything. Constantly.

July 17
The End of the Road
Is it true that the Chinese use the same symbol for disaster and opportunity?

August 13

Stuck

Modern society has purged us of our ability to cultivate a healthy emotional life.

If Bergur weren't gone, I could steal that sentence from him for my own book.

September 22

Confusion

Ívar stayed with his father overnight for the fifth time. I'm trying not to worry about him, but I'm still feeling worse than I did the first time. His nose is still all stuffed-up. What if something happens and Bergur makes too little of it?

September 23

Paradise

Ívar made it through the night. Now just Saturday to go! Tried to forget everything and went with Mamma to have our eyebrows waxed and get pedicures (she's going to look so sexy in the hot pots this winter). It was great until Jóhanna phoned Mamma and accused us of leaving her out.

Mamma says she's long reconciled herself with the fact that her firstborn sacrificed her outward appearance for inner peace. She hardly has the means to fix up both her toes and her mind, but in her opinion, pedicures are more important than mental health.

Now they're not on speaking terms, but they both call me. But I don't want to deal with them. All I did was give Mamma a ride in exchange for a pedicure. She wanted to give me a treat because of the divorce.

"Well, that's your life in a nutshell," Jóhanna says, discernibly bitter about the last entry.

"Sorry. About the pedicure thing."

"Ah, don't let our mother play games with you," she says petulantly. "I've told her time after time that it was a joke, but she refuses to listen."

"But I remember you called, and you were really hurt—"

"Ah, Jesus."

"What?" I ask, a little taken aback.

"Just—just—Jesus fucking Christ, where is our mother?"

I don't say anything. I feel guilty.

"It's not your fault, Saga," she says as if she's read my mind.

"Are you sure?"

"Yes, my lovely, lovely Saga. But you know what?"

"No," I say flatly.

"If we find our mother in one piece, I'll buy you both a wax and a pedicure. It's about time, no?"

"Wait—so you're telling me that our mother is out in the snow with furry legs?" I gasp and Jóhanna half laughs, half cries until the sound slowly dissipates. She's so full of feelings, she needs a wider rib cage to fit them all in. Now she's cradling herself, crossing her hands over her chest, tightening them as if she's consoling herself. Then, to my horror, I ask the question, the words that can't be taken back. "Why did Mamma go?"

Jóhanna slams her hands down. "Are you seriously me

asking that?" Her blue eyes darken as she looks through me. She doesn't move a muscle.

Out in the park at Kjarvalsstaðir, I can make out the shape of trees in the darkness. There, between pine and birch, I see someone stumbling in the wind. It must have rained; there's a slick crust over the snow. The trees bend under the force of the gusts, unprotected in the elements. Are birds being tossed around in the darkness too? I wonder. But there's no way out from under the enormous question Jóhanna has latched onto.

"You say you don't remember anything that matters—fine. But now you're asking me about something that you have never, ever wanted to have anything to do with," she spits.

I raise my eyes to her. My heart hammers in my chest. I'm panicking, but I want to understand what she means.

"Saga, I know you know that our mother has run off before." She glares at me, but I don't answer. "And it was always around this time of year when it happened. Remember? The freezer was always full of fresh lamb Pabbi bought from the farmer. He didn't know how to make anything other than kjötsúpa, and he'd just reheat it again and again until we got her back."

"I remember the warmth of his soup. He said something about that just today. Strange coincidence."

"*Is* it a coincidence?"

"Why don't you just get to the point, Jóhanna?"

"Well, do you trust me? Are you going to listen?"

"I don't know what you mean. Of course I trust you."

"Are you sure?"

26

Distant mountains draped in glacial cloth have shed the otherworldly purple of late summer evenings. The fjall-konur we know so well, deep wrinkles of snow lining their cheeks, snowdrifts padding on their plump bellies—they look out over lava fields all the way to the sea, ugly in the winter wind. The waves seethe behind the aluminum plant Jóhanna once tricked me into believing was a stranded cargo ship, full of monsters covered in green slime that steal little children from their parents.

We coil closer and closer toward the city, farther from the outskirts, near our old home: a house that looks over vast plains of ancient lava.

The bluish tones of winter gloaming play around us. The day is windy. In summer, our neighbors had begun to build a small garage, but it wasn't complete before autumn arrived. Iron beams and a scattering of wooden planks froze with the first frost; thick chunks of cement began to disintegrate, leaving little but sand. The sand blows into our eyes in the autumn wind, beating against the windows of nearby houses already caked with mud.

Outside the kitchen windows, which are always immaculately clean, the lava fields paint a kelpy-brown canvas dotted with gray flecks of ice. If I stare long enough, the mossy-green tones run together with the red clay of basalt, merging into a shifting gray that finds its source in the sea bottom. In the driveway is a LADA Vesta Sport, shiny and red like lacquer, but with a rusty, gray tail pipe. My father waxed that car every weekend. The light from the kitchen is comfortable; candlesticks placed squarely between two handsewn curtains of delicate lace illuminate the panes. Elínborg gave the material to my mother as a housewarming gift before they stopped speaking. She said she did that because my mother is a woman who never gives herself anything decent.

"Should we go inside?" Jóhanna asks in a voice as silvery-clear as a child's. I tighten my grip on her hand. We approach, open the doors, breathe in the scent of our childhood: cleaning chemicals, percolating coffee, zinc baby lotion in a pink bottle, fresh laundry from the washer in a tub, Salem Lights, sizzling cutlets in a pan. It all runs together into a singular sense of home.

"Where is everyone?"

"Mamma is heating up dinner, but she says she doesn't really have an appetite. She went into the bathroom, and she hasn't come out yet. She's been in there so long that dinner's burnt," Jóhanna says indifferently.

"Is she waiting for something?"

"Nighttime. She really wants to sleep, but she can't."

"Why's that?"

"Because she has us. You, me, Guðni."

"Why does she want to sleep?"

"You already know."

My head is so heavy that I can hardly turn in her direction. I can't move; I'm held fast inside of myself at this horrible place. This place is so terrible but so wonderful that I feel like I'm going to cry. I need to, but I can't. The wind is picking up, howling so loudly that I can't hear a word, even though we're inside. What did she say?

"What did you say?"

"You already know!" A little girl's face flashes over Jóhanna's. "You're just being an idiot."

"But I don't know," I wail.

Then she hurries me into our parents' bedroom. Their bed is broad, with two large orange baskets of clean laundry, mostly from us kids, at its foot. On my father's side is a bedside table with a clock radio and two books: *Candide* and a thriller by Alistair MacLean. On my mother's side is the changing table loaded with neatly folded children's clothes, powder, baby oil, cream. In the window, she's hung curtains made of the same fine material that Elínborg gave her as a gift: dark pink with white stripes, not tied in the middle but on the sides. They've already been pulled across the window.

I sit with Guðni in my arms under a down comforter with green stripes. It smells of our mother and her youngest child. He seems as big as me; he's heavy and it's difficult to hold him steady, even though he's only one year old, much younger than I am. I'm now four years old and have to watch over him.

"Jóhanna, I don't want to be here, I can't," I beg her tearfully.

"You promised to trust me!" she says, perturbed.

Suddenly, I hear a piercing sound, something smashing, and Mamma crying out.

The wave of sound fills our mouths with mud, gums up our cold veins. My heart pounds, beating too quickly or too slowly, I'm not sure. Time does not want to pass, but it passes; minutes inch forward. I don't want to exist. I call to Jóhanna, but she can't hear me.

"I'm going to help her," Jóhanna says quickly.

"No, don't go," I beg her.

"You have to watch Guðni. I'm going to help Mamma so that he doesn't kill her," she snaps, hushed.

"Jóhanna, wait!"

"What?"

"How do I know that it happened like that? You were just a kid."

"I can only remember what I remember—nobody else can tell you anything. Nobody!" the adult Jóhanna bites, even though she's trying to remain calm for her little sister. She seems to be aware of the heaviness of her own words when she lets go of my hand and drops her face into her palms. And there we sit, two sisters, silent, on our parents' old bed in a room on Miklabraut, condemned by circumstances to sit alone, as if our entire lives have led up to this moment.

"What happened?" I ask after a long pause. The words get stuck to the lid of my mouth. I feel like I don't have control over them; they've become glued to my tongue like during the last seizure.

"He attacked her, just like he always attacked her when he drank."

189

"Always?"

"Yes, but he didn't drink that often," my big sister says. She was so little when she saw him sneak out to the house to buy landi from the local taxi driver, who lived right by us in a shack. The yard was full of rusted iron, broken bits of wood, and hubcaps. She remembers all too well what had happened the last time our father dashed over there like an ashamed dog; so much had happened that she could hardly believe he'd ever go back. She'd prayed that the taxi driver would end up in a terrible accident and disappear, but it didn't matter how hungry she was to control it; she could not bring it to an end. Her home was a doomed airplane taking flight, a warning light blinking.

Our father was good. He was amusing and kind when he was in a good mood. He told sidesplitting anecdotes and fooled around like a little boy with his kids, who loved him just as much as they loved their mamma. But when he drank, it was as if he were possessed, our mother had told us, and Jóhanna agreed with her: he had been drinking himself into an early grave, and she believed that he would understand that he couldn't drink anymore after he went berserk when Guðni was born. And so came The Day. She had long waited for it: show-and-tell, when all the kids in her class brought their favorite toys to school. Of course, she brought Dísa, her doll, in actual children's clothing: a purple cotton onesie with a cloth diaper and pink leggings. The sun came out early that morning; the sun and the snow gave the day such a blinding brightness that it almost *had* to turn out well. But then the sky turned gray.

Ice in the air, Pabbi in his thin linen shirt, exhaling steam when he snuck to the taxi driver's. For the last few weeks, he had been volatile, so she had avoided crossing paths with him. He would often scold her for nothing or for something he himself had done, like losing the car keys or forgetting to put the cheese back in the fridge. She had long ago begun to suspect that he was sneaking over to the house next door again; she watched him attentively, although she didn't want him to know, while she helped Mamma take care of Saga. Jóhanna was the least well-behaved of all of them, but she was always beside herself when she got in trouble, as if she could have done anything differently. She was only trying to take care of them.

Her internal seismograph told her that the strain was getting to her father, even though he wanted to be good—she knew that he wanted to.

But the tension ratcheted up until it took over and he lost control of himself.

The reality was as immutable as the iron that had frozen to the earth with no way out. I empathize with the little girl, but I almost can't bring myself to ask: "Did he hit Mamma? Wasn't it just a bunch of arguing?"

"I remember him standing over her—he was terrifying, and he screamed at her when I tried to stop him," Jóhanna says weakly. "The year before, I remember hearing a bone snap when he hit her, or I think so, anyway, but I was so small. Sometimes I thought he might—"

"What?"

The little girl disappears and Jóhanna, my adult sister, is looking back at me, looking queasy. "Sometimes I was afraid that he had forced himself on her," she says finally, swiftly. She falls silent, then hesitates, tells me that sometimes she thinks she can still hear the sound, but she doesn't know for sure. She'd always imagined the worst when she heard that sound, the sound that conjured horrors in her mind.

"I don't know what I heard," she says, "just what I think I heard. But I believe I saw more than I can remember."

A profound anger takes hold of me, and it's so sharp that I want to hit her. Shove her. She has no right to imply such disgusting things when she can't even say for sure if they happened. But Jóhanna doesn't even notice my revulsion, or maybe she's just determined to tell me. She says that when she wanted to talk about the violence with Mamma, many years after it happened, Mamma told her to stop talking nonsense. Pabbi had stopped drinking by then; Mamma couldn't bear to remember.

"I knew they fought," I say impatiently, "but nobody knew—"

"Someone did," Jóhanna protests. She says that our aunt Elínborg knew about it. On top of everything else, our mother had confided in her, at least to a certain extent. But she regretted it bitterly. Jóhanna acknowledges that it's impossible to know what Mamma told Elínborg and what she herself should have told her. "Mamma always pretended that it was all in her mind, that it was maliciousness in Elínborg to make something like that up. But Elínborg helped me remember it and asked me to never forget the violence," Jóhanna says.

"You know she could never stand Pabbi," I say brusquely. "She was always jealous of him."

"So Mamma says."

"She *was*, Jóhanna. She was always saying something ugly about him."

"Yeah, you say that, but you were only four years old when they stopped talking. Elínborg wanted Mamma to marry someone else when she glimpsed what he was like when he drank."

"So *you* say, but you weren't even born when they met!" I say. Suddenly, I feel the violence that's sitting in my extremities, an unbearable urge to strike my sister. I feel like she is trying to force me into her memory to make it my own.

Mamma, are you sick? Jóhanna cries, but I can't get myself to move. I stare at them, transfixed, while the blows shake the door. He is going to break it to get to us. Mamma says, *Soss, soss, svona, elskan,* to Jóhanna, who is pretending to be asleep. A loud crack as the door gives in and the door-frame sends splinters of wood flying. We scream. Guðni is tiny, pressed tightly to my mother's breasts, which are so heavy with milk that it's soaked through her nightgown.

Get away from us! Mamma screams. *The kids are here, goddamnit!* But it's like he doesn't see us.

When the next child was born, Katrín Bjarnadóttir, Mamma didn't try to lock herself away with the children but instead threw herself into the lion's den in the hope that we wouldn't see him mistreat her.

Was it really like that? I try to puzzle together an image from Jóhanna's words. I feel the horror drawing closer, a fear that still eats me from the inside three decades later. In some difficult-to-understand way, I feel that my reaction is just like it should be in precisely this set of circumstances, as if I've gone to an acting class to learn how I should feel if someone told me a story like Jóhanna's.

But one is truer than the other, though I pause to consider it. I squeeze my eyes shut and open them again, stare into the darkness without turning away. Baby feet squirming in light-pink leggings. Mamma crocheted those leggings and I get to play with the little feet in them, and as I do, something ancient and lost inside of me begins to laugh. I count the toes in the leggings: ten little toes. I laugh louder and breathe in her scent, the sweet smell of a newborn, baby powder. I can only see the foot. I can't see Katrín's face. Katrín, my new sister.

My strength is dwindling. I can't look. I look down.

"You remember her, don't you?" Jóhanna whispers, sorrow lighting up her dark eyes. "She was so beautiful and so tiny, but she had so much hair and little hands, almost two months old. We squeezed her until Mamma chided us. We loved her so much. I remember the first time you said: *I love Katrín.* We laughed so much, then, us and Mamma. And she let you hold her; we helped you support her head. We loved how she smelled—you must remember!"

"No," I say, but I remember.

Tears swell and smart in my eyes. My chest is already heavy, a painful stab.

Pabbi is in a rage, standing astride my mother, above her. She's lying in a pile on the floor; cement walls surround them as he draws back his arm to hit her again. *No!* I call out. Somebody wraps their arms around me. Jóhanna? A newborn whose face I can't picture is babbling near me. Is that Katrín, or have I imagined it? Jóhanna has to protect her little sister, lying in her cradle. Her sinuses are clogged so we have to keep her head elevated, keep a pillow under her mattress.

Mamma has already taught Jóhanna to suck the mucous out of our sister's nose with her mouth—not using too much force, only just enough—and my sister isn't put off by it. We just think it's funny. Sometimes, we suck the mucus out of Guðni's nose, too; he's just over a year older than Katrín. *Just think, what nonsense, they're almost Irish twins!* Mamma fusses teasingly, although there's seldom an opportunity to sit over a Salem Light and a cup of coffee with Gurra next door. Now, Katrín's nose is so blocked up that all I hear is Jóhanna's constant attempts to suck it all out, and it isn't amusing. Guðni is crying and I'm crying. It's always like this when Mamma and Pabbi fight. The horror makes my stomach seethe.

"Why can't I see it like you?" I ask.

Jóhanna strokes my cheek. "Because we have to forget in order to move on," she says affectionately. "And we all did that—everyone except for Mamma. She disappears every autumn, right when the days start to get shorter."

"Yes," I say, feeling certain. I want to pull myself to Jóhanna, but I can hardly move.

"It was about this time of year," Jóhanna says. She hesitates just a little, gathering her thoughts before she continues to relate the night my father snuck off to the taxi driver's house and she knew, without a doubt, that the night would be bad, even though he hadn't done anything to harm us in a long time, not since Mamma was carrying

Katrín. She sits quietly for a moment, wipes her eyes.

She smiles, full of understanding, when I risk the question, "How was the night bad?"

"You had to watch both of the kids because I had run off to help Mamma," she says. "You tried to do everything just like me, you told me after, because I was the only one who understood you. You kneeled on the bed next to the cradle to keep your balance so that you wouldn't fall while you tried to suck the snot out of her nose just like I had always done, but you were so little yourself—you were terrified of hurting our little sister. But the sound wasn't coming from her nose. How would we have known that? Guðni was crying in our parents' bed, and you were trying to figure out how you could put him back in his crib, but you realized that you were too small to do it, and so you turned back to Katrín and ordered her to breathe regularly. You shouted, but it all came to nothing, so then you tried to call out when she started to wheeze like a dog's whine, hardly breathing anymore, but nobody heard you. I'd told you to stay quiet, to stay in the room, while I tried to save Mamma. Pabbi was out—dead, dead to the drinking. Katrín was trying to drink in oxygen with her muscles, she couldn't breathe, she had exhausted all her energy, but how could you have possibly understood what was happening? You tried to comfort her, but you had to try to calm yourself too. Guðni was screaming and crying while you struggled to support her neck at the proper angle so that you could hold her. Her lips turned blue and you called for help, but nobody heard."

27

We are stranded in Jóhanna's memory, our memory. I fight tooth and nail. I don't dispute her version of events, but it's a quagmire; the further I slog, the deeper I seem to sink until I am submerged. I will die if I cannot get out. The tightening in my throat is going to choke me. But I can't escape the regret in her eyes. She remembers what I survived, she remembers for me, she suffered for me. I feel the anguish of compassion for my sisters—the one who died and the one who lived—because she should have been the one protecting them.

"Mamma pretended not to see me," she says, distant. "I know that she wasn't herself. When she finally spoke, she hissed that I was never to leave you alone with Katrín."

"You were innocent."

"Maybe, maybe not. I wasn't allowed to go to the funeral."

"I never thought about that."

"No, you didn't, Saga. They went alone, and in the evening, they each disappeared into their own room. After that, it was like Katrín had never come home to us. Mamma keeps a crumpled photograph of her in her jewelry box, did you know that? But there aren't any other pictures. Nothing—except the guilt. Guilt was the survivor."

I stroke her cheek, just like she stroked mine when we were little.

"Children warp things in in their imagination, I know that. I have two kids," she says, looking expectantly out into the night. "But I can still hear the bone breaking. I hear her whimper, *Don't, Bjarni!* And I can still hear him going at her relentlessly, even though, more than anything else, I wish that the sound had just been a figment of my imagination, created by dread. I'd seen a movie in which a woman was raped and the sound was the same—maybe I saw it much later and it reminded me of the same sound, even though it wasn't. And maybe I've imagined it all, Saga. Maybe." She stares at me, her eyes bloodshot, and mumbles, "I hope that it was just a figment of my imagination, just like they want it to be. Because I love Pabbi just like I love you and Mamma and Guðni."

"Our father is a good man," I say, trying to hold back tears. I'm falling into a wormhole of some type. I'm tired enough, curious enough, not to resist.

28

I collapse into the mire, forced under by the rush of thought. We're standing on the threshold of Elínborg's home, our fingers laced like little-girl hands, our bodies shoulder-width apart. I am very still and very quiet as Jóhanna steps forward to ring the doorbell.

I never really liked Elínborg, our mother's sister. But now she's right there with her strong perfume, the coiffed curls that she styled with a hot iron, the chicken pox scars on her forehead. She is imposingly tall, elegant and lithe in her movements, and she wears fashionable clothes and red lipstick. She has an anachronistic way of speaking, even though she's only five years older than our mother. *How tremendously childish you are, starry-eyed like a newborn lamb.* I don't remember her visiting us, but I seem to recall visiting her with my mother when I was young. After that, I always went with Jóhanna.

But she's here now, a vision welcoming us from her doorway, thin and chic in polyester pants and a matching blouse, a silk scarf wrapped around her neck like a flight attendant. We say a shy hello in tandem, then Jóhanna speaks for us both, asking if we can come in.

"Of course," Elínborg says, moving to the side as we squeeze past her into the little apartment on Barónstígur, where she lives with an old Siamese cat.

"Our mother is lost," Jóhanna says to Elínborg.

"I know why, even though she's stopped talking to me. I haven't told her anything she doesn't already know," Elínborg says finally. Still, she visibly misses my mother, so she veers away from this tack and invites us to sit at her kitchen table, which is only intended for two, but we're small and make space in the bright kitchen. Elínborg's blue Turkish vase catches my eye, filled, as always, with flowers.

"We know why Mamma is lost, too," Jóhanna says.

"We do?"

"Yes," my sister says. "You know."

"Because your father is a bastard," Elínborg says, "but you can't do anything about that now, elskurnar."

Her hands tremble as she cuts a slice of lemon cake and moves it to a square crystal dish.

"Pabbi has been good for more than thirty years," Jóhanna says, taking the slice of cake.

"Good? Ha!" Elínborg snorts, slapping a slice of cake down on a plate for me. Nodding her head toward Jóhanna, she remarks, "You never needed to encourage *her* to eat."

I'm offended for my sister but launch into a defense of my father: "He was young and angry. He had never been loved before he met Mamma—he was left to fend for himself with some distant relatives, abandoned by his mother and his father dead."

Jóhanna looks astonished—I infrequently share her opinions—and eager to hear more, so I let it all out. "He was so lonely when he met Mamma at that sveitaball—was it in Reykhólar? They were just teenagers. Then, all of sudden, they had a kid."

"All abusers have a story. Don't feel sorry for your father," Elínborg says. "He beat your mother, and, in my view, he killed your sister. What more do you need to know?"

"Katrín could have died even if they weren't fighting."

"They weren't *fighting*, Saga. He was beating her."

"Maybe she died of SIDS? We won't ever know what really happened," I say. "Jóhanna isn't sure about anything."

"Your father stopped drinking after that night, so he must've felt responsible for something," Elínborg retorts. Her Siamese cat slithers against her calves.

"Well, if he was so drunk, could he even remember what happened?" I say, which sounds ridiculous as soon as it leaves my mouth.

"*We* remember how Katrín died," Jóhanna says.

"Listen to Jóhanna," Elínborg says.

"I really only know what you've told me," Jóhanna says then, expression murky. "Yes, I know, I know—I heard the noise. But I can't really be sure what I heard, whether he was just ranting or . . . and you don't know either, Elínborg."

"I know what I know. I know that my sister would cover the bruises with makeup. I know that I no longer know my sister because she's married to a pathetic monster."

I've had enough. I get to my feet, push past Jóhanna's

chair, and say, "Listen, Elínborg! Mamma was bad to him too. She was so nasty!"

Jóhanna reaches for another piece of cake.

"Oh, gæskunar," Elínborg says. "There are few things on earth as clearly unforgivable as beating the person you claim to love."

"Your generation just doesn't understand psychological abuse," Jóhanna says. "She really does have a tendency to belittle Pabbi."

"Try getting punched in the face and then talk to me about psychological abuse," Elínborg says coldly, "and stop eating so much cake, or I'll stop offering you sweets."

"Have *you* been punched in the face?" Jóhanna looks furious.

"Why, yes. Your grandfather, elskan," Elínborg says. She turns to me and says, "I'd offer you each a glass of sherry if you didn't have your father's blood. But can I offer you a cuppa?"

She hands me a polka-dotted coffee cup—I remember that she bought these cups in London, and that I thought they were so beautiful. I reach for the cup, but her outstretched hand shimmers and fades.

• • •

I shake myself back into consciousness, breaking the surface of the water in a sharp, urgent gasp. I've got one of the sorest throats I've ever had, and the pain is traveling down to my chest. My head is heavy—or my neck is weak? It's hard to hold up. An image catches my eye: our old changing table. I blink and blink again, but it's still there.

Maybe I blacked out and missed something. I'm here, I'm trying to listen to Jóhanna. Katrín is looking at me, but I only see tiny feet.

"She was a fantastic woman, Saga. I think so, even if you don't. I believed her—and Amma Bogga. When I visited her at the nursing home—you know, Grund, in Vesturbær—Amma said almost exactly the same thing as Elínborg."

"Now you're confused, Jóhanna," I protest. "Amma was senile and ate up everything Elínborg told her, which is why Mamma had to cut them out of our lives."

"No, it's because she couldn't live with two truths, so silence became her reality. You know that she never talked about Katrín to Pabbi? She was cold to Pabbi, distant with us—you remember. And he became softer than her, stricter with us. I always wanted to ask what Katrín died of, but nobody would tell me—except Elínborg. Of course, Elínborg's word isn't gospel, just a fraction of the truth, and she wasn't there that night. I was young when I told Elínborg everything I knew. I didn't realize that some people believe only what they choose to believe. I didn't understand that she would dress up my memory, add details from her point of view, and repeat it to others. After a bit, the story of that night ceased to be my memory, my account, and became hers. I won't ever really know what I witnessed and what Elínborg created," Jóhanna concludes, "and that haunts me."

I look into her eyes, world-weary: "It doesn't matter now. You did all that you could, I am certain of that."

"You can't be sure."

"You took good care of me," I add, surprising even myself. I feel a wave of gratitude swell in my throat. "Please don't forget that!"

"It was abuse, Saga," she says, her voice cracking, "but I don't think I will ever know how bad it was. I've blocked out most of it. I remember feeling fear before the door broke and feeling pain after, screaming . . . but I don't have any picture in my mind of the incident, except when he kicked down the door. I will always see that clearly, maybe because it was in my nightmares for so long. But I *couldn't* have seen much more," she says, "because he dragged her into the hall."

"It was abuse," I repeat, a bit astonished by my own affirmation, this new belief, as a fissure forms in my chest and everything begins to move and quake. A magmatic discontent gushes out of the wound, red as fire; I am so alive that I am dying.

She wants me to hold her and protect her, just like she protected me. But my body needs to flush out this burning anger with brute force; I need to pummel something—*sparka, sparka, sparka*—and I have to smother my fury to keep from hitting my sister.

"But it still matters to me to know exactly what happened—how far Pabbi actually went and who is to blame," Jóhanna says. "Did he cause our sister's death? I have to know."

"And if he didn't . . ." I say, tear-drenched.

29

Water pours out of the spout into the bathtub. I bend toward it, fill my palms with tepid water, splash my face. I turn to the mirror, drained. As streaks of water run down my forehead, my cheeks, my chin, I feel its weight on my senses, as if somebody has flattened me with a rolling pin. Jóhanna told me in no uncertain terms that I smelled and needed to take a bath. It's awkward to tell somebody they smell, but I haven't taken a bath since the seizure, unless somebody washed me at the hospital. It's strange to get used to your own stench. I imagine I smell of stress hormones, layer upon layer of sour sweat. I'm ill-attuned to any need, apart from the primal instinct to sleep, eat, kiss my son. Meanwhile, my sweat glands secrete the reek of my reality, of my being. Ívar is swamped in the bad smell of his mother, who cannot take a bath by herself, who can't bathe him alone.

A light knock at the door. Someone pushes it open before I manage to answer.

Pabbi looks in, his eyes glassy with exhaustion. He turns toward the mirror to talk, at least giving me some small amount of privacy. "I couldn't sleep, but I tried to take a nap," he says, resigned. "It's been a long time since she last ran off, and she's in no condition for it. I'm so scared she's lying in a ditch somewhere." Then he stops to contemplate me, the horror in the mirror, before he proceeds to ask, "Are you okay, Saga?"

"No," I say.

"Can I do something to help?"

I'm certain that I'll never be able to speak to him again—not really—about anything other than my son, or debts that need to be dealt with, or the lack of true democracy in Iceland, even though he will try to have conversations for our ears only about the pain of separating with the father of my child. Is it painful to be you? I could ask. But I would never do that. The thought alone makes me even more tired.

"Are you crying, Saga?"

"No."

"I'm sorry, vinan, I'm just so scared about your mother," he says, his voice tinged with hope that I'll say, *Nonsense! She'll be back.* But what do I know? He'd be better off asking Jóhanna.

But still I say, "It will be fine, Pabbi."

"Will you also be fine?" he asks then, placing his hand on my shoulder.

I jerk.

"Did you just startle?"

"No, I'm just tired," I lie, shifting out from under his hand.

"Understandable," he says, looking at our image in

the mirror, downtrodden. "She's so afraid for you, your mamma. I should have known that she was in trouble as soon as Ívar got lost. She can't tolerate the stress of things like that. I'm afraid for you, too, Saga—we all are. It's awful to see your face bruised and swollen."

I swallow something so thick and knotted that it gets stuck. I don't want to lash out at anybody, I just don't want him to touch me.

I find love reflected in his dark eyes in the vanity mirror as he says, "Now, we can only hope that Guðni finds your mother soon."

He disappears back into the hall, leaving me behind in my unshowered scent. I am nothing but this scent, and I breathe it in, *feel* the scent of my fingers, my armpits, and I remember Bergur, shivering in a thin shirt out on the cold balcony with a cigarillo pursed between his lips. He exhaled smoke, looking pleased with his own arrogance when he said, *We aren't fully what we present ourselves to be, but rather playing with the idea of ourselves . . . or fumbling for it in the fog.*

I shed the memory, then my T-shirt, then my cotton pants, underwear, socks, flinging them all into the washing machine. The naked woman in the mirror looks okay, I think—slender with soft nipples and toned biceps. I wince when I look at my face, nose swollen, eyes sunken.

The woman in the mirror isn't going to let me go. "You are badly bruised, love," she says tenderly. "Your attacker really let you have it. Not for the first time, and not for the last time either. Bones cracked—he threw you to the floor, the child crying. He shook you so that spit frothed between the gaps in your teeth. You wet yourself, shit smeared down your thighs to your ankles, you screamed like the dark force that lurks in all of us. It is him. It is him that rules your body. He owns you. You think that he comes at you from behind, but he's crouching inside you, in the body you trust, that you force yourself to retrust each day so that you can function."

I touch my face and smile at the girl sitting on the edge of the bathtub, playing with Ívar's boat. Her dress is soaked; the edges seeming to float on the water, just like the dress Elínborg sewed for Jóhanna one Christmas against our mother's wishes: lilac with a ruffled skirt. Red hair cascades down her shoulders; she has hair like I used to have. She shakes it out of her eyes and I can see her face, chiseled unlike a child's should be: eyes turbulent, and cheeks high over a little chin. I look at her eyes. It's as if I'm looking into my own face, the one true image of myself, but it's Katrín who looks up at me from the boat, bright with life.

"I see you," I whisper to this girl I have always missed. The words make me dry heave.

"Saga, are you okay?" Jóhanna calls.

"Yes," I say, retching. "I'm running a bath."

"Wait, don't go in until I'm there."

"I *know*," I shout. Of course I'm not going into the bath when the attacker is hovering around me. He could drown me. I'm not an idiot.

"Where do you keep the towels?"

"In the hall closet."

Did Mamma say that to Pabbi? That she wasn't an

idiot? Did he make her feel that way? No, she must have said that he was a fool. That sounds more like her.

I told Bergur he was an idiot. I don't remember when, I only know that I did. Maybe because he fastened Ívar into his safety seat the wrong way. I said that he was an idiot because I had so many thoughts darting around in my head. Stress is my heroin; I was always on high alert when I worked in the movie business, watchful with the cutting cold of the glaciers where we regularly shot foreign advertisements and postapocalyptic scenes for American films. I just didn't know that the stress of losing the income I'd gained from working for a bully of a producer would be anything like the stress of watching over a sick child. Now I'm awake, alone, and my husband is gone. I might have called him an idiot one too many times.

I believe, although my belief is disputable.

The memory floods my veins like the water reaching the rim of the bathtub, the words cold with contempt.

Our son doesn't matter to you! I said, blind with rage at Bergur, who slouched closer to his laptop, not daring to look up. *You promised to make him an appointment at Domus Medica!*

I forgot! he said, his eyes penitent, desperate.
Do you want Ívar to die?
Stop it, Saga! You're not in your right mind.
Forget about me. Think about yourself!
This is abuse, Saga. I don't know who you are anymore.
Compared to what? Compared to me at seventeen?
Before Ívar was born.

Oh, you've got to be kidding me! Are you really going to blame our baby for your problems?

I'm not blaming him, I love him more than anything, I'm just . . .

You're so selfish. Such an idiot that—

That what?

That I wish we'd get a divorce.

"Saga, the water is overflowing!" Jóhanna shrieks, pushing me aside.

I land in a naked bundle on the toilet. She turns off the tap, throws herself to the floor with two bath towels, and begins to soak up the water.

"Did you have a seizure?" she pants, visibly shaken.

"No."

"Then what? What happened?"

"I got lost."

"Isn't that what a seizure is?" she asks more to herself than to me. "Let's get you into bed."

"Look, I just need to take a bath," I say, supporting myself on her arm as I climb into the bath. An orange boat floats on the surface of the water when I look down into it, too resigned to turn my back when the teenagers burst in because they heard a cry.

Jóhanna hurries to hide my naked body from view. "There's nothing to worry about. We just got carried away," she says, and they seem to accept the explanation because they head back downstairs.

I am really sick, I think to myself, cool and certain. It doesn't matter anymore if I'm naked or dressed in front of people. Jóhanna rubs the knots out of my tense shoulders, soothes them with expensive, imported Weleda baby oil that I would've never bought for myself but always have on hand for my son.

She hums as she rubs my muscles, nurses my skin with her soft palms, and her hands ignite a memory somewhere deep inside of me: I'm a little girl again, my sister washing my hair because I would never let our mother do it. Jóhanna teaches me a song; she was a little mamma who knew what song she needed to trick me into obeying, into letting her wash my hair. I never cried in front of her, but now I can't control the tears landing like raindrops on the surface of the bathwater. She continues to hum the half-familiar song—maybe it was a song she came up with to calm Hallgerður and Grímur when they got soap in their eyes. My sister, who I've always found coarse, is good.

I soak in her little tune and close my eyes again. I awaken in a forest of downy birch, saturated in the golden light of autumn. Soft-black basalt, fringed with woolly moss, rusty krækiber bushes, purpling brush. A short distance away is a decaying bridge over a rivulet, and I can see Mamma standing a few steps from the porch of a timber house. I can't quite make out the color of the house—brown or blue.

We went there in August in search of krækiber and bláber—Mamma, Ívar, and I—in red rubber pants and matching raincoats, trudging around tussocky ground under a fine mist of rain, releasing the smell of wet growth with each step. For a good hour, we wandered around that place, out east in Grafningur, in the soft violet of late summer under a stretch of rainbow that Ívar chased hopefully. We made our way into the sparse forest in the hope of finding birch bracket mushrooms that we could fry up with butter and cream and garlic, and it was there that Mamma said she wished she had a summer house where she could live every weekend of the year. Her tangle of hair fell out from under the red cap she knitted herself as she rubbed the dust from the windows to peek into the interior of the little house. Then, she did something that I found very strange; she got up on the tiptoes of her rubber boots and pawed after a key on top of the doorframe.

She found it and stuck it into the lock.

Mamma, what are you doing? I had gasped. She fidgeted, resolved to unlock the door, and it gave in with a quiet click. She put her full weight against the door and pushed it open, releasing a gust of mildew.

She looked triumphant, weather-worn after a long day. She was disheveled in her light-blue lopapeysa, but the glimmer in her eye and the loose locks framing her face were almost complimentary. She was so singularly happy that I hardly recognized her. When we snuck into the house, she reminded me of an ornery teenager, grabbing old copies of *Vika* and even older copies of *Andrésblað*, the Icelandic translation of *Donald Duck*, amid cookie tins and old-fashioned china, the kind you'd find in a charity shop. She reclined in a straight-backed armchair, her tired but well-cared-for hands on her knees as she looked reverently, even longingly, at a teakettle resting on a coal stove in the corner. *Imagine how wonderful it would be to drink your morning coffee looking out at all this beauty!* she had said, impassioned.

The memory of a kettle on a coal stove, vintage copies of *Vika* magazine, and endless stretches of colorful leaves is itself an admission that despite everything, I know my mother. When Mamma comes across a conceivable escape, a ticket to a dream, she keeps it behind her ear.

"Jóhanna, I think I know where Mamma is," I say, groping for a bath towel.

30

Mamma made herself a shelter in the room that was meant to be Guðni's, and instead of filling it with the things of childhood, she made it her dreamy retreat, with pale-pink blankets of light wool and the curtains Elínborg had given her when they were still speaking; they waved in the gentle breeze of the open window. Inside was a narrow bed, a bedside table for a glass of water, an alarm clock, and the latest *Vogue* ordered from abroad because the act of ordering American and British fashion magazines had been her special indulgence since she was a teenager.

For the first few years, a cradle was to the right of the bed for Guðni. She hardly glanced away from him, except in the dead of night. When he turned five, he moved into the room I shared with Jóhanna, much to our dismay. Mamma had clung to her private room; she wanted to stay there, she told us. She needed to sleep because she was so often ill. At her worst moments, her body was so tender that you could hardly touch her, even though she tried to hide it, and then we knew that she needed to sleep for a few days, and Jóhanna understood her well enough to care for us when our mother was debilitated by chronic pain. We knew, too, that on the few occasions when Mamma wasn't working, she needed to lie down after she'd seen to the chores that were her own protected lands and cared for Guðni. Her daughters were in the way; her worry over us was unceasing, but she wanted little to do with us. Sometimes, it seemed like it was too much for her to be near us. But she tried, and whenever she managed, there was nobody as good, nobody as clever, and nobody who understood better, so we did everything to make her spend time with us. Jóhanna saw to it that we made ourselves as little trouble as possible throughout the course of the day, so that life would stress Mamma out as little as possible, while I tried to make our mother happy with ill-conceived antics, like stealing fashion magazines from the waiting room of the doctor's office for her and fluffing the pillows on her bed until she snapped at me to leave her alone. I took the rejection to heart. Since then, I've let her come to me first. I became sparing in our interactions, and I feel disgusted with myself for it right now.

After the incident, Pabbi had sought shelter in a circle of male friends. They were a kind of brotherhood of former drinkers who'd done bad things. He didn't go to those meetings for long—I believe he had difficulty trusting the others with his private life, although he felt even less confidence in the man he was when he was on his own, without the support of other former drunks. But he stayed dry. He couldn't remember what he had done, he said—the night was a black hole that had sucked all memory into it, but he wore his guilt and shame like a scarlet letter: Katrín's death was his fault. They never spoke about whether they could have saved her, but he was full of grief. Culpable.

They needed to take care of their other children, and they didn't know how to do it without one another, these delicate creatures who had been a couple since they met at a sveitaball and share a common origin story. Both were displaced at country homes, where work makes the man. Pabbi never managed to connect with the other children at the farm in Króksfjarðarnes; they were mostly sweet, but they were all younger than him and had the right to something that he was mooching, given that he had family. Sometimes, he thought of his biological brothers, but they had all eventually left their mother, who became more bitter with each passing year—she felt such miniscule kinship with her sons that they became estranged, even from one another. He was alone when Mamma took him under her wing. Her love was meant to heal him, offer him a family of his own, but his fear of having her withdraw the offer overwhelmed him. After a few sips of landi, he'd rage at her with the fury and hurt meant for his mother, blinded by a venomous sorrow.

Mamma and Elínborg, meanwhile, had grown up on a wealthy farm in another county under the thumb of a loud-voiced neat freak of a mother who had deployed her caregiving in the service of cleaning rather than coddling the children. Their mother was commanding and stern; it seemed she could control the weather, the farm animals, and her family with her eyes when her piercing voice no longer sufficed. Their father was distant. In fact, he hardly ever paid them any mind except when they fought for it,

216

in the same way that they competed to get the rare word of encouragement from their mamma. During the long polar nights, their father would sink into a depression, lost in the blizzard of his mind, and would occasionally disappear in town for days. When he was gone, the children quietly threw themselves into chores to keep their mother distracted. They didn't want her to raise her voice.

The sisters had three older brothers, all as indifferent to the girls as the girls were to them. Jónas became a sailor after high school, evaporating from their material life seemingly with ease, but he took care to write postcards to them all and still writes Mamma to this day. The second-oldest brother moved to a distant county and avoided all contact, and the youngest took up goat-and-salmon farming in Norway.

The sisters were close but cruel. It sometimes seemed like Elínborg only visited Mamma to gather evidence of family discord, so she could later cut a straight path to the retirement home to gossip with our grandmother. She profited from how impossible everything was for Mamma and Pabbi. Because the siblings didn't get along, Elínborg seemed unable to accept that Mamma had found someone who she wanted to spend her life with.

Their love was shot through with spite and jealousy, but they missed each other so much that they'd spend entire afternoons gossiping about one other. When Katrín died, Elínborg wanted to be a good sister, to help out, but she interfered so much that Mamma hated her. Ultimately, Mamma needed to protect her family, the family that Elínborg intended to tear apart with cruel words. Besides, now that he wasn't drinking, Mamma could control our father with her eyes, a power inherited from her mother. Pabbi enjoyed the suffering of letting her take control, grateful she bothered with him at all.

• • •

In the old album on the bookshelf in Mamma's room, there are a few pictures of them from the old days, as they could have been their entire lives: Young people leaning against a Bronco with a red stripe, Pabbi's arms wrapped around her waist, Mamma standing barefoot on the gravel, a gamine in a lemon dress that eddies on the wind to reveal her long legs. In her arms is a basket with knitting supplies and a thermos. He's in a green-striped work shirt, a thirsty expression in his eyes, like he won the lottery to get to be with this woman. She is sun-kissed and freckled; her smile says she won't *ever* become her mother, no, she will adore her husband and never, never shame him. Back then, he'd told her that he wanted to travel the world and see every country. She'd smiled without giving anything away because she simply wanted to get a good job, build a home that would be truly lived in, and have lots of children with this man. Once married, they worked hard; Mamma was a secretary by day and cleaned offices in the evening until she pushed her way, with brute force, through the trade school examinations with a child at her breast. Pabbi was a sought-after electrician, the kind that folks could reach on weekends, and sometimes he'd even work in exchange for a cup of coffee, a tradition that harks back centuries in Iceland, if he felt the person *didn't really have anything*, as he put it.

Thinking of this photo now, my parents appear to me in a new light—or rather, I see them in the darkness. They were neglected kids who had found their family. They'd had four children and one of them died. Always and forever, refuge is inside the home they made with their children.

31

A memory bobs to the surface of my consciousness. A painful memory, but my mind lets it enter.

You have to come! I am shouting to them as loud as I can because her snuffles and snorts have transformed into a hissing rasp. She is tired from the exertion of trying to breathe, the rasping sound waning with her diminishing strength. I run to them, but they are screaming too loudly to notice me. Pabbi is accusing Mamma of speaking with some man in the wrong way, thundering that she is a lying whore.

Listen to me, Bjarni! She is doubled over in her wrinkled terry cloth robe, faded after a thousand washes. *I swear it, Bjarni!* Jóhanna is yanking on Pabbi's shirt.

I screech, *Katrín is blue!* and they freeze in the middle of the scene. The spell is broken, dark eyes again becoming human. Pabbi retreats as Mamma scrambles to her feet and runs with Jóhanna at her heels.

The doctor couldn't do anything. They waited too long to call the ambulance. He traveled a long way to get to us, tried everything he could to save her, but by the time the ambulance arrived, she had died.

I see them bent over, crying over her. Everything is gray as stone, but I hear the sounds, all of these horrible sounds, and I stare into an empty water glass on my bedside table, numb as I try to gather my senses. What is that sound?

They're here, the teenagers, in Ívar's playroom, waking me. Jóhanna went home with Pabbi after she put me to bed. Are they going to find Mamma? These sounds, they remind me of something—as if they're comforting each other. Then, a moan.

So animal, breath quicker and quicker; I hear them tumbling in the bed among Ívar's Playmobil men and Lego blocks, their sounds sneaking into my awareness and filling me with revulsion. I would have never let them stay here if I knew that they were going to have sex. What next? Is he going to ejaculate on Ívar's new Lego fire station? A teenage girl calls her friend under the guise of helping me, but really so they could fuck. They conned me. They could attack me; they're almost certainly going to rob me.

I reach for the cord of the lamp and the sharp light bites my eyes. I hurriedly turn it off and stare out the window to calm the pain, fix my gaze on the dull light of the streetlamps.

I want to tell them to get lost, but now I'm afraid to make them angry. It's two against one. Idiot. I should have listened to Jóhanna; she's the sensible one. Fear stabs me in the stomach. I can tell that I'm panicking, spiraling, but I can't tell if that is a rational response to being alone with two strangers in my home. Focus, Saga. I must hold onto the smell of him, I am going to recover my memory, I remember so much now, even things I had long forgotten.

A lifeline: the telephone rings.

It's Guðni, with news. "I didn't know if I should wake you, but I wanted to tell you that we've found her. She's fine. I'll fill you in tomorrow. Gotta get some sleep," he rambles through a yawn. Even exhausted, my brother is the steadfast servant of duty.

32

My phone is ringing insistently. I fumble for it under the blanket.

It's Jóhanna. She's excited. I tell her that Guðni broke the news last night.

"No!" she cries, irritated and disappointed. "I waited to call because I didn't want to wake you!" She brightens when I let her recount the events: Mamma was found at two thirty in the morning. Guðni and two of his friends drove on black ice through the storm to Þingvellir. When the car couldn't handle the terrain, they parked and trudged on foot toward the mountains—enormous shadows at that time of night—through snow up to their thighs, gusts of wind slapping their exposed cheeks. They were driven by nothing but Guðni's sister's nonsensical theory, then: a glimmer of light. Trampling toward it, they made out the shape of a summer cabin that should've been completely buried in the snow, but wasn't because somebody accustomed to the routine trials of the countryside had plowed a path to the door and left a light in the window.

"And there she was!" Jóhanna concludes, astonished. "Huddled on a cot in a sweater and old snow boots. I just thank god she didn't end up with hypothermia. She'd brought along our old Primus stove. She could have set herself on fire!"

"She's a lucky one," I say. "Do we know how she got to the cabin?"

"Já! She *hitchhiked!* It's lucky that she didn't have an accident, or get injured when she was walking, or—" Jóhanna is massaging the grim possibilities, but when I don't join in, she modulates to a lighter tone. "Get this! When Guðni and his friends woke her up, she offered them coffee. She started to set the table!"

"Well, did they accept?"

"Not according to them." Jóhanna laughs, then snaps back into serious mode. "Listen, we can't forget how fragile Mamma is right now."

"No," I say hesitantly.

"Remember last time? She disappeared right after you had that seizure on an escalator at the mall. Was that your junior year? Or am I getting it confused?"

"I think it was," I say. "And we found her at Hótel Borgarnes, remember?" I'm feeling extra pleased that this memory surfaced without effort.

"I'll be damned!" she says.

"We managed to reboot me," I joke.

But Jóhanna doesn't laugh. Brusque and officious again, my sister says she'll pick me up around lunchtime so we can visit Mamma.

I feel like a guest in my own home as I trudge down

the stairs. I'm reluctant to say good morning to the teenagers. I don't remember them asking to spend the night and, after last night's parade of awkward events, I wish they hadn't, but I can't help but head toward the smell of freshly brewed coffee. Lilja Dögg is standing in my kitchen in a blue-striped apron, frying eggs like the matron of the house. I move into the dining room. Someone's laid my Indian runner on the table and lit a fir candle. The table is set with colorful dishes and a blue-and-white ceramic pitcher, a curated picture for a lifestyle magazine.

I perch at the table, my hands flat in front of me, and stare at my spidery fingers and red palms. They're workworn, like my mother's. They may have even begun to swell. My imagination is the only thing that's right. Out the window, the beginning of a faint sunrise stirs me. I feel a long-desired hope, newly woken from a restless sleep, sore in my body from everything my sister and I discussed the night before. I'm marooned under the weight of my own existence, and yet a shard of hope breaks through the morning blue of winter. My emotions play with dark clouds, far off in the distance, like balloons that slip from a child's grasp. I can hardly sense myself anymore. Have I become nothing more than a sneaking suspicion? These hands are surreal, but they belong to me. Nobody else. I examine them through tears. I'm thawing; fine particles of ice scrape my insides, and still I'm craving . . . eggs. Hunger is a good sign.

"Katrín, I need to eat," I say quietly to myself as the teenagers make their way into the dining room. Lilja is holding her pan carefully, as if it were a three-tier wedding cake. She slices the omelette in two—for me and for her—because Óðinn has opted to eat fruit cocktail from the can. She brings a bottle of water to her lips, and I notice how white and cherubic her cheeks are, like a child's. She is beautiful in her way; seriousness lends her a certain grace.

I tell her that my mother has been found.

"*Really?*" Lilja says, looking at me expectantly. "What happened?"

"Well," I start, but I find it difficult to find words. "Uh, she went to a cabin and must've forgotten to let us know." I aim to sound authoritative, like an adult, but my voice is shaking.

"Já, well . . ." Lilja trails off with a kind smile. She doesn't press the issue, which is nice.

"Saga," Óðinn says, "I found something on the internet you might think is interesting."

"Let's show her." Lilja races to the kitchen and then sits back down across from me with a little package of papers. I smooth out the papers next to the dish and dive into a printout from the science section of BBC Online:

> . . . *Nobel Prize-winning neurologist Professor Susumu Tonegawa of MIT researches memory "plasticity," wherein negative memories can be transformed into positive ones and new memories can be fabricated, simply by stimulating neurons. . . . Memories about the location of an event are stored in an area of the brain called the hippocampus, but memories about the nature of the event, whether it is positive or negative, are stored in the part of the brain called the amygdala.*

"It's basically about how complex and unreliable memory is," Óðinn interrupts. "Which is inconvenient at the grocery store, but when relying on eyewitness testimony in a court case, memory's tricks can be *deadly*."

I almost laugh when he says that last line, he sounds so melodramatic. "Saga, it's pretty amazing. This doctor, Tonegawa, triggered memories that correlated to specific regions of the living area of a set of mice," he continues in a sincere tone. "In some locations, the mice were given delicious food to instill a positive memory but in other locations—"

"Wait, how big is the living area for these mice?" I joke. "I'm starting to get jealous."

Óðinn presses his lips into a frowny smile and makes eye contact, like I'm a troublesome teenager and he's a patient teacher. "In *other* locations, the mice received a shock, to create a negative memory. Mice sought out the areas where they recalled receiving food, which is positive, and avoided the places where they had felt pain. Are you following?"

"I am," I say.

"*Then*, and this is the part that relates to you, Saga," he says. "Dr. Tonegawa electrically stimulates the hippocampus of these mice and, the next thing you know, they wander unperturbed through shock locations they had previously avoided. He does it again and the mice are suddenly terrified to be placed in the corner of the enclosure where they had been given food." He pauses, eyebrows raised, expectant; he rests his case.

To end the staring contest, I glance back down at the

article and my eyes land on this sentence: *"The brain is able to alter the memories it stores, suppress consciousness of past trauma, and even create false recollections."*

"So, it seemed to us that if you tricked your brain into thinking that the bad things are actually good things, you'd have an easier time of remembering your life," Lilja says while Óðinn nods.

"Precisely," he says, comically professorial, at least to me. "You can't be afraid of your memories, Saga. Instead, when you think about something that bothers you, try to think about it in a positive light and sort of game the system."

He's intently fussing with the bit of beard that's grown out of his teenage chin, as if he's cracked the Case of Saga's Seizures with a single Google search. I decide not to cheat them of their moment, though; I was once seventeen and believed I knew everything. Actually, this conversation reminds me of Bergur and his eternal struggle to get to the bottom of everything, as if it is his role to understand everything that mankind can't yet make sense of while being astonishingly out of touch with his own wife and child.

This is Bergur in a nutshell, I think: author on an isolated, homogenous island who boasts of having traveled the world a "few" times, but lets his son end up with a rash because he is so engrossed by a Danish public radio debate about the autobiographic works of Norwegian savants, who were allegedly autistic, that he forgets to change Ívar's diaper. Once he tried to comfort me after a monumental fuckup at work by telling me that the "I" I was blaming didn't exist, that "I" was nothing more than a narrative device.

Whose narrative? I had asked, confused and irritated by his esoteric style. *Aren't the thoughts my own?*

Well, you are your own fantasy, Bergur had said. His idiotic logic had, I assume, helped him forget the scathing criticisms of his books through the years.

Another bon mot from Bergur: he wrote somewhere that *we are all guilty because we were condemned to forget and, because we forget, we are guilty.* I'd laughed at his circular logic, but now I know that everything I've forgotten is the very stuff that made me into myself. I *am* the sum of my forgetting, and I will continue to forget. God, I'll completely forget myself any day now, I'm sure of it. But forgetting does not erase what has happened; the events continue to live in their own wake.

Anger is welling up inside of me now. It's directed (pointlessly) at Bergur, but also these kids who are just trying to help me. Am I really this irritated about being compared to a lab rat? No, I'm just angry. Of course. I'm furious. I can be furious!

"Óðinn found that yesterday," Lilja interrupts my rage reverie.

"Thank you. It's a helpful article," I force myself to say. They smile back expectantly, as if waiting for a more dramatic reaction, but I just smile and try to calm myself down. I take a bite of the eggs, still beaming as I chew and swallow. "You did really great, Óðinn."

I take another bite to avoid saying more. We chew in silence. I think they can feel my irritation. The silence is tense but better than chatting. I refill my coffee cup and, as I sip on it, I begin to recover my composure.

"Have you spoken to your parents?" I ask abruptly. "Do they know where you are?"

I hadn't really thought about it in all of the chaos. My guilt subsides when Lilja mumbles that her mother lives for long stretches in Oslo, where she is a nurse. "She can work anywhere in the world. And she has a Norwegian partner who works at the same hospital."

I have the feeling that something is bothering her; maybe it hurts that her mother left her behind in Iceland. I'm getting the impression of a tough life for her mother, one in which she has to work abroad to eke out her existence—and with an epileptic child. Or perhaps she found it safer to have her child in the Norwegian healthcare system. I avoid putting Lilja in a position of divulging more by asking her about her father.

"He wanders," she says matter-of-factly, which I take to mean he's homeless. "Like a lone wolf. He's never really known how to exist."

God, she's so calm and sagelike, I'm almost speechless. I wasn't so mature at her age. I ask, "Where do you live when you aren't with your grandma?"

"My mother has a basement apartment on Grenimelur. But I'm with my grandma a lot, next door to you. She's pretty much in her own world, but I can always eat at her place."

"What about you?" I ask Óðinn.

He answers, "I live on the Old West Side."

"And your parents?"

"They're around," he says, sniffing.

He looks beseechingly at Lilja, who smoothly transitions the conversation. "Saga, we were thinking—"

"Yes?"

"After my sister has a bad seizure, she always eats food that's full of good fats. You know, salmon with pine nuts and avocado salad. We'd like to make you something like that for dinner this evening."

This thoughtful bit of care melts the icy feelings I had about them squatting in my home. "So you'll be here for dinner, then?"

"Sure, if you want."

"Yes, I think that'd be for the best."

"Óðinn can tell you all about that too," she says, looking at him with the proud grin of a tactful wife.

"About what?"

"About fats that are good for the brain. He's read so much about the brain."

"Well, now."

He nods shyly and says, "I can print out a few articles for you, if you want."

"Sure, why not," I say, finding no reason to decline the offer, and they're so lovely, both of them.

"Great. Hey, Saga, could we have a little money to buy ingredients?"

"I only have my debit card," I say. "I'll need to run to the ATM."

"We can go for you too," she offers.

"Já, we'll figure it out," I say. I'm hungry again, and I turn back to my eggs when the telephone rings. I shove a bite into my mouth before I run for the phone.

• • •

My doctor, Elliði Tómasson, wants me to come to his office as soon as I can. Jóhanna is at work, but after a little prying, I discover Óðinn has his driver's license. He says that he took the test a few weeks ago, and he's excited to drive me wherever I need to go in my old clunker. Jóhanna calls me from her work desk, which I know is covered in coffee cups, and fervently disagrees with this plan.

"Fine, go with him if you want to risk your life for a checkup," she says, chortling at her own rather spiteful joke. She's in a good mood now that Mamma's home. "I'll see you at Mamma and Pabbi's after lunch, then. Can he drive you there too?"

"I think so," I say, taking stock of the boy clad in the sweater too short for his arms and one of the unnecessarily colorful hats Mamma knitted on his head. He jingles the keys as Lilja stomps to shove her feet into her boots.

In my car, Óðinn initially has the satisfied grin of a tomcat out on the town. His expression becomes stressed determination as he spins out on the ice, and I have to pull myself together to navigate as we jerk toward the hospital. Lilja is stoic in the back seat, leaning against the window with her keffiyeh covering her mouth. She doesn't even look up when Óðinn tries to merge twice—both times, unsuccessfully—and I grab the steering wheel, making us both squawk in terror.

His deep, pubescent voice leaps to a high-C: "*Never* touch the wheel if you're not the driver! Don't you know that?"

"Jú, I do know that, I'm sorry," I pant. "I do stuff sometimes without thinking. Not sure you knew that about me."

Lilja chuckles. The drama blows out of the exhaust pipe.

33

I once allowed myself to believe that I would never sit here again. Elliði Tómasson's office has moved several times, but his face and the framed posters of the human brain on the wall behind him remain constant. He's pale, marked by striking features. His blue eyes have such crystalline intensity that I would have readily cast him in a film about a psychic—or a psycho. He seems to stare through my scalp and skull all the way into the secretive mechanisms of my brain.

"I meant to come sooner, as soon as my son turned one, but—" I say, flustered.

"Well, taking care of children is time-consuming. Maybe that's why you let him wander off like that," he says, pretending to chide me.

"Ha." I chuckle to be polite, but the thought horrifies me.

"We'll do our best to stop it from happening again," he says, glancing at his computer. "Þormar increased your dosage, I see. Hmm. To be honest, your EEG doesn't show any unusual activity; it's similar to what we've seen on your other EEGs. How is your memory now? Are things becoming clearer?"

"I believe so," I say. "My sister has helped me remember a few things."

"Memory problems after a seizure are pretty typical," he says. "I was more surprised by the next note from my colleague. He said your memory loss is specific to thoughts that are in some way upsetting or challenging to you— is that accurate?" His expression is trained, careful to mask the skepticism he must be feeling. I know he tries to remain open to the curiosities of the body, but he has limits.

"Those things—the hard things—are coming back," I say. "But it's strange. All sort of odd memories—musings, really—seem to pursue me. Things from my childhood, even. Difficult memories that I've tried to avoid thinking about, very triggering memories. I suddenly have total recall of incidents that I'd convinced myself had never happened—or that I never thought of." I am talking fast as I confide in him. I'm bursting with all these sudden memories, and in truth, there's no room for them in my life or in my sore mind. Vagrant words spill out of me as I attempt to describe the correlation I see between these bad memories and my physical symptoms.

At the end of my recitation, he smiles. "One's emotions and one's identity . . . both can be greatly upset by a shock to the system," he says, calm as ever. "I can tell you, though, that confusing or even disturbing memories are better than experiencing total erasure. There can be permanent memory loss—brain damage—when a person suffers multiple grand mal seizures in quick succession."

"Those around me seem to know more about my experiences than I do because I don't remember the seizure. I remember a short period before, and I can perceive the strange reality after the convulsion—its aftershock—when the moments began to arrange themselves and I become, again, an entire self."

"Þormar's hypothesis is interesting," Elliði says. "It doesn't actually sound so farfetched that these are functional symptoms. After all, the Emperor truly believed he was well-dressed, even as he walked naked in the street."

"Are you saying that I'm imagining these"—I search for the word—"these *redactions* in my memory? The migraines that descend when I try to recall why my husband and I are not living together?"

"Well, as you say, you've just gotten divorced, and you have a young child," he says instead of answering me. "You are no doubt under stress."

I nod and remind him about Ívar's illness and my own sleep deprivation.

"Remember, Saga, fear causes stress, and high stress levels disturb the functions of the body. It can affect your heart and brain. Lack of sleep also affects the memory."

"I know."

"And you also know, of course, that alcohol consumption exacerbates stress, sleeplessness, and memory . . ."

"Já, já, já," I say, a little offended by his tone of teacher repeating the same old lesson to his dumb student.

"We'll see whether your memory sorts itself out, but nobody can guarantee any of these symptoms won't happen again. Instead of upping your dosage again, I want to try a simple experiment." Elliði falls silent, twiddling his thumbs as if he's about to say something momentous. "Let's try reducing your stress levels."

"It's not so simple," I say.

"You need to take stock of your circumstances," he says. "Work less—find a job that's a better fit. Sleep at least eight hours a night. Exercise. Eat healthy meals at regular intervals. Watch your breathing, try not to panic, relax. Ask for help when you need it. And you need to get someone to stay with you for the duration of this experiment."

"How long is the experiment?"

"Until the next seizure, if there is one."

• • •

The kids are waiting inside the car like faithful companion animals.

Now to follow doctor's orders and refrain from grabbing the wheel. I have to trust the driver, I say to myself as I march toward the car. Lilja seems to be asleep against the cold window, but Óðinn is hunched over something that, upon closer inspection, turns out to be a paperback that Bergur left in the glove compartment: *How to Be Alone*, a collection of essays about man and modernity by Jonathan Franzen. The sight of it reminds me that I must get around to cleaning the car.

"Did the doctor say you're still you?" Óðinn asks as I sit in the passenger seat. I wonder if he's a closet philosopher or just endowed with a dark sense of humor. I pretend to laugh, but there's something creepy about his fascination with my mind. Or is there, really? Maybe it's a boy thing. Maybe one day Ívar will pore over science articles on the internet, when he's not following girls into strangers' houses.

Then again, Lilja is just as interested in my problem as he is. She's opened her eyes and now she's yawning while cradling herself and shivering. "Did it go well, Saga?"

"Yes," I say, fiddling with the heater to try and warm her up. I'm grateful that she's here, this mysterious guardian angel.

"Does it matter what you don't remember, as long as you recognize everyone you love?" Óðinn asks. It's a thoughtful question.

"What do you mean?" Lilja asks before I can.

"Just that we're constantly downplaying everything that actually matters, especially our relationships. As a result, our many realities run together and become nothing, fed willingly into a black hole that consumes and consumes and consumes all meaning. We'll all become amnesiacs if there's *nothing* to remember."

I'm confused. Is he high?

He turns with the paperback in his hands, leans toward me—careful that we don't touch—and places it in the glove compartment. I can smell that his hair could do with a wash.

"I still don't get it, Óðinn!" Lilja pops her head between our seats in search of clarity. "What do you mean?"

He looks pleased by the question. "Just what you say yourself," he answers.

"What do I say?"

"You told me that a world where adults hurt children can never be just. In that world, there is no distinction between right and wrong, just grotesquerie."

"Sounds about right," I interject, glad that I have a spiritual mini-me in the back seat. I turn to face Lilja, who's leaning back in her seat, nodding, looking rather pleased with herself.

"I think I'm right, too, then!" she says. "But you know what, Saga, I heard once that a brain with dementia was like a computer with a working hard drive and a broken keyboard. The information is there—you just can't access it."

"Another interesting theory," I say.

"Dementia is on her mind because her grandma's losing her memory," Óðinn says, looking affectionately at Lilja, who seems annoyed that he's speaking for her about a private matter. He continues to explain, oblivious to her discomfort, "We've read a lot of articles that compare the brain to a hard drive, but I think it's more accurate to liken a human being to a flower, rather than a computer. A computer is just depressing."

"A flower," I repeat, smiling at him. I had forgotten how sincere depressed teenagers can be.

"A flower that must be watered," he continues, blushing, reminding me for a moment of my son when he chatters about something he finds beautiful. There's a twinkle in his eyes as he drones on about a book that was reviewed on some science website. "The work is by a German author and it hasn't been translated yet, so none of us can read it, but the author says that dementia can be triggered by lack of physical and emotional nourishment. Like, if a human lacks security, warmth, and love, the brain becomes malnourished, because the brain is nourished through the heart. Scientists are going to introduce a tiny chip soon that can capture the movements of brain cells and preserve memories," Óðinn continues, "so you don't have to worry too much,"

"Me!" I exclaim. I had been sure we were talking about Lilja's grandmother. "I don't have dementia!"

"Oh, right, sorry," he says, withering.

"Of course, if it turned out that I *did* have dementia," I joke, "would I even know it?"

"Saga!" Lilja exclaims, "I almost forgot! We found something on Óðinn's phone while you were inside."

"What? More news about dementia, I hope?"

"No, no, no, look!" She forces herself between the seats, blowing her bangs out of her face, and leans over Óðinn's shoulder as he fumbles for his phone. "Come on, you have to show her!"

"It's an ancient article, Lilja," he says reluctantly, opening a page on his phone.

"What does it say?" I ask, though I'm becoming tired of hanging out in a cold car, Googling things.

"You have to read it!" Lilja says.

She pokes Óðinn, who begins reading quickly: "*US scientists have discovered that the same technology used to predict earthquakes can be retooled to predict epileptic seizures.*"

Now I'm interested.

"Well," he says, scanning the text and paraphrasing as

240

he goes, "their research shows that the longer the interval between seizures—and earthquakes—the longer each successive interval will be. There are apparently similarities between minor earthquakes that indicate a major earthquake and, um—wait, misfires, I think—yes, flaws in the electrical functions of the brain just before a seizure. So, maybe one day we'll use seismographs to predict seizures."

"I wish!" I joke, seeing no reason to stifle the well-meant curiosity of these kind souls who have made it their mission to solve my troubles. The time has come for me to let go of my skepticism, to let myself fall freely through air and time and sensation.

For thousands of years, magma built up pressure below the earth's surface until unseen chambers could no longer contain the tension. In that instant, lava ascended through conduits torn like wounds in stone. This great quake rives the ground apart, forces fossils and fragments of silvery crystal to the surface, antedeluvian histories petrified in basaltic memory gush from uncharted reservoirs. Lava, hot and volatile, oozes elemental over heath and valley. Everything is made new. The landscape is forever changed. I stare down into the fissures in my own life and hear the foundation fracturing everywhere around me. I let myself free-fall forward.

"Thank you," I say, dazed. "I'd like to get a printout—it sounds very exciting. Um, should we go?"

Lilja beams triumphantly at Óðinn, who struggles to start the car.

Elliði's comments reinforced the hope I woke to this

morning. All at once, the day is bright and vast, like the midday sun under a cloudless sky, so sharp in its blueness that I don't dare stare too long.

I could stare my way out of my body, as I did when a child during an absence seizure, dumbstruck by something almost hallucinogenic, like the patterns etched into each leaf in late May that blend together into a foresty haze. I felt contentment until my mother delivered the blow: "Does she have to be so absent-minded?"

We speed toward Hafnarfjörður and my mood stays lighter than air. Óðinn has the right view. I don't need to remember everything because I remember that I love my husband (although I should call him my ex-husband) and I love our son with his eyes. I might soar in certainty of the love I contain, of my body working well for me, the cells I never see but are steadfast in their purpose, that fire my pounding heart. That conviction makes it seem as if the winter sun is kissing the heads of citygoers. A warmly bundled man pushes a stroller down a bike path next to the road, and his wife (I assume) strides past him on the icy surface, walking stick-in-hand. I see the trio as a positive omen, the shape my little family once took and can take again. Ravens wheel circles over the snow-covered trees lining the path to Nauthólsvík, where the sea glitters gold and silver in the midday sun. The shards of a shattered mosaic have arranged themselves in the right pattern using the magnetic strength of the same neurons that mislaid my memories. Now they've strengthened my senses. The most crucial pieces found one another: us three.

I just have to check on Mamma and then I can run to Bergur, who is almost without a doubt sitting sloppily at his desk in jeans and his robe. I'm sorry, I'm going to say to him, then open the robe, crawl into his lap, and wrap the belt around us both. I'm sorry, Bergur, I can't remember everything, not yet, I'll say, pushing myself up against his chest, sweaty from coffee and puzzling out the world's riddles, but I remember at least enough to know that we should be together, my love, and that we will forgive each other.

Óðinn parks the car at the shopping center while I dash over to the ATM to withdraw cash for the grocery store. I can't bring myself to ask them to give me a lift to Bergur's. I'll go alone.

34

Our childhood home, the backdrop for so many memories, is perched on the edge of endless moss-covered lava fields, sometimes clay-red, other times peat-green, dotted with clusters of fragrant blóðberg. As a child, I'd stare out the window at these fields until the patterns blended together and I disappeared into the muted bliss of coalescence.

Its white-painted walls are adorned with pictures of Jóhanna, Guðni, and me at various ages. The heavy wooden furniture of my earliest memories—the lamps with a vintage fringe, the velvet sofa set, and the stocky dining room table—give way to slick IKEA furniture. Colorful pillows and blankets—my mother's handiwork—fight with the new objects in the room, revealing that the minimalist interlopers do not belong here. A hideous, gray-and-brown painting still hangs above the bright new sofa, oppressing it: a boat sailing through a veil of fog on a Scandinavian or German fjord. Its dullness contrasts bluntly with Iceland's actual nature—the mountains that erupt from time to time and the mantle under them that lies in wait to break apart in jagged rifts. Perhaps Iceland itself is epileptic.

Iceland has changed in recent decades, softened and brightened, shooting out tendrils of connection to the world. As a kid, our spice shelf consisted of blóðberg, salt, and pepper—staples to season meat, nothing else. Now, sizable bulbs of garlic mingle in the old apple bowl and the window ledges are a tangle of fresh herbs almost all year round.

Still, some things don't really change—my parents, for instance. Always unaffected by the zeitgeist, they didn't follow their peers, who have adopted new habits like yoga and taking courses in web design at night. Still, they strike me as reasonably hale, as if they are growing a bit younger after acting like eighty-year-olds for most of their lives. Today Pabbi is playing solitaire at the end of the kitchen table with a light-green deck of cards, his eyes bloodshot and tired, a plaid work shirt rumpled over slouched shoulders. Mamma is standing at the counter, flipping through the paper, freshly set hair and wearing a bathrobe over her clean, cotton nightgown, as if she'd simply returned from a trip to the health retreat in Hveragerði.

I come up behind my mother and do the unthinkable: I embrace her. She startles and then tries to hug me back, weakly, as if it hurts. It looks to me like she has scratches on her face that may have been from something sharp, maybe frozen branches; she must've put on her makeup this morning, her face caked in light foundation that can't conceal the evidence. I dash over to Pabbi, breathe his scent in deeply, and say, almost angrily, "I love you—both of you. You have to know that."

"Oh, well, your mamma will be happy to hear that," he

says, struggling to conceal his discomfort while my mother rushes to busy herself in the kitchen and avoid another sentimental outburst from me. Some women seem incapable of existing unless they're doing housework. I feel sympathy for her, but her theatrical tidying is so annoying that soon I'm struggling against the urge to throw her to the floor. There are so many secrets in my crumpled existence that I suddenly have the urge to uncover.

"Pabbi," I say, launching in, "you cosigned a bond for me, right?" I'm trying to mask the unsteadiness in my voice. I am certain that somebody guaranteed my debt, though I don't know much more about it, except that it was him. Pabbi looks up from his game.

"Yes, I remember something like that."

"You haven´t gotten any notices from the bank, have you?"

"Something, but you said that you were selling the house, so I wasn't really worried about it. I was a bit annoyed that they'd write me about an old loan, but I didn't want to trouble you with it. You couldn't work much after Ívar was born, and I know how hard life as a contractor can be."

Mamma, relieved the conversation has moved toward problems to solve, adds, "Yes, you two were going through a difficult time staying on top of everything when you packed it all in at the theater. Bergur, the aspiring *author*, couldn't provide much help."

That seems a bit harsh. When Ívar was born, neither of us were entitled to maternity or paternity leave, so Bergur began to freelance as a translator for scholarly publications and taught writing on the side for more than two years. His "book"—I can still hear the quotation marks my mother adds to it—was only now becoming a reality.

"Bergur might not sell as much as some authors, but his readers send him adoring letters riddled with references to his jokes, and they buy everything he writes," I say, defensive. "They bang on the door to get an autograph, praise his ability to decipher the signs of the times, as if this graduate of Réttarholtsskóli is a mystic. Famous writers mention his influence on them in interviews. People that get him love him—like I do. They'll love the new book. It's called *Cryptograms*." I hadn't intended to channel Bergur's fan club, but their judgment has triggered my adrenaline. "You weren't going to lose your house because of me," I say, "or Bergur."

Quick to smooth this over, my father says, "I think very highly of Bergur, even if he isn't my type of author. I respect anyone who takes up the pen and writes well in Icelandic."

He turns back to his cards, leaving me with a mind full of claustrophobic arguments: Bergur can take on more now that his book is out, and I'm going to go back to work, I know I need to work, I can't afford a normal day job with the Icelandic tax authorities looming over me. I am afraid of causing my parents to lose their house. Of course, we got a good price for the place on Ránargata, but we were idiots to buy this big apartment just because it had a room for Ívar and an office. Why didn't we consider the dizzyingly high tax bill that Pabbi would have to guarantee, as he'd guaranteed our other debts? Still! We'll figure it out. Maybe I'm searching for security in worldly things like Mamma does, but only because I have to manage the home and make sure that we have enough for Christmas and remember birthday gifts because Bergur even forgets that the trash needs to be taken out. It was just so difficult to live when we didn't have enough money for milk and diapers; I was so stressed that I didn't feel like myself anymore, shoved B vitamins and castor oil and D vitamins down my throat just to function, and I was still doing everything that normal people do every day: care for a kid with a cold and calculate the costs. I don't have to argue. I am so dizzy, I am so unwell, I am becoming like my mother, in a never-ending whirl of illness, and—

"—Saga."

"What did you say, Pabbi?"

"Just that you're my baby, Saga," he says, eager in his clumsy way to deflect the stress of this conversation. "I trust you. More than I trust myself."

Mamma is scrubbing the sparkling clean sink. She looks natural in this family environment, it's hard to believe she'd been AWOL just a few hours earlier. I peek into the living room and find my brother. Normally, Guðni's going in circles, opening the refrigerator at least five times an hour, but he's sitting, looking rather defeated, in Pabbi's TV chair, his feet on the old ottoman where Mamma stores her knitting.He thinks his role is to save everyone, otherwise he's worthless. He needs to protect people, his family, those out in the street. My brother, the loner. I want to say, "I wish I knew you better." I know that he enjoys hunting, rambling about politics with my father, and playing the piano he bought for his near-empty apartment in Grafarvogur. I wish he had children and a wife who knew him in a way that nobody else knows him.

Guðni looks up and catches me looking at him. He smiles when he notices me. "So tired."

"Understandable," I say, smiling back. "How are you?"

"How are *you*?" he asks, paternal.

"Better than before," I say, winking at him.

Back in the kitchen, Jóhanna's hardly taken off her jacket and she's already performing her practiced role: oldest child, martyr, the one who knows best. It's as if she'd never taken my hand the other night, led me out of the play.

"Are you sure you're okay?" she asks Mamma, who has abandoned her scrubbing to leaf through an old copy of *Vogue*.

"Good as gold!" Mamma lifts a plastic flap in the magazine to inhale the dissipated scent of perfume and turns to me. "Are you sure *you* are okay, Saga?" she asks in the same suspicious tone Jóhanna used on her just a moment before.

"Yes and no," I say, slipping into the chair next to Jóhanna. The coffeepot completes its task with a loud hiss and Mamma hops to her feet, giddy for the chance to fuss over pouring coffee.

Pabbi, still sulking over his cards, calls over to me, "Saga, what did your doctor say?"

"That I should get myself some Adderall," I respond.

"Why, is that the latest treatment?" Mamma asks, brow knitted.

"I'm joking." She likes when I tease her.

249

"You never know with these doctors," she clucks. "Don't they prescribe amphetamines to badly behaved kids these days?"

It's apparent—to me, at least—that Mamma is in the most denial of all of us, no matter how fervently Jóhanna hopes that she will help us piece together that horrible night in its entirety. Now Mamma is back at the sink, removing cups from the dishwasher one by one, drying them with a dish towel, even though they're already dry. Stop acting like an idiot! I want to scream. I want to shake her, shake, shake, shake and hold onto her and make her accept my embrace. She would wriggle in my arms, but I would tighten my grip, tighter, tighter. I could crush her.

She held *me* in the hospital last week; she must have. She always held me when I was in the hospital. When she comes to the hospital, we never have to squawk about fashion or local politics or sneer at Bergur's grandiosity. We are just *us*. It's such a comfort.

35

A memory: It was almost time for the evening news. Like always, we sat down at the kitchen table, each of us in our place, but there's no hint of the usual commotion: Mamma jabbering, Pabbi grumbling, kids whining. There was nothing. Just the man on the television rattling off everything that happened that day, things that didn't concern us.

Mamma had given up trying to teach Guðni manners, so he splashed milk on my haddock mash. Meanwhile, I played my own game with my food, dipping each bite in ketchup and staring at it for thirty seconds before placing it into my mouth, as if to confirm that it was real. It was dark out. I could be staring out the window into oblivion. I could free myself from the waking state and escape myself: Saga, Jóhanna's little sister, Guðni's big sister.

I didn't understand why it was so trying to be me. It felt bad to exist. I wanted to tell Mamma something nice and cheer her up, but I sensed she didn't want me to say anything at all. Jóhanna didn't pick up on that. She talked a lot, loudly, even when she chewed her food, but nobody listened to her. I chewed on a mashed-up fish cake quietly.

I knew that Mamma wouldn't rebuke me, even if she did hear chewing noises; I wondered if she would ever chide me again.

Mamma won't always be so down. Jóhanna's voice pierced the moment. *I promise.*

Then a loud crack when Mamma slapped her. *Bang!* Guðni cried out, slamming his baby fork down on the tray of his high chair. After, Mamma retreated back into herself, her hands trembling as she fiddled with her cutlery, then she stood and said she was a bit tired, playing normal.

But everything, apart from the setting itself, has been filed away into the folder labeled NEVER HAPPENED. The slap in the face was imagined, even to Jóhanna, who had stared at her plate in silence as tears ran down her cheeks.

36

My parents know how to seek shelter in one another, even after they've cut such deep wounds that they will never heal. They don't trust the outside world to understand that a *good man* can do all the bad things my father did when he drank himself into a stupor. *He can't be judged based on a single period in his life!* They sentence themselves to silence because uncareful words might splinter their relationship. The wrong question could puncture their fragile bubble.

Mamma wants to do something nice for me, fry an egg or serve me beans on toast, but I just want to ask her what I never have: "Where did you go when you would leave us, Mamma?"

She avoids my eyes. The egg carton shakes in her swollen hand. She says she just wanted fresh air; she's entitled to it, just like anybody else. Jóhanna looks encouragingly at me, about to add to the interrogation when Guðni appears in the doorway, suddenly shaking his head at us so that Mamma doesn't see.

"Mamma, I need to head out soon," he says.

"Guðni, don't you want me to fry up an egg for you before you go to work?" she asks.

"No thanks," he says. *What is wrong with you?* his eyes say to me, and the message in Pabbi's expression is crystal-clear as well: *Saga, cut the crap!* And although Jóhanna wants me to talk, talk, talk about all of it, the vibe is now so oppressive that she hurries to conjure a way to clear the air.

"Are you seeing someone, Guðni?" she asks.

"What? Where'd you hear that?" he tuts, waggling his eyebrows. "Are people talking?"

"No-o-o, but someone saw you with a girl at the movies," Jóhanna says. "My friend, Gréta, saw you and—"

I can tell she's about to launch into something juicy because Pabbi injects himself into the conversation. "Come on, Jóhanna. Leave the boy alone!"

"Sure, but who's the girl?" I say. I can't help antagonizing him.

"Just some girl. Mamma, I'll have an egg. Do you have tabasco?" The request prompts her to spin around to the exotic spice shelf and escape back into artifice. She wants to make her boy happy with a drop of the spicy red sauce in the tacky bottle. Guðni grins at her. She looks thrilled.

I smirk at his smile; there's no reason to say anything more. Words turn to dust and crumble between those smiles.

"You know what I want to say," I whisper, and I see her. Recognition crosses her pale face, her lilac dress still sopping wet. She smiles shyly, but her expression is too serious for a child. I see her feet dangling under the glass table, kicking, and she's wearing jeans under the dress. Knees, dirty. Wool socks, yellow. Leather shoes, worn. This must be her seat at the table, I think. She always sits there with them, even though they pretend that no one is there. I find comfort in the knowledge that she will always be around, no matter how much they want to forget her. She grew up with us but hasn't aged herself, and I suspect that she's just as Mamma sees her. She watches us, absorbed. It's well past time that we step into Katrín's world so that she can be with us. I struggle against the urge to yell at my parents: But Katrín—what if Katrín were with us? What would she say? How would she see us? How would we look at one another if she were sitting here today, at the head of the table?

They would stiffen at the memory we've turned away from all our lives, and then Mamma would put the issue to rest by asking whether I'd like an egg.

I have a vague recollection of all those hours when Mamma was gone and we waited, anxious for Pabbi to fill the silence with one of his stories. Then she came back, and we were as well-behaved as we could be so that she wouldn't leave again. She left; she came home. And the years passed, more than a decade, and then . . . today.

I want to shake them both, but I can't be without them. I'm no longer the only one of my kind—I'm one of them and they are me and all the tumult within me, even though we are damned to run away from one another's words. We're all aliens, an extraterrestrial family, and we communicate telepathically, the only option we've been left with since the youngest in the family died. I have to go.

"I spoke with Bergur about stopping by his place and then heading over to leikskóli to pick up Ívar," I say, pulling this fib out of thin air.

"I'll drive you," Guðni says. "I'm ready to go."

"No, it'd be better if I just took a taxi to his place so that we take the same car."

"So Bergur will keep an eye on you?" Pabbi asks.

Jóhanna wears the same doubtful expression as he does.

"Yes, of course!" I say, a little too exuberantly.

Pabbi looks at Mamma, who's all but wringing her hands with anxiety but *determined* to be cheerful. "I'm so happy to hear that you're doing this together," she says, ready to swallow any happy fiction.

"I was just about to say that," Jóhanna echoes, but her poker face tells me that she'll be calling sooner rather than later. "Oh! While I'm thinking about it," she says, "I forgot to tell you something—forgive me, Saga, there's just been so much going on."

"You've piqued my curiosity," I say. "Tell me."

"It's just that the flower shop made a mistake or misunderstood, or maybe his mother doesn't know white roses are for mourning," she says, shaking her head, "so the roses you got—they should have been a different color."

"What do you mean?"

"Because he survived, that kid that you saw get hit by a car. I read more about it in the paper yesterday. He *was* hurt, but not so seriously. In fact, his mamma is quoted saying he'll start up again with soccer soon."

"G-good. Thank god," I sputter. "What a relief!"

I head out, buttoning my parka all wrong in my panic

to get out the door. I unbutton and button again. My head starts to burn, but I go out of sight before I dare bring the heels of my hands to my temples. One side of my head feels like it's on fire.

What the hell is Jóhanna talking about?

37

I once dreamed that Mamma was driving a white car. I recall this within the taxi to Bergur's as a white Škoda passes us on Laugavegur. An older man is at the steering wheel, but I can't shake the feeling that it is her car, a childish inner logic that argues that if she has a white car, then all white cars are her car. Ever since I had that dream I-don't-know-how-long-ago, any white car makes me think of her.

Now I conjure another scene of a child who was hit by a car—I see a small, yellow moving van and the boy straining to breathe, his teeth broken, his cap wet with blood. I crouch beside him and spread my coat over him while we wait for an ambulance for what seems like eternity. A mailwoman in an orange sweater is next to me, holding my shoulders, as if feeding me the strength to watch over him.

I lived inside of the delusion that it was all a dream.

When I came home from the hospital after the seizure, I had this strong feeling that *something* had happened, something that caused me dread. I experienced fragments—surreal images of a child running into the street and a car swerving—flashing against the back of my eyelids like a rapid parade of shadows, but they didn't quite feel real. They didn't cohere into an actual memory.

A ghost within me had whispered that it was an invention of my imagination, but I now push myself to concentrate on the event itself in all its horror, as well as my own body: I stood at the window on Miklabraut. I dropped a full glass of water in my rush to reach him, treading barefoot in the snow, holding my jacket and boots. He seemed to be dead in the road; the mailwoman walked me home. I was sobbing, shaking in a cotton shirt, my jacket lost in the sea of EMTs. Like a dream, it happened somewhere I couldn't quite make out again and again, a long time before, although I'm quietly conscious that the accident took place the day before the seizure. Everything is now righting itself—the boy lived. I am remembering.

I count myself lucky that my brain has protected me from reliving this event until this moment, since I know now that he didn't die and I can remember the events without gasping for breath.

With the faucet of my memories now turned on, they run to my husband. When did we end? He was always out running or reading, and I was tending to the garden when I had a spare moment; rather than speaking, we made very little of each other's work. Why didn't we ever go to the movies or the mall as a family? Were we too highbrow for that? We could have gone for a hike with Ívar, even around the lake at Elliðavatn, just outside of town, and for a swim after. What stopped us from doing that?

I recall that in the hospital after giving birth, I eyed my husband with horror as he tossed our fragile newborn up and down in the air. How could someone that sturdy be so clumsy? The busybody nurse picked up on my disdain and told me I had to *trust the father*, and hatred swarmed inside me—hatred of him and of her, this nurse at whom my attractive husband was gazing gratefully. He quoted her when he did anything risky with Ívar. He never remembered to support Ívar's bottom until I screamed *babies can get hernias*; way too young, he gave him slices of bread to choke on. Once he even lost him at the library—just as Ívar was learning to walk. Another time, he forgot to fasten him into his car seat because he was preoccupied with lecturing me about an article he was writing about free expression, prompting me to lose it.

Oh, fuck it! I'd shouted.

Fuck what? Free expression? Bergur had asked, puzzled by my low regard for what he regarded as the foundation of democratic society.

Actually, fuck you! I'd snapped.

During those early moments of parenting, I was exhausted. I did not care about the increasing weight of the words I shouted at him, just as I didn't care about my disheveled hair, my unwashed clothes. The scales tipped with the heft of my words in the garden of my own neglect. My work, my exhilarating work in film that I had always loved, I had now begun to hate. I no longer had any interest in adventures. I didn't dare look away from my son. If I left for the evening, I wouldn't know that he'd thrown up in bed because Bergur had confused a jar of pesto with a jar of homemade apple-spinach baby food, or that Ívar had bumped his head and Bergur hadn't noticed. I needed to be vigilant.

Yes, in Bergur's eyes, I was constantly crying wolf, elevating regular bumps and mishaps to life-or-death drama. At a certain point, the only thing I talked about with my husband were the thousand-and-one ways our son could come to harm, however unlikely—and the few moments that I felt free of fear about the fate of our child, the space seemed to fill with my anxiety about our household budget, which took a hit each time I had to duck out of a well-paid gig because a flu was going around at the leikskóli. For the first time in my life, I was burdened by the insecurity of my freelance work, my dread of accident or illness.

Bergur said he no longer recognized me, the happy, carefree woman that I had *always been*, the woman who seemed to do everything effortlessly, without thinking twice, without mood swings. Well, I didn't recognize Bergur in this man who casually, obliviously endangered my child.

Take the evening that Ívar nearly suffocated: I had gone to sleep, even though I felt in my gut that his ragged breathing might be something more significant. But I didn't want to seem neurotic, and I intended first and foremost to become a normal mother in my husband's eyes, a woman who could handle it when her child got a cold, who lived up to Bergur's expectations: *You can't be so afraid. You'll tear us all apart.*

And so we slept.

We slept until Bergur gasped, *Wake up, Saga, something's wrong with Ívar!* Then he was holding our child in his arms on the landing, waiting for the ambulance. Is that when the hatred really took hold of me? He had tricked me into going to sleep! I wanted him out.

A few days later, when Ívar had been discharged from the hospital, I told Bergur to leave.

Fine, I'll go! he'd said. He was angry, too, but he didn't believe that I could really be kicking him out. He made as if he knew better than me, going on about my hysteria, even though he despised the word.

I couldn't feel anything but a persistent horror that my son had nearly died from a benign illness. The only way to move forward was to anesthetize myself to everything around me except for Ívar.

The doctor said that croup was very seldom harmful, and there could have been something else wrong that had exacerbated the issue, that Ívar might have an anatomical defect in his throat that had worsened the croup, and he recommended further testing. He wrote a script for an EpiPen to have on hand. We made the appointment for an endoscopy so they could put him under anesthesia and slip a scope down his throat, but the waiting list was long, and the waiting time doubled because I—yes, I—had written down the wrong date. Rescheduling caused a delay.

The wait became unbearable when Ívar got a cough or cold. He sounded like an old drunk with sleep apnea. I slept lightly and fitfully out of fear that I wouldn't wake up if his throat swelled and he couldn't breathe. I had to remain attentive so that I could discern the sounds in his sinuses from the sounds made in his windpipe.

This is not a sniffle anymore, it's a whine, a grating whine, I thought to myself every time he made a sound. I kept guard over the sounds in my child's chest, listened so intently to his breath that my own breathing became too much for me. But I was going to stay awake. I watched, red-eyed.

For me to be in control, Bergur had to be gone. Why should he care? Without our marriage, he could surround himself by women who gobbled up the truths imparted by supermen who ejaculate superseed from their super-pens. At some point, he'd realized I was serious. He left.

Now, I shudder at the rupture of our family, the rift I caused. How cold—how shortsighted of me. Now we are even less safe.

Oh, Bergur. I remember that Jóhanna said I was lucky because not all fathers are as thoughtful as you, Bergur. She had seen you dress Ívar for leikskóli and was impressed that you had carefully chosen each garment, making sure he would be neither too hot nor too cold. Yes, I saw that you nurtured your little son. Perhaps I saw it so often that I forgot it, or I took it for granted. I remember how you snuggled up to each other, and he laughed when you played with him. I forgot that *I* had put him in slippery socks when he ran across the kitchen floor, that time that he fell and bonked his head—or when I fell asleep on his arm as we were cuddling on the couch and cut off his circulation. His arm turned purple. You laughed and massaged his little wing; you made a joke so I wouldn't blame myself.

"I'm sorry, Bergur," I say out loud.

"What's that? Should I turn here?" the driver asks. He is young, clean-shaven, the conservative radio station playing quietly in the background.

"Yes, turn right on the first street," I say. "Here."

38

"Saga." Bergur looks surprised as he opens the door, and not especially pleased. "Uh—what brings you here?"

I'm tongue-tied with all that is inside me. My mouth—and time itself—is too small for the effusive eruption of feelings inside me. I don't know where to start. Do I tell him that I've been resurrected and now I see everything in a new light? I run my tongue over my teeth and smile in the hope that words aren't needed. He needs to say something to clear the air, which seems to me to be something only he can do. C'mon, darling, smile a gentle Bergur smile and wink at me; no words needed. He'll probably get a kick out of hearing about Lilja Dögg and Óðinn and all of their theories.

He takes measure of me, tilting his head just a little. I want to run into his arms, but something holds me back. As I anticipated, he's wearing the expensive wool robe I got him a few Christmases ago, his usual outfit when he works. I can tell that he's been lost in thought, pulling his mop of hair without noticing. When he works, he talks to himself, both of his hands gesturing as if he's grasping after the right rhythm, wriggling impatiently to get his thoughts on paper before they evaporate into oblivion. He chomps on nicotine gum, even though he only smokes the occasional cigarillo, just to keep him sitting at his desk. I know his quirks.

He breaks the silence: "Um, how did you get here?"

"I took a cab," I say. We're off to a banal start. I want to blurt it all out and catch us up with each other.

"I see," he says, looking out the door as if he's hoping to retrieve the taxi for a return trip. "Is everything okay?"

"Já! Everything's fine."

"Well, come in." He steps aside. Think, Saga! Organize yourself. I want to tell him about the boy that lived and my amnesia. The words make their way to my teeth just in time for me to close my lips. Maybe I already said something to him about that without remembering it. My ears are ringing, my thoughts spiraling—I'm losing my thread.

"Did—um—did you see some roses at my place?" I finally ask.

"Jæja," he says to my immeasurable relief. "I was picking up some clothes for Ívar—you were in the hospital. I saw on the card that they were from that guy who found you after your seizure—Hafliði, I believe. Very nice of him. Didn't you see the card?"

"I did, yes," I lie. A strong disquietude rushes over me. I thought they were from the boy's mother? Isn't that what Johanna said? I'm not confident that I know what I should remember. I have to focus so that I am able to tell Bergur everything I came here to tell him, but the ringing is unbearable. I have to sit down, sit down.

"So . . . how are you otherwise?" Bergur asks.

"I'm fine," I say. "I went to the doctor."

"And?"

"He basically told me to relax."

"Now I could have told you that," he jokes. "Do you want some coffee?"

"That'd be great, thanks."

I follow him into his rather spacious kitchen, its delicate fixtures painted apple-green and white. It looks good, cozy and artful, much more like a home than when I picked Ívar up here the first time. A flowerpot on the windowsill, curtains to match the cabinets. He bought an apple-green drying rack, too—a nice touch. Next to the kitchen clock, he's hung a framed picture of Ívar at school—I have the same photo, except mine is in a paper frame that Ívar made himself and Bergur's is a cheap one from Flying Tiger. Never in a million years would I have thought that Bergur would shop at a store dedicated to frivolous plastic tchochkes.

Pictures that Ívar drew hang all around the frame. Some are just paint splotches, while others are more like sketches. A bowl teeming with fruit is perched on the low table in the middle of the room: apples, oranges, lemons, bananas, mangoes. That's new. I always had to force Bergur to eat fruit; the bowl must be for Ívar. The thought warms me, reminds me to stay connected to this idea of Bergur, the nurturer. Looking around, I'd love to brew a pot of coffee in this kitchen. His apartment is little but bright and decorated so tastefully, like the apartment on Ránargata—certainly good enough until we find something better, especially if Bergur can rent an office space else-where. Maybe we should move here temporarily while the old apartment with windowsills covered in ash and sooty memories is on the market; it's only ever brought us bad luck. Maybe the air there wasn't clean enough for Ívar. What do I know?

"Bergur!" I say, my heart beating fast. "I need to tell you something. Jóhanna and I finally talked about Katrín."

"Katrín," he repeats, looking at me as he shovels coffee beans into the grinder. "Remind me who Katrín is, again?"

"You know, my sister who—" I start, but my words drain back down, inaccessible. He waits for me to complete the statement and shrugs his shoulders when nothing more comes out, then he turns on the coffee grinder. I feel sick to my stomach, disgusted by myself.

I'd never told him. In Bergur's world, Katrín doesn't exist. He and I met as teens, but I wasn't the kind who spilled family secrets—that didn't happen in the environment I grew up in—and by the time we met again as adults, I had become a full-fledged liar. Have Bergur and I really always been alien to one another, this *alone* together?

He'll be surprised when he hears it all, I remind myself, and he'll remain level-headed. Just tell him. Where do I start?

Bergur takes his hand off the grinder. "Listen, you might be interested in this article I came across today."

"Oh yeah?"

"Jú, it was fascinating," he says. He pats the ground beans into a moka pot, screws the thing together, turns on the stove.

268

"What's it about?" I ask unsteadily, trying to force away the nausea as I search for a stool to sit on. I'm dizzy.

"It's called 'Forget about God,' if I recall correctly," Bergur says, lighting up like he always does when he's sharing something he finds remarkable. "It considers whether the white light so many see just before death is real, even if it's not proof that there is life after death. The author posits that it's the brain's way of settling us with death. The brain intensifies our awareness of the insignificance of our ego just before it dies. For one brief moment, we realize that the 'I' doesn't matter and now, reconciled to our own meaninglessness, we experience greater happiness than we've ever known."

I feel a pang of irritation. Typical of Bergur to go on about some ridiculous theory when I've come to tell him that I love him. He must realize that I'm not here to say hello.

"What about the light for people who see it—what is it?" I mutter, disinterested and sad. I don't want to engage in this theory when my thoughts are hovering around Katrín and everything that Bergur and I could have said to one another.

"Well, the bottom line," he says, smiling, "is that when your brain freaks out at the moment of death, some people report seeing a light, and this writer believes that near-death experiences might actually be a type of seizure. You should ask your doctor about that—Elliði."

"Right," I say.

He looks at me as if he's expecting more of a reaction.

"I hear you. I'm insignificant in the grand scheme

of things," I say, "but I'm afraid of what Ívar would go through if I were to die. How could it be 'true happiness' to lose your connection to a child?"

"I'm speaking in terms of the physiological processes of the body as it dies," he answers, defensive, "not challenging your conscious emotional relationship as his mother."

"Okay, understood, but you're not a scientist. You're a writer on the west side of Reykjavík who spends his time reading unverified sources and pretending you know everything," I say. Adrenaline is flooding my body; I'm furious that he doesn't know what I've never told him.

"I forgot how constructive our conversations are," he mutters, turning back to the coffee heating on the stove. A deep breath, then: "I'm sorry, Saga. I don't know what got into me. I was going on like a jackass," he says, suddenly contrite. "I guess I wanted to talk about seizures as if they're something intellectual, to make them less frightening. I know they must be terrifying. I've been so afraid for you."

The adrenaline moves to another part of my brain, and for a moment, I feel that I can tell him I love him, but I stay silent, on the edge of tears. In the end, I smile at Bergur, who smiles back. He moves closer, perches beside me, and rests his arm on my shoulders. Impenetrable—the same smile I've loved since we were kids. I want to kiss him. Maybe that's enough: to kiss him.

"Saga," Bergur says, "I want you to know that I am happy you've stopped by."

I scoot closer to him. "This is good. Honestly, Bergur. For all of us."

He pulls me into a hug, as if he's trying to comfort us both, but lets go as soon as I lean into him, leaving me behind with his all-too-familiar scent: gum, cologne, and something that I can't quite put my finger on. Something that's uniquely him, the base note of his smell.

"There's so much I have to tell you," I begin meekly.

He still seems to have his guard up when he says, "What's that?"

"Well," I continue, determined not to lose my nerve. "Sit with me!"

"I'm making coffee."

"It's not going to boil over."

"I prefer to stand."

"Bergur!"

"Saga."

"I want to talk to you," I say, getting up.

"Does it have to be now?"

"When else?" I ask, confused by his reaction.

"Maybe it can wait. It might be better if we talked another time," he says opaquely. "I'm sure you understand."

"No—I don't understand. You just said you were happy to see me."

"And I am."

"But?"

"You know I'm not in a position to have this conversation."

"I don't know anything."

He looks at me pleadingly. His boyish eyes once begged me for love, and I had ample love to give. And I still do! Just as much as he can accept. And he must feel it, too, he must, because he suddenly pulls me toward him and we kiss, all messy and clumsy. I press myself to him again, chasing an urge to disappear inside of him. Love is on the tip of my tongue, burning between my thighs, but he ends the kiss.

"Saga, we've already tried everything."

"But I couldn't explain to you why I was afraid. I can now."

"There's nothing to say, Saga. We stopped being close a long time ago. Your endless fears were so . . . oppressive." Tears fill his eyes and he looks away for a moment, then meets my gaze. "I don't think you understand. You've never understood that I love our son just as much as you do. I haven't always known what's best for him, and I haven't always known how to handle things at home as well as you—"

"Bergur," I start.

"No, let me finish!" He lets out a deep breath. "I'm no less a parent than you are, but you insisted that I was. And I don't know if I can forgive you for that, Saga."

"I never intended to make you feel that way," I say, trying to take his hand, but he pulls away.

"I know that you didn't intend to cause any harm," Bergur says, his eyes full of sadness. "But you can't love someone you're afraid of. You have to love someone for who they are. You are still the most wonderful woman . . . but that magical girl, the one who had a sense of humor, has disappeared. In the past few years, you've spoken to me with such contempt. You challenged everything I did. You acted like you were afraid of me. You killed us."

"Hey, Bergur!" a shrill voice interrupts from the entry-way. "Who's here?"

The voice is familiar.

"It's just Saga," Bergur responds, walking past me.

Just Saga? My head starts to spin.

39

Here she is. Standing in the entryway, tramping her little boots on the Persian rug Bergur got as a wedding gift from his uncle. Some thread of memory tickles into my brain, like a dream I had forgotten. I begin to inch mechanically toward her brightly forced smile, her barely concealed astonishment, her quick look at Bergur, as if to find out how best to approach this sensitive situation.

Then, the clouds of memory pour down rain. Of *course* I know her. She was the fucking director of infant care at Ívar's first school. I remember how grateful I was to her for her conscientious approach to Ívar, how comfortable I felt leaving him with her. We'd called her the baby whisperer in the car on Ívar's first day of leikskóli, astonished that we'd left our child in the hands of a stranger. We'd decided to get a hearty brunch at the café by the harbor. Our eyes had been glued to our cell phones, waiting for bad news. But they never rang.

I had often thought about her as I adjusted to Ívar being in daycare. I calmed myself by imagining her bright smile and warm eyes, her dark brown ponytail as she glided across the playground in purple snow pants with a group of screeching kids in her wake. We were overjoyed to have her; we mourned her departure but cheered her on when she broke the news that she had gotten into the creative writing program at the university; she wanted to try to realize her dream, and she'd already written a children's book. She *loved* Bergur's books, she gushed, which elevated her further (in his eyes). How could I have forgotten *her*?

"You two hardly need an introduction," Bergur says stiffly. They've both put on well-meaning expressions, full of pity, because they need me to understand.

"No," I say, blinking to fend off the pressure building behind my eyes, the colors in the room suddenly so dreamlike that I wonder if this whole scene is all in my head. They gaze at me and move closer to each other on the Persian rug where Ívar learned to crawl. I look down, and the colors on the rug run together.

I see them, see that he's short with sleepy, chocolate-brown eyes. She's gentle, dark, and short like him. I see they want to weave their fingers together to steady one another, but they are too tactful to try it in front of me— comfortable with one another, lovers that speak without speaking. Is he going to tell her about our kiss? Of *course* he will—him, the champion of truth, in his deep Bergur voice as she strokes his cheek gently, tells him that she understands, that it's natural to kiss, that it doesn't always mean something. She understands him, unlike me, who hardly listened.

Why didn't I anticipate that Bergur would hook up with some woman who'd play house with Ívar?

Stepmother—like hell! Here's Bergur—take him! I've lost him, but I'll never, never lose Ívar!

"I was surprised that you took it so well when I told you about us—we thought that you would think it was too fast." Bergur sounds oddly casual, as if it had never been just the two of against the world, and then the three of us.

As if we had never had the entire world, our son, one another.

"Do you remember?" he presses gingerly. "I told you about us last week, the day before the seizure."

"No," I say as the skin drips from my bones. My bones crack, my mind melts into a mush that oozes onto the Persian rug—a putrefied, stinking puddle at their feet, eyeballs and tiny nerves quivering and flailing for everyone to see.

But then I *do* remember. His expression of discomfort, the frustratingly loving voice feeding me cliches: Sometimes you can't choose who you love, Saga. You will find love again too, Saga.

The house shakes at its foundation. The sky crackles white. Then, as now. I am burning alive, can't they see that? Obviously, they can't; they're waiting for some sort of response.

"Did you take the food processor?" I say, severe. "I came to get it. I bought it. Remember?"

"The food processor," Bergur repeats. It's a dramatic non-sequitur, but he notices I've given him an exit. "Yes, of course, what was I thinking. Just a sec!" He turns on his heel and disappears into the kitchen, leaving me behind with her. I smile sweetly until he reappears with a plastic contraption that, to be honest, I never figured out. He shoves it into a linen bag and says, "Here you go!" He is chipper as can be. Chipper because from here on out, all of our interactions will be scripted, and we both know that.

"I'm picking Ívar up from school today," I tell him from the doorway. I seem to fit there—out the door. He's already made his new reality, this man who lives in the present by modern rules, eternally upgrading with apple-green accents; otherwise, we become obsolete in a society that's founded upon our ability to adapt. I dash out in time to conceal the tears forming at the corners of my eyes.

I need to find a dumpster where I can toss the food processor. I deposit it next to a flower shop, a meaningful distance (I hope) from his house. As I saunter away, I remember that there are sharp blades in the machine. If some kid were to find it . . .

Out in the street, I finally find a trash can next to a streetlamp and toss the machine into it with a crash. I run back along Hringbraut, past the National Library. I have to get a hold of myself, for Ívar's sake! Clouds of breath pump out of me faster than I can breathe, I need oxygen, I can't catch my breath, I have to breathe. I have to breathe now!

I have to sit down. I have to think clearly.

I've never felt that my body belonged to me. It wasn't mine. It owned me. I am owned. I am stuck.

I need to talk to Lilja Dögg and find out if she can stay with me and Ívar, like an au pair. I should be able to pay her, overdraft my account; maybe it'll all work out somehow. Goddamnit, Bergur! I won't give up. I can't even think of it! Jóhanna always helps me, and . . . I'll get a hold of Elliði as soon as I can. This is evidence of my condition, right? There must be a psychological reason that I couldn't remember what happened with Bergur and Ívar's teacher. Maybe Elliði can refer me to a psychologist. I have to own up to the fact that I can't remember my life reliably, that I can't always tell what is life and what my imagination spins for me, but I still have everything under control. Tomorrow, in fact, Lilja and I will pick up Ívar at his new school. I'll make hot dogs for him and mashed potatoes, the best he's ever had, and I'll buy him a froskafrostpinni dipped in chocolate. I'll hold him and kiss him and kiss him and listen to him laugh.

I must gain control over my body. Nobody can liberate me from that. I have to find freedom within it. My body is not bad. My son is the progeny of this body. I owe him my love, and this body can forget that I love his father. Maternal love is a part of our biology, built into our organs. I can't forget that love. "Goddamn love!" I shout into whirls of snow as I plod past unrelenting traffic. The shock of lights cuts my eyes, dirty with tears. Freezing wind stings my skin. And it's good. It's good!

I move my feet on the earth, one step forward at a time. Forward! I'll manage it. I can't be afraid. I can maintain my forward motion.

40

Cheers to the savior of the universe: Saga! Tedda had raised her glass and winked at me before plunging her hand into the gigantic birthday cake we'd barely touched. She shoved handfuls of caramel cream and marshmallows into her mouth and her girlfriend leaped to lick the sugar off her lips. I stumbled to the bathroom, thinking to myself that this new girl was going to get hurt. Tedda always pushes people away in the end.

How are you doing? Tedda had asked me, looking me straight in the eyes to divine my true state.

Fine, I'm fine, I lied.

I didn't quite know why I wasn't being honest with her. I'd avoided the truth since everything started to get so cold and relentless and—I guess since Ívar first became ill. I hadn't told her how serious that trip to the hospital had been; I also hadn't told her that I could hardly sleep because my heart, heavy though it was, was always beating as fast as a rodent's, or that sometimes I woke up crying, and I was no longer the fun-loving Saga I had been, that I wasn't myself anymore.

I didn't tell her that earlier in the day, I had spread my coat over what I thought was a dying child just a few minutes after Bergur came and went, that he'd dropped by to give me a book for my birthday and to sort out some boring papers, and then, out of the blue, told me that he'd met someone. Of course, we had separated pretty recently, but *life is just that way sometimes—ha*. They'd met at a lecture and just *clicked*, but he had to tell me because of Ívar and because I knew the woman. Bergur had left and then the car had hit the child, and then Tedda knocked on my door with a bottle of pink Cava and sugary cake and this new girlfriend, giggling through a chorus of the birthday song, and then I drank champagne and ate cake because I couldn't find the words to explain what I had just gone through.

I couldn't tell her that I hadn't slept more than a few hours at a time for days because I needed to listen closely to Ívar's breathing. I knew that sleep deprivation could trigger a seizure, and I dreaded going to work the next day and trying to convince my colleagues that I was fine, but I couldn't take sleeping pills because who would watch Ívar? And I absolutely should not drink under these circumstances. But I said nothing.

The champagne went straight to my head, and I wanted to keep drinking. When we ran out, Tedda produced a bottle of gin and something else with tequila and announced that since I was now officially single, the time had come for me to get proper drunk again.

It was the first time I'd had hard liquor since my twenty-fifth birthday. I was thirsty to forget everything, but most of all to forget that Ívar wasn't with me—he was with his father, with a cold, and I couldn't do anything if something happened while he was sleeping. I lusted after oblivion.

Tedda called a cab when her girlfriend passed out in the bathroom. They stumbled out into the night, transferring their revelry to the taxi. I was alone in the sudden stillness. It was just as well because I needed to wake up early the next day; I had to be alert when Bergur brought Ívar back. I'd promised him we'd build a snowman if there was enough snow on the ground.

41

Ívar, my Ívar, skips toward the park, his hand slipping in and out of my own, extravagant in his enthusiasm for fresh snow, powdery on the sidewalk along Miklabraut. His bright laughter runs together with the whiteness enswathing our world and charges it. Gusts of wind swirl the crystal blanket around his legs, frolicking with him as if it were a living playmate.

We stop at the crosswalk and wait for the green light, a little man like my Ívar, always taking the same stride; I hold his hand tight, but his patience is still an unformed thing—and he lunges forward to scramble across the street, through the fast gaps between cars. The blood in my cheeks flashes hot. A balloon of pressure behind my forehead sends a shock down my forearms and it concentrates in my fingertips as I panic and crouch to meet his eyes, to make sure he's still here and whole. I steady myself on his shoulders as I find his gaze. His pupils swell and swallow his irises, dilate

constrict

dilate

constrict

I am lost inside this surge, and then just as suddenly, I am waiting at the crosswalk by the bus shelter on Miklabraut, Ívar clasping my hand as cars careen past.

A double-decker bus—fire-engine red—stops for us to cross, HOP ON! painted in yellow letters on its side. When we're safely across the street, I point my finger toward the bus, still holding onto my son's hand. "Look, Ívar! Look at the big bus. It has two stories!" He laughs with joy, and I laugh, nestled inside the purity of his happiness. And as I laugh, the world seems to lurch—forward and backward, as if the track of a rocking chair—and I see myself outside of myself, climbing into the bus. Her thicket of curls and gait—one shoulder shrugs forward more than the other— give her the appearance of a woman askew, as if one side of her is exhausted, the other still vital. But she's more whole than me.

This mother has a child, this wife has a husband, this homeowner has a home.

She hesitates on the steps into the bus, snaps her neck around to face me. I recognize each laugh line and each mark of worry in her face. But she can't be me, can she? She's whole. I am a mother without a child, I am a wife without a husband, I am a homeowner without a home. I'm still holding onto Ívar's hand; I can feel the warmth of him, even through my strata of knitted mittens—he must be here, he must be holding onto his mamma, we're going to make a snowman, we're going to go to the park and then we're going to drink hot chocolate and meet Jóhanna and Amma and—

The colors around me are whirlpooling into a blitzwhite that's more actual than any other color; the omnicolor makes itself in waves. My breath is fast—my breath is moving faster than my thoughts, or my thoughts are moving faster than my breath, I can't tell. I stare out at the world, helpless, in search of this shadow self who disappeared inside the bus, but all I see is my son as I watch my body fall. I reach for him in a cacophony of color, try to hold onto him, fat fingers stretching as far as I can stretch them. I resist gravity, will myself in his direction, and graze him. I am no longer inside myself; I am up on the ledge now and below is a beauty so sublime that I feel dizzy. I feel sand under the soles of my feet. The snow has melted and frozen into a sheet of ice; his dark eyes reflect in the mirror of its surface, and his milky-white teeth are bright, and I smell the sweet, fresh scent of my son in my arms.

"It will be okay," I hear myself say. Nobody contradicts Saga. "She is smart—she wanted to be smart," I whisper as I reach for her. Dikes of spar cut into stone glitter white in the bottom of the canyon; I stare into the stern faces of mountains warmed by the sun and I see, I see it all at once: the world in a flash, and it hurts. I blink and the sun splits into twinned coals that smolder as solidly black as the tube in my vision. The two suns scratch my corneas as they burn themselves out. I see now—after it all—that the trick was to let it all burn, let it burn off inside me. But everything leaves a mark, a track. Guðni, Jóhanna, Ívar, Guðni, Jóhanna, Ívar, Saga, Saga, Saga watching Katrín I
   cannot crash

         never

            you will be with me

I try to overpower the surge, but it becomes too much.
I am waylaid. I cannot go back, I cannot get back in, I
am trapped outside of her, quaking as the atmosphere
fills with our child-heads; they make and unmake themselves like fixed flashes of filmstrip: Jóhanna, Guðni, Ívar,
Jóhanna, Guðni, Ívar. Mamma? The projections shatter,
spilling glass in reds and blacks and oranges over the
blank ground. My hands stumble after them, but the sky
is tumbling over them
                              my love

You laughed, and because you laughed, I'm as high as the
sky on the edge of a cliff, boulders crumbling into an abyss,
all this beauty before us
                              the waves
                                        will never
                              paint over our steps

Helicoptering you in circles, your edges blend into the
only color now left—

        I would never

                    lose

    you

285

Translator's Note

Icelandic is a precious language, in part because only around three hundred and fifty thousand people speak it at all. Iceland—an isolated island that was ruled by Denmark, Norway, and Sweden in turns for most of its history—is a basaltic time capsule for the language known as Old Norse, which has changed remarkably little in the island's 1,200-year history. Icelandic bears lineage in common with Norwegian, Swedish, Danish, and Faroese, but remains the closest to Old Norse—or simply *norrænt mál*, the northern language as it was once called—and is intelligible to most speakers of Icelandic. I have not tried to read Old Norse, but my Icelandic electrician once told me that I occasionally slip into an Icelandic that sounds, well, Viking, which I took to mean I have found home.

I met with Jennifer Baumgardner, founder and director of Dottir Press, in Reykjavík during July 2019, having completed two-thirds of a draft translation of *Quake* by Auður Jónsdóttir *(Stóri skjálfti)*. Because she doesn't speak Icelandic, Jennifer still hadn't read the full book Dottir Press had agreed to publish. In truth, I was beginning to glean that I did not understand the book yet myself—its spirit. I could decipher the words, but I had not discovered the language that would bring *Quake* to life in English.

Translation of literature consists of much more than meaning in a strict sense; it somehow births something that has a past, and teaches this reborn creature how to tell its story in another language. And then teaches it *again* how to tell it well. During this time of gestation, my friend Gunnhildur Jónatansdóttir would read the book with me, helping me to refine phrasings in Auður's floating, feral Icelandic that I didn't quite understand. We occasionally sat together while I translated, as if my frantic typing were a spectator sport for linguists.

In December 2020, almost a year into the pandemic, I worked in isolation from my fourth-floor apartment overlooking Faxaflói Bay and Esja, our mountain. Gunnhildur had moved away, but I completed my first full draft of the novel within a few weeks and began revising in February 2020, just as the earthquake swarm began in the south of Iceland. That swarm became significant to this translation. In Iceland, buildings are engineered to withstand seismic activity. When the ground beneath a structure shakes, as it does in an earthquake, the building sways as the energy of the quake rolls through it. On the top floor of a building, such as where I live, you feel the wave of energy acutely, like you are the tip of a wheat stalk. The movement itself was not frightening to me—it reminded me of an airplane during ascent—but its sound made me feel helpless.

The sound an earthquake makes is stratified. Teacups clinking in the cupboard, radiators rattling against cement walls—these are the top notes. Beneath that: heavy furniture trembling on hardwood floors. And the base note: a sort of unidentifiable, unfolding thunder, like the lowest note of a cello or the vibrations of a tam-tam. These sounds, I later discovered, are captured in Páll Ragnar Pálsson's symphonic rendering of the chief conceit in Auður's *Quake*, just as they are now captured in my own.

It was in this state of constant quaking that I began to understand *Stóri skjálfti*, to feel compassion for the book and its spirit. Once I began my revision, I completed it very quickly, correcting dozens of clumsy errors made in the haste of inexperience and depression—but even as I sent the book (now ninety thousand words, as Icelandic tends to expand in English) to Jennifer, I knew it was still a rendition, not yet a living creature with a soul.

I decided I needed to spend time with Auður, to be "with" her and her text in the sense of Wallace Stevens's "qualities of a poem"—"interesting / indigenous to a person / with / . . . contagious."* So I went looking for her. I sought her even when we were not together, working in the corridors of Kjarval. For instance, I discovered "fallandi konur," a series of paintings by Helga Ástvaldsdóttir, when I was searching for the spirit of *Quake* during this last phase. Each work depicts a woman falling in a different position, different tones, and for a different reason. Grayish-nude skin contrasts with silver leaf; a parchment body is carried by deep ocean currents; and desire, a deep brown rust, drips down an inverted amber body. These

*From *Wallace Stevens: A Poet's Growth*, by George S. Lensing

women seem to be expressions of a disturbance similar to the one Saga experiences in *Quake*, what she describes as "the anarchy of the body." Alongside an intense and productive three months of revision with Jennifer, I spent a great deal of time with Auður. The joy of those two relationships was a necessary part of a third and final phase.

Right off the bat, Auður gave me permission to translate with my instincts, to make changes to the text, to assert myself as an author. She has maintained this throughout our relationship. "The translator is *always* an author," she told me. And this text is very much changed. This English *Quake* is both mine and Auður's, and we have been open with one another about this in a way that I have rarely experienced in my practice as a translator. As she puts it: "I have to trust you. It's as if I'm a passenger in an airplane, and I have to let you land the plane."

And although the text is considerably shorter, the changes themselves are, for the most part, not dramatic or material but stylistic. Icelandic as a literary language is much more permissive of, for example, the use of adverbs and adjectives to color in a scene. English uses a greater variety of verbs (I say this anecdotally) and can create action with fewer words. Auður's voice is digressive in a way that is captivating, and rendering that fluidity—her Auðurisms—into English took a great deal of experimentation. Conversations and trains of thought were tightened to streamline the narrative in English, to pull the thread taut but not snap the fiber.

The final chapter of the English edition is, in fact, a composite of text that had been excised from earlier chapters and the original ending, insights from neurologist Kári Stefánsson, and my own imaginative writing with Auður's guidance and her explicit permission and encouragement. In August 2021, as we looked through the near-final translation, Auður said, "One should always be translated by a poet." A generous thing to say, and my favorite Auðurism.

I want to thank her for sharing her voice with me. I would also like to thank my brilliant editor Jennifer Baumgardner, my aungvinkona Gunnhildur Jónatansdóttir, Vala Benediktsdóttir of Forlagið, and all of my kind reviewers and editors for their support and criticism. Finally, I'd like to thank my sister, Windy, for helping me to understand the brain and body.

—Meg Matich
Reykjavík, 2021

Glossary

afi: grandfather

amma: grandmother

ástin mín: my love

Besti flokkurinn: political party founded by writer and actor Jón Gnarr, mayor of Reykjavík from 2010 to 2014 (literally, "Best Party")

bláber: blueberries

blóðberg: wild arctic thyme

bókaflóð: annual surge of books, published just in time for Christmas gift-giving (literally, "book flood")

leikskóli: government-subsidized "play school," attended from infancy until about age six

elskan: darling

fjallkonur: plural of fjallkona, meaning "ladies of the mountains," female personifications of Iceland

froskaís, froskafrostpinni: popsicles with a chocolate-brown bottom and a froggy-green top half

Frumba: cute neologistic nickname, meaning "firstborn" or "firstie"

gæskunar: "my darlings," an old-fashioned term of endearment

hæ: hi

heilsusafi: "health juice," a juice blend of apples, oranges, and carrots

já: "yes," pronounced *yow*

jæja: "yes," "no," "okay," "sounds good," "whatever," "I agree," "sigh," "duh" . . . so many things

jólasveinn: "yule lad," one of the thirteen tricksters said to visit homes in the days leading up to Christmas

jú: "yes" in response to a ". . . right?" or ". . . no?" kind of question

kennitala: Icelandic Social Security number, which is publicly available

kjötsupa: Icelandic lamb soup

kleinur: plural of kleina, twisted, diamond-shaped donuts

krækiber: crowberries

landi: extremely strong Icelandic moonshine (literally, "the fellow countryman")

lopapeysa: wool sweater with a decorative yoke design at the neckline

prumpa: passing gas

saga: story, as well as a fairly common name

smørrebrød: Danish open sandwiches

sparka: to kick or punch

sveitaball: country ball, which is a dance or mixer

tja: "Well . . ."

Ugluspegill: The Icelandic translation of "Eulenspiegel," infamous trickster of German lore

vinan: an affectionate term for a female friend

PLACES

Barónstígur: a street in Reykjavík, directly west of Domus Medica

Domus Medica: a clinic in Reykjavík

Elliðavatn: a lake in greater Reykjavík

Grafningur: a region east of Reykjavík

Grenimelur: a residential street in western Reykjavík

Harfnarfjöður: a port town of nearly 30,000 (Iceland's third most populous) six miles south of Reykjavík

Hveragerði: a town in south Iceland

Kjarvalsstaðir: art museum in the center of Reykjavík, adjacent to Miklabraut

Kolaport: Iceland's largest flea market

Króksfjarðarnes: a rural town in Iceland's westfjords

Miklabraut: a segment of Route 49, a major traffic artery in Reykjavík

Nauthólsvík: a geothermally heated beach in southern Reykjavík

Nørrebro: a hip part of Copenhagen

Snorrabraut: a street in Reykjavík, directly east of Domus Medica

Ránargata: a residential street near the Reykjavík Harbor

Reykhólar: a village in Iceland's westfjords

Tjarnarbíó: a century-old theater right on the lake in downtown Reykjavík

Vesturbær: the west side of Reykjavík

Þingvellir: a valley national park northeast of Reykjavík and the site of the first parliament

Auður Jónsdóttir is one of the most accomplished authors writing in Icelandic today. The winner of the Icelandic Literary Prize, Icelandic Women's Literature Prize, and a finalist for the Nordic Council's Literature Prize, Auður is renowned for her wry poetic voice and dark humor. Director Tinna Hrafnsdóttir's film adaptation of *Quake* was featured at the 2021 Toronto International Film Festival.

Meg Matich is a poet and translator in Reykjavík. She earned an MFA from Columbia University and has received support for her work from the Banff Centre, PEN America, and the Fulbright Commission. Among other projects, Meg has collaborated with poet Magnús Sigurðsson on an anthology of Icelandic poetry and translated his collection *Cold Moons*, translated a book of essays in honor of former President Vigdís Finnbogadóttir, and translated the 2021 novel *Magma* by Thóra Hjörleifsdóttir.